A.S. FENICHEL

FOOLISH BRIDE

Foolish Bride

Sadly ever after... unless some dreams really do come true?

Elinor Burkenstock never believed in fairy tales. Sure, she's always been a fool for love—what woman isn't? But Elinor knows the difference between fiction and truth. Daydreams and reality. True love and false promises... Until the unthinkable happens, and Elinor's engagement is suddenly terminated and no one, least of all her fiancé, will tell her why.

Sir Michael Rollins's war-hero days seem far behind him when, after one last hurrah before his wedding, he gets shot and his injuries leave him in dire shape. He wants nothing more than to marry Elinor, the woman of his wildest dreams. But Elinor's father forbids it... and soon Michael is faced with a desperate choice: Spare Elinor a life with a broken man or risk everything to win her heart—until death do they part?

Edited by Penny Barber

Cover design by KaNaXa

This book is dedicated to those of us who have lost their better half.

One day the sun will rise again.

For Dave Mansue, my sunrise.

Acknowledgments

So many people affect the writing of a book and in ways they probably don't even realize. This book is very personal, maybe more so than some others. The entire Forever Brides series is near and dear to my heart. First and foremost, I must thank my sweet husband for his bravery in fighting and beating prostate cancer. Special thanks to all the doctors, nurses and techs who helped us along our journey.

There is a long list of women in my life who keep me grounded and moving forward. To Mom, Linda, Amy, Kim, Nancy, Karla, Llonda, Heidi, Sarah, Stephanie, Sabine, Karen M., Kristi, Karen B., and Shelley, I don't know what I would do without each and every one of you.

Cancer takes so many.
We've been lucky at times and devastated at other times.
Do what you can.
http://www.cancer.org/cancer/prostatecancer/

Prologue

"I was not out yet when the earl was engaged. I only know the rumors." Elinor wished Sophia would change the subject. She had hoped for a nice quiet walk in the elaborate gardens to get away from the ballroom.

Sophia patted her dark hair into place. "And, what was the rumor?"

Elinor cringed. How she hated gossip.

"Never mind, Elinor. You do not have to tell me."

It wasn't that she didn't trust Sophia, but talking of such things reminded her of the newspaper article that had nearly destroyed her. "I hate rumors. They are often exaggerated, and none of us really knows the truth. Well, except those involved."

"Yes, of course you're right."

The bushes to the right rustled, and Michael stepped out of the shrubbery's shadow.

His dark hair hung over bright blue eyes, and he was rumpled from hiding in the garden. "Forgive me, ladies."

"Michael," Elinor whispered.

"I was trying to wait until I could speak to Miss Burkenstock alone. I hope I didn't startle you." He fidgeted, which was unusual. Michael was always in control.

All the waiting, and now she couldn't stop her tears from falling.

"Shall I leave, Elinor?" Sophia asked.

She'd forgotten Sophia was even there. "Thank you, Sophia."

"Are you certain you will be safe?" Sophia crossed her arms over her chest.

Michael's smile was warm. "You have my word I shall not harm her in any way."

"Elinor?" She narrowed her eyes.

A wave of lightheadedness swamped her. "I will be fine."

Sophia nodded and walked away

"Elinor." He said her name like a prayer.

"Yes, Sir Michael?" Pretending she was unaffected by him, she looked away. She wished she could be more like Dory. Dory was excellent at pretending she didn't care.

"I was watching you dance." Taking a step closer, his gaze locked on her. "You seemed to be enjoying yourself. Especially when you danced with Travinberg."

"Are you jealous, Sir Michael?" She turned away from him and examined a yellow rose. Leaning down, she sniffed for its sweetness, looking for anything that would help her keep her composure.

He closed the gap until he was so close, his warmth spread along her back. "I am beside myself with desire for you. I hate every man who even looks at you and even those who only glance in your general direction. The last week has been torture."

All her torment of the last week bubbled up in her belly. She faced him. "Then why did you leave town, and leave me to deal with the scandal all alone? You left me with only a note to keep me company and not much of a note at that. What was I supposed to do?"

His smile widened. "My God, you are even more beautiful when you're angry."

Damn her fair skin for not concealing her blush. "Do not change the subject. I may not be the smartest girl in London, but I know that what you did was terribly unkind. I might have been ruined if not for my good friends."

His voice remained low and calm. "I did not run from you. I ran to try to make myself into someone you can be proud of."

It was impossible to stay aloof. She wanted answers. If not for the kindness of her friends, she would be ruined now, and it was all his fault. "Where did you go?"

He took her hands. "I am going to be worthy of you, Elinor. I promise that I will, if you will just wait for me."

"Wait? For how long? Mother will not allow me to wait if another offer is made. And what if the gentleman is titled?" Panic tightened her chest until she struggled for breath. She would need to make a list of ways to stall Mother's plans.

He pulled her closer and nuzzled her neck. "A few months is all I ask, my darling. Just give me a few months, and I will have enough money to come to your father and make an offer. Surely you can hold off your mother for a few months."

"I suppose I can, but why? I have my dowry. Certainly that will be enough for us to live comfortably."

Breaking away, he looked down at his feet, which he shuffled from side to side. "I do not want to marry you for your money, Elinor."

Her heart beat wildly. "But is that not why you pursued me?"

He kissed the tip of her nose. "I will not deny I came to London this season because I needed to marry to restore the money that my father squandered." He kissed her cheek. "I had every intention of finding a rich bride to enable that plan." He kissed her other cheek. "Then I met you, and you were the perfect solution to my problems."

She tried to pull away, but he held her close and kissed her lips. It was only a peck, but the thrill of it traveled to her toes and hit everywhere in between.

His body filled all her curves as he hugged her and spread kisses along her cheek and neck. "I knew you were the one, Elinor. So beautiful, charming, and sweet, I could not resist you. I want to be worthy of your love, and in the weeks we courted, I found a way to get enough money to repair my country home and still have enough to make a good start to the marriage. I made the deal on some grain. It will take a bit of time for my plans to pan out, but in a couple of months, I should be able to show your father that I am worthy of you."

It was difficult not to let his lips distract her from his words. She heard him say he loved her well enough, though. She breathed normally again, though her heart still raced. "I would gladly have given you my money."

Stiffening, he frowned. "We can take your money and put it away for our children."

"Children." The notion of raising babies with Michael made her sway with joy.

"You do want children, don't you?"

She looked up at him, holding back tears of joy. "Oh yes. I want a house full."

"I have a very big house." The strain around his eyes eased, and his grin spread wide.

"Good." Tears trickled down her face. Elinor had never been so happy.

With his gloved thumbs, he gently wiped the moisture from her face. "You will wait for me then?"

"I will wait, Michael."

Kissing her deeply, he tightened his arms, leaving no space between them.

Her mouth opened under his, and she melted against him. Visions of Michael and a house full of children with his marvelous blue eyes filled her head. Her heart beat so fast, that when he pulled away, she gasped for air.

"I have to go before I really do ruin you." Out of breath, his eyes flashed with passion.

"Must you?" She didn't want him to go. What she wanted was more of his kisses.

He laughed and placed a chaste kiss on her forehead. "It will not be long, my love. I shall return to London as soon as possible, and we will be married."

Once again, loneliness pressed down on her. "Don't go."

"I must, but I will be back. I promise." He took one step away.

"Michael."

He turned.

Straining against emotion, she pushed herself to ask, "Do you love me, Michael?"

He wrapped her in his arms as if he'd not seen her in years. "I love you more than life, Elinor. I will not betray you. Please trust me."

She tentatively kissed the skin behind his ear. "I do trust you. I just want..."

"Yes, my love, what do you want?"

"I want...I do not know." Her tongue touched his ear.

Grabbing her bottom, he pressed her roughly against his arousal.

Surprised but not afraid, she arched against him.

His lips found hers roughly, and he caressed her everywhere. He pulled her deeper into the thick garden shrubs. His breath came hard. He kissed her ear, her neck, then moved down to her throat. He caressed the top of her bodice, then tugged gently, releasing her nipple.

The cool air was odd and delightful on her sensitive skin.

He grazed it with his thumb, then his mouth covered her. She pulled him closer, wanting something but not knowing what she needed. Everything spun the way it did when she drank too much wine. It was wonderful and terrible all at once. She gripped his arms tighter, never wanting to let go.

He pushed her away. "No."

Longing for more, she clutched at him.

He fixed her dress and pushed a stray curl behind her ear. "I must go. It is too difficult to be here in the dark alone with you. I will not be able to stop myself."

"I did not ask you to stop." She surprised herself with her boldness.

He grinned. "No, you didn't, but I will wait and take you when you are mine, my love. We can wait for our wedding night, and I promise it will be worth the wait." He kissed her nose, then was gone.

Chapter One

See the dressmaker
Find just the right gift for Michael
Ask Mother for pin money
Write to Michael so he will know I am thinking of him

Elinor had many more items to add to her morning list. A knock on her door forced her to put down her quill. "Yes."

Mother stepped inside. "Your father wishes to see you in his study, Elinor."

"Why so formal, Mother?"

"The matter is quite urgent." Virginia Burkenstock folded her hands and grimaced; her sour face much different from her normal serene expression.

Elinor placed her list inside her desk, stood, and shook out her skirts. When she reached her father's study, nerves twisted her stomach. She entered, her mother close at her heels

Rolf Burkenstock scratched his belly where it hung over his trousers, then tugged on his morning coat. He pointed at the chair near his desk. "Sit, daughter."

She obeyed.

"You will not marry Sir Michael Rollins." Clearing his throat, he fiddled with a document on his desk.

For a full thirty seconds, Elinor couldn't respond. It was so outrageous for him to be canceling her wedding a mere month before the much anticipated day, she was sure she had misunderstood. She stared at him for some sign that he would say more or make her understand. "Father?"

"We'll say no more on the subject, Elinor. It's bad enough that we will have to deal with some gossip about breaking the engagement. The man should be left with some dignity." Her father's new earldom meant that Sir Michael Collins was now beneath her, but she never dreamed that either man would go back on their word. Recently raised to the rank of Earl of Malmsbury by the crown, Rolf had a new sense of his own worth. He stood prouder, had lost much of his natural modesty, and lived in fear of gossip and scandal.

Lady Virginia's eyes were puffy and her nose red. She bit her lip and sniffed, which she always did when trying to contain her tears. Several strands of her blond hair had escaped her usually neat chignon.

Father hadn't cried, of course. His imposing height and piercing pale blue eyes usually intimidated Elinor, but now he wouldn't make eye contact, looking from a spot on the wall to one on the carpet. As a diplomat for the crown, he met with kings and princes on a regular basis, but his own daughter made him uncomfortable.

"Has Sir Michael cried off?" Elinor was calmer than she would have thought possible.

Now neither of her parents would look her in the eye.

"Father, what is going on?" Her voice gained an edge.

Mother spoke. "He has been injured, Elinor."

"Injured? When? How? Why was I not summoned to care for him?" Panic rose in her chest. She rushed away to gather her wrap and have the carriage take her to Michael's townhouse.

Both of her parents shouted in unison, "Stop."

She spun, gaping at them. Her place was at Michael's side if he required care.

Mother sprang forward like she might leap over the table to reach her. One hand covered her mouth and, with the other, she reached toward Elinor.

Hands outstretched, Father strode across the room with his hands like claws about to physically restrain her if she persisted in her efforts to leave.

It was almost comical.

Father pointed one fat finger at her. "You are forbidden to see Sir Michael. You will not care for him. He is nothing to you, as you are no longer engaged. I will be dissolving the contract immediately, so there is no reason for you to be in his company ever again."

"Father—"

"I will brook no argument, Elinor. You will obey me in this." Returning to his desk, he pushed a pile of papers to one side and plopped a heavy glass ball on top of them.

The entire world had gone upside down. Her parents had lost their minds. It wasn't possible that she couldn't marry the man she loved, after a year-long engagement. Her emotions boiled to the surface. "Will no one tell me what is going on?"

"Elinor," Mother scolded, "you must not raise your voice like a scullery maid."

She stared at her and forced her mouth closed. Everyone had lost their minds. She took a deep breath. "Mother, I have been summoned, told that I am no longer engaged, and informed that I am not to even see Michael again. What reaction were you expecting?"

"I expect you to act like the lady I raised you to be." Mother straightened her back and folded her hands in her lap.

"Then tell me what has happened to Michael."

"Sir Michael," Father corrected.

"As you wish, Father." She continued to stare at Mother as if seeing her for the first time.

"It is just as well. He is beneath you now anyway. I was only allowing the wedding because the agreement was already signed, and I did not wish to renege. It is a shame that a true patriot has suffered such a fate, but you can certainly do better now that you are the daughter of an Earl." Father was mostly talking to himself, but she listened for some bit of logic that would make this sudden change of plan make some kind of sense.

"Mother, what is going on?"

Father cleared his throat. "I'll leave you two ladies to have a chat." He practically ran from the room, his morning coat flapping as he went.

Most people in London society thought Elinor was silly and senseless, and she would admit to her closest friends that she rather liked the low expectation her ignorance afforded her. However, at that moment she wasn't concerned about what society, her friends, or her mother thought of her intelligence. "Mother, I demand to know what is going on."

Mother sat in the small chair, then leaned forward, putting her head in her hands. The pose imitated the one she'd taken just over a year earlier, when the paper had reported Elinor's certain ruin. She and Michael had been caught kissing in a library at a ball by Lady Pemberhamble, the most notorious gossip in London. The kiss had been brief and passionate. It had been foolish really, but she couldn't help herself when she was with Michael Rollins. Then, when Michael had escaped town after the report became public, she was only saved by her friends' support. She hated causing Mother any pain but needed to know what was going on.

"Elinor, please take a seat," Mother whispered.

She perched on an armchair facing Virginia. Whenever summoned to her father's study, she snuggled into the soft cushion. Usually, the chair was warm and cozy, and no matter what silly rules her father set out to impose, she would snuggle into the chair and listen to him with half an ear. She waited for her mother to speak.

And she waited.

Mother held her head, fidgeted in her seat, and looked up and back several times at the Persian rug between them.

After a full three minutes, it became clear that Virginia might never speak if not prompted further.

"Mother, I can see that you are upset. Shall I ring for tea?" Though tea was the last thing in the world that Elinor wanted, it might put her mother at ease and thereby speed up the dissemination of information.

"No, dear. That will not help today."

"What would help, Mother?" The question came out less kindly than she intended.

Mother looked up, and a weary sadness dulled her usually clear blue eyes. "What I am going to tell you is not easy for me, Elinor. These kinds of things are just not discussed. Your father had much difficulty in his explanation to me, and I dare say probably left out quite a bit. Now, I will tell you, but at this point who knows where the story has gone wrong with so many people between the source and you and me."

Elinor couldn't think of a single response.

"Sir Michael was in an accident of some kind while

working on behalf of England. He was in France." She looked up at her daughter hopefully.

"He did mention that he would be traveling on the continent for a few weeks. He promised to return a week from now and told me that I should not be concerned about his missing the wedding. He said it rather jokingly, and so I took little notice." Michael often went away on some business for the crown. Never asking the nature of his business, she'd accepted him at his word.

"Yes, well, I do not know the exact nature of his business in France, but I do know that it was official and important, according to your father. I also do not know the exact nature of the injury or how he obtained it. I cannot tell you exactly where he was in France. I do not know when he returned to England."

"Mother, what do you know?" Elinor's frustration leaped to her breaking point.

A deep sigh shook Mother's shoulders. "It would seem that his ability to be a proper husband has been compromised."

Elinor waited for her to continue. This couldn't be all the information she would be receiving.

Virginia took a deep breath and her expression eased, as if satisfied with her explanation and would say no more.

"What is that supposed to mean?"

Her mother's frown returned. She pulled her handkerchief out of the waistband of her skirts and dabbed her bright red cheeks. "It means that you cannot marry him."

"But why? You have not told me anything." Hysteria was one more bit of strange conversation away. Her skin itched, which meant red blotches were appearing all over her neck, arms, and face. It happened whenever she was hysterical, and there was no way to stop it.

"I have told you enough," Mother said.

"No. You have told me nothing." Elinor stood and walked toward the door.

"Elinor, stop."

She faced her mother. "Tell me what has happened, or I swear I will go directly to Michael and ask him myself." She scratched her neck making the blotches worse.

"He is no longer able to father children," Virginia screamed.

Elinor stood still and let what Mother said seep into her mind. "This is certain?"

"Your father had it from Lord Marksbury at his club. I cannot imagine the earl would make up such a tale." Virginia pressed two fingers to her temple, which meant she was developing a headache.

It was difficult not to sympathize, but she had to get to the heart of the matter. "Perhaps his Lordship was mistaken. Where did he hear this news?"

"I do not know. You know how fast news travels in London, dear."

"And how in error those rumors often are." Anger welled up from her gut.

Virginia stood, walked over to her, and placed an arm around her shoulder. "I understand that you would wish the rumors were false, my dear, but I am afraid we must look elsewhere for a husband for you."

Her life was once again turned upside down by the will of London gossip. She shrugged off her mother's embrace and stormed across the room. "Look elsewhere. You make it sound like we are purchasing a dress. I will not be looking anywhere, Mother. I will marry Sir Michael Rollins or no one at all until I hear from his lips that he does not want me. Father can do as he wishes, but I will not cry off. I am not quite sure how anyone could know whether or not my fiancé is capable of producing an heir, but I am certain that London's gossips will not stop me from having the man I am in love with."

"Do you mean to disobey your father?" Virginia's eyes were wide and her skin pale as death.

To actually state such a thing would be foolish. Her father would likely lock her in her room, or worse, exile her to the country estate. She must be smarter than them. "I will think on all you have explained to me, Mother. I realize I have become overwrought. I would prefer to go to my room now, if that is acceptable to you."

"Quite understandable, dear; you will need some time. I completely understand. We will not accept any invitations for the remainder of the week. Monday will be soon enough to begin again. I do hate the thought of starting this whole marriage business again. We were so close." Sighing heavily, she closed her eyes.

Elinor left her mother, curtsied to her father, who hovered outside the door, and rushed up the steps to her room. She had to have a plan.

Sitting at her desk, she pulled out her journal and made a list. Perhaps the most important one of her life.

Get out of the house unseen
Transportation
What to say to Michael
Would he require care when she saw him?
Find the address of the best surgeon in London
What if he refused to see her?

The last item sat her back in her chair. *Then what?* Tears filled her eyes. Elinor wiped them away, but more came.

All her shock at the news she wouldn't be married to Michael overwhelmed her. Gasping for breath and shaking uncontrollably, she tried to move herself to the bed. She had to write a letter to Michael. She had to know if he had truly thrown her over. It was obvious that she wouldn't be able to go to him, at least not immediately. It would take time to plan a clandestine visit to a man's townhouse.

Once the tears began, she couldn't stop them. Writing was difficult with the flood coming down her cheeks and blurring her vision. After several failed attempts, she gave up and put her head on the desk. Racking sobs shook her body.

There was a scratch at the door, but Elinor did not answer.

She woke to a dim room hours later without the slightest recollection of being undressed or put into her night clothes. The fire was warm and kept the room from complete darkness.

Had the entire evening been a horrible nightmare? The dread in her chest spread down her arms. It had all happened. If her father had his way, she would never be Mrs. Michael Rollins. Fresh tears filled her eyes.

At her washstand, Elinor splashed her face with cool water, wiped it dry, and went to the small desk strewn with a dozen crumpled and torn pages. She opened one of the tear-splattered attempts at writing from the night before.

Michael, why have you deserted me?

Even to her grief-stricken mind, the note was pathetic and selfish. He was injured, and she was only thinking about herself. Had she even asked Mother about the seriousness of her fiancé's injuries? She couldn't remember.

She began a new letter. It took her the rest of the night to compose the correspondence, but once done, she was satisfied. Once he responded, she would know how to proceed.

What if he were too ill to respond?

Taking another sheet, she wrote a second letter addressed to his mother. This was even more difficult than the first. The sun peeked through the heavy drapes by the time she'd completed her writing.

She rang for her maid.

Josephine popped her head in a moment later. "Miss, have you been up all night?" Her tone was near scolding.

"Josephine, can you take these two letters and see that they are delivered without my parents' knowledge?" Elinor's voice was higher than normal even with the scratch of a sleepless night.

Josephine took the letters and stared at them. She scrunched up her nose and frowned.

Elinor was grateful Josephine couldn't read.

"If you will promise to take yourself to bed immediately, I will see them delivered. I'll not have you becoming ill."

Elinor grabbed her in a quick hug. "I will sleep for a while. Just see that those are delivered, Josephine. It is very important."

"Yes, Miss." She tucked the notes in her apron and bundled her mistress into bed.

Knowing that Rolf Burkenstock waited below stairs, Michael fought the pain shooting down his legs and up his back until he was somewhat upright.

His mother, Tabitha, tucked several pillows behind his back. "Are you sure you are up to this, Michael? I can send his lordship away. I'll tell him to come back in a week. It's impertinent, his coming at this point in your recovery."

Closing his eyes, he waited for the sharp agony of his wound to subside to a dull ache. "Another week will not change what Malmesbury has to say. Tell him to come up, please."

A deep frown crossed her face. "As you wish, but I think he could wait a week or so."

Forcing a smile, he pushed the pain to the side. "Your objection is noted."

She brushed his hair back from his forehead. "Do not let him overtax you, or I will become cross."

"Yes, ma'am." It had been years since Mother had ordered him around. Hiding his amusement wasn't an option.

With a nod, she left the room.

Michael's hero status might have kept the bill collectors at bay after his father's death, but nothing would stop Malmsbury from having his say. No amount of money or deeds done would help him now.

Hands flat against the mattress, he pressed himself more erect and endured the jolt of pain, clenching his teeth to keep from crying out.

As the door creaked open, Michael steadied himself and hoped his expression was mild and calm. "Come in, my lord."

His face burned bright red as Rolf Burkenstock, The Earl of Malmsbury, entered the bedroom. "Sorry to bother you while you are still abed, Sir Michael."

It was probably a lie, but Michael forced a smile. "It's all right, my lord. I expected you would come at some point. Would you like to sit?"

Rolf trudged around the bed and stared up at the coffered ceiling, then ran his hand along the gold-trimmed chest near the window. "This is a fine house you purchased, Sir Michael. You should be proud of what you accomplished in the past few years."

Wishing Malmsbury would just get on with it, Michael stifled a sigh and resigned himself to enduring the next few moments of his ruined life. "I was happy Stonehouse came available for me to purchase. Though, I can take no credit for the décor. Your daughter and my mother are responsible for filling the rooms with charm."

Clearing his throat, Malmsbury clenched his hands behind his back. "Yes, well, they did a fine job. It is not your fault what's happened."

"Are we speaking of my injuries, my lord, or something else?" Michael longed to get out of the damn bed and face his foe, but longing was all he was capable of.

"Elinor is the daughter of an earl now."

Michael had seen this coming. Of course, her father wanted to marry her off to someone at or above his new station. His injury was the perfect excuse. "I am aware of your recent good fortune, my lord."

Rolf puffed out his chest like a pigeon on the prowl for a mate. "It was an unexpected boon from the crown."

Another lie. Burkenstock had lobbied for the prize and won by kissing more ass than a royal courtesan. It made no difference. "I assume your admiration of my new house and your good fortune are not the reason for this visit, my lord."

He bristled and walked closer to the bed, still keeping his distance as if Michael's wounds might be contagious. "I regret this outcome, more than I can say. I have my daughter's future to consider. She is our only child and such a delicate thing. I saw Lord Marksbury at Whites last week, and he is in the confidence of Mr. Church, who knows your surgeon quite well."

Evidently, the nature of his injuries had become part of

London's gossip. It was only a matter of time. Michael wished he'd had a bit more. Elinor's sweet smile and musical voice floated through his mind. "My prognosis is still unclear, my lord."

Malmsbury gripped the back of the chair, his fingers biting into the red velvet fabric. "I am sure you wish it to be so, but word is you will never be the man you were. Even if the rumors are false, I cannot have my dear Elinor exposed to such harshness."

More likely, the earl feared the gossip would hurt his political aspirations and relationship with the crown. He was in too much pain to risk any sudden movements, but the sting to his heart might have outshone the rest of his wounds. "I see. What does Elinor say?"

Malmsbury's cheeks and ears flushed red, and he crossed his arms over his barrel chest. "Lady Elinor is a good girl who does as she's told. The matter has been discussed with her."

"Has it?" The notion that she knew of his inadequacies hurt almost as much as losing her.

"Of course. Her mother and I explained it this morning. She was upset, but she knows her duty. We'll say no more on the matter. I assume you still care for her and wouldn't wish to hurt her reputation."

Fury burned his gut and twisted his mind. "You might find a willing duke to take my place, my lord. Wouldn't that be a treat after nearly having to put her on the shelf last year?"

Malmsbury gazed at the ceiling, oblivious to Michael's sarcasm. "Oh my, wouldn't that be something." He cleared his throat and shook his head, returning the concerned crease to the space between his eyes. "My family and I wish you a thorough recovery."

"I would like to speak to Elinor." She would be better off without him, but he couldn't stop himself from asking for one last sight of her. Skivington was available. She could be the Duchess of Skivington within the year, a far step up from the wife of a knight who'd stolen a kiss at a ball and ruined her. Maybe she would laugh at the folly of the memory.

Backing toward the door, Malmsbury shook his head. "You wouldn't want to confuse the girl. You know how she is, head always in the clouds. The kind thing to do is to make a clean break. She understands the situation. She's a good girl."

"Of course." Michael's throat closed around the words.

Malmsbury opened the door, bowed, and clomped down the hall.

Michael clenched his fists and pummeled the mattress. Pain shot through him. His legs jerked with agony, and he rolled to his side.

Thomas Wheel rushed into the room and eased him back onto the pillows. "Hang on, Mike. I'll get your nurse with some laudanum."

Gripping the arm of his oldest friend, Michael shook his head. "Just wait. It will pass. I hate that stuff. Give me a minute."

When he opened his eyes, Thomas sat in the chair Elinor's father had avoided. His eyebrows raised and his legs spread in front of him, he looked ready to either relax or run for help, whichever was needed. "Better?"

Michael steadied his breath. "I lost my temper. It was foolish even in the privacy of my own thoughts."

Nodding, Tom leaned forward. "I passed Malmsbury in the hall."

"He came to inform me of the dissolution of my engagement. Though, he never actually said the words."

Thomas pounded the chair arm. "Cowardly to come at this time. You had a contract. He at least could have waited until you have properly healed. Bad form to hit a man when he's down."

"He's only protecting Elinor." Saying it out loud made it a bit more believable.

"If that were true, you wouldn't have nearly killed yourself with the loss of your temper. You would die to protect that girl. What does she say about it?" Tom stared at him with intense green eyes, his military training looking for any tidbit to twist in their favor.

"She wrote to me this morning asking after my health. She made no mention of her father or her wishes. I assume she will be happy to find a more appropriate husband now that she comes from a titled family."

Tom leaned back. "I doubt that's the case. Elinor Burkenstock is devoted to you."

The agony shooting down his legs was nothing compared to the pain of losing Elinor. It was his own stupidity that led him to this. He should have stayed home and never taken one last assignment. "Devotions change in the face of power and money."

Tom pounded on the chair again. "I will not believe that. Look at all you have accomplished. Your father left this world and you with more liability than any man can overcome, and yet you paid off his debt and even managed to save the family home in the country."

"I appreciate your loyalty, but I have not done much. Stonehouse is a nice townhome, but it cannot compare to what an earl or a duke can provide for Elinor."

Tom shook his head. "Write to her. Tell her how you feel and see if she feels the same. Do not let your chance at happiness slip away because Malmsbury is a greedy fool."

"Elinor deserves a better life than I can provide, Tom. Even if my finances were enough, the doctors say it is unlikely I'll ever father children. I can never be a proper husband to her."

Tom fidgeted, but kept his gaze locked on Michael. "You should trust her enough to make that choice on her own. Give her the opportunity to show you how much she loves you. I believe you will be happy with her."

It was too much. "You should go now. I am tired, and perhaps a draft of laudanum is just the thing I need."

Tom touched his arm. "I can stay and keep you company, Mike."

Even shaking his head increased the misery that took over his body and soul. "It will be better if I am alone. Besides, I cannot get my mother to leave Stonehouse no matter how I try. Go now. I'll be fine."

Tom rose and squeezed his shoulder. "I will return tomorrow to check in on you."

Michael closed his eyes and waited for the door to shut behind his friend. He sank down into the pillows as his despair enveloped him.

Mother arrived with his draft of bitter laudanum. He took it without argument, letting the drug blot out his sorrow and make him forget his desperation.

The pain in the lower half of his body persisted, but his care about it fuzzed and faded until he no longer focused on anything and oblivion took him away.

Chapter Two

Elinor should have been a bride that morning. Instead, she stared out the window at the street as drizzle soured her already miserable mood.

Virginia entered, pulling on her gloves. "Why don't you come and pay a few calls with me, Elinor?"

"No, thank you, Mother." The last thing she wanted was to plaster a fake smile on her face and pretend everything was okay. Elinor made several lists, but her malaise continued.

Mutual friends informed her that Michael was out of his sick bed.

Even Mrs. Rollins had been kind enough to send a note expressing her regret and understanding.

Elinor had written back thanking her for her kindness.

She sent letter after letter to Michael, but received no response.

When she left for the country estate, Mrs. Rollins sent a second note assuring Elinor that Michael was healing nicely. She did mention he remained in a particularly bad temper, but no longer required his mother's care.

After several attempts with her mother, she still didn't understand the nature of his injury. While relieved that his long recovery was near its end, she hated him for not writing to ask after her wellbeing. Didn't he care that she was devastated? He only thought of himself.

Typical.

"You cannot just sit in this parlor indefinitely." Mother put her fists on her hips.

Elinor had to push down her temper or she'd shriek her rage. "I am in no mood to frolic around town as if nothing is wrong. I will not pay calls today, or tomorrow, or the day after that. If that is not satisfactory for you, Mother, you should rethink your position on my marriage."

"I have no idea what has gotten into you."

"Really? I would have thought it quite clear."

Mother huffed, and her face turned red.

The housekeeper peeked around Mother. "Lady Marlton and Lady Dorothea to see you, miss."

"Oh, thank goodness," Virginia said.

Elinor wished everyone would leave her alone. She stood as her closest friends entered.

Virginia curtsied. "I am sorry, ladies, but I was just leaving. I am sure you will enjoy a nice visit."

Dory and Sophia expressed their regret for missing a visit with Elinor's mother, then sat as Virginia exited.

"How are you, Elinor?" Dory asked.

"Fine."

"I am sure this is a difficult day for you." Sophia leaned forward and kept her voice low.

"I am fine." Elinor smoothed her dress and stared out at the clouds rolling in over London.

Dory sat next to her on the settee. "Elinor, we are here because we know you are hurting, and we are your friends."

Holding her tongue had gotten her nowhere, and holding her temper even less. "I do not need your pity. I am fine."

Sophia said, "Dory, perhaps Elinor would prefer to be alone today. We can come back another time, when she is more herself."

"Of course." Dory got up. "If you need anything, Elinor, send for me."

Elinor bit the inside of her cheek to hold back the sharp comment building inside her.

With a brief goodbye, her friends left her alone.

Emotions were like a kettle on an open flame. Elinor tried to cool them, but to no avail.

If Michael wouldn't answer her letters, then she would go to him and see if he could as easily ignore her face-to-face. It was improper, but she brushed aside thoughts of society and right and wrong. She wrote a note addressed to Dolan, Michael's butler, and told her maid to have it discreetly delivered to Stonehouse.

In return, Dolan wrote, "I shall make the arrangements."

Elinor lay across her bed, reading the same paragraph of her novel for the tenth time. Her attention would not focus on the words on the page. The lace coverlet distracted her, and she stared at the intricate pattern.

"Elinor, your father and I are leaving now." Virginia stood in the doorway.

Elinor looked at her mother. "Enjoy your evening, Mother."

"Are you sure you would not like to change your mind and join us, dear?" Draped in royal blue, Mother was stunning. Virginia was perhaps a few inches taller than her daughter, but they both had warm golden hair and sky blue eyes. She rubbed the sapphires around her neck. Of course, Mother was uncomfortable; everyone in the house had tiptoed around her throughout the cursed day.

"No, thank you, Mother. I will likely retire early this evening. You and Father enjoy your night. I will see you at breakfast." Elinor fought back tears. She had to be brave. Now wasn't the time to lose her nerve.

Mother's voice caught. "All right, dear. Good night."

Elinor waited for the carriage to pull away, then jumped up from her bed and dressed. She had sworn her maid to secrecy, as well as the footman who would put her into a hack.

Nervously, she watched in the mirror while Josephine arranged her hair. Once dressed, she donned a heavy dark-blue mantle with a large hood that would conceal her identity. If she hadn't been so anxious, she might have enjoyed the mystery of the clandestine behavior. As it was, she was so anxious it was only anger keeping her from running back to her bedroom as the footman handed her up into the hired carriage. Luckily, the servants liked her better than her father. Of course, if he found out they could lose their posts.

Her father wouldn't find out. And if he did, she would find a way to protect them.

She twisted her gloved hands in her lap and repeated a list of things she had to speak to Michael about. Before she knew it, the driver yelled down that they had arrived.

At the door to Stonehouse, she tapped lightly. It was just after eight, but light shone from within. Perhaps he was in bed and still unable to take callers. Her legs shook, and when the door opened with Dolan looking serene, she chided herself for being a ninny. There would be no ghost swooping out to claim her. She pushed her shoulders back and took a deep breath.

Dolan raised his brows. "Are you all right, my lady?"

"Yes. Fine, Dolan. Just a bit on edge."

He was perhaps thirty years old and had been with the Rollins family since he was a teenager. His long nose and sharp eyes could assess a person's character in an instant. "Sir Michael is in the library, Lady Elinor." With a bow, he disappeared behind the servant's door.

Everything she was doing went against her upbringing. She would be ruined if word got out that she had gone unaccompanied to Sir Michael's home in a hired hack in the middle of the night. Well, it wasn't so late, but that wasn't the point. She was risking everything, and she didn't even know if Michael wanted to see her. She suspected he did not. It didn't matter. This wasn't about him for once. He had broken her heart without so much as a note of explanation.

It wouldn't do.

Inching down the corridor toward the library, she secured her mantle in case any servants were watching. She stepped past the round table she'd ordered for the alcove beneath the stairs. It would look better several feet to the left, but she checked herself and left the table as it was.

"This is not your home now," she whispered as she continued down the hallway to the right.

The library lay behind a pair of doors. Elinor raised her hand to knock, then took hold of the handle and opened the door without announcing herself.

"Go away, Dolan. I left word not to be disturbed."

Her breath caught, and she had to clutch the wall. He was beautiful. Wrapped in a black robe with his back to her, he did not look sick. He stood tall, though perhaps thinner than the last time she'd seen him. His shoulders squared, he stared out into the dark garden.

"It is not your butler, Michael." Her voice shook, and she could have kicked herself for the weakness.

His back stiffened before he turned around. His eyes were

as blue as she remembered, but there were deep shadows beneath them. His dark brown hair was tussled as though he had been nervously raking his hands through it as he did when he had a lot on his mind.

"What are you doing here?" His shout shook the walls. "Where is your father? He let you enter here without him? If it is money he wants for your dowry, well, I will see what I can do. I am not made of money as you well know, but I suppose it is expected."

Money? Had he lost his mind?

He stared at the bookcase, then studied the intricacies of the Persian rug she had picked out three months earlier.

"You think that I have come for money?"

"Where is your father?" His voice was rough and cold. When he looked in her direction, his gaze did not meet hers.

"My father is not here." She took two steps into the library, then closed the doors behind her. She pushed back the hood of her cloak.

"Your mother is waiting?" He crossed his arms and watched the door.

"I am alone." Hands shaking, she untied the knot at her neck and placed the cloak over the back of a chair. Her simple blue dress had been the most appropriate for a meeting of this kind, but its low neckline left her feeling exposed. Putting the cloak back on would appear cowardly.

His eyebrows rose and then narrowed to a point between his eyes before he turned back to the window. "Go home, Elinor,"

She stepped closer, amazed that her legs held her. "Not until I have what I came for."

He scoffed and stepped into the center of the room. There was a limp to his gait, and his jaw tightened. "I told you, if it's money you want, I do not have much, but we shall work something out."

A tear escaped down her cheek. She dashed it away, and the anger replaced her sorrow. "I do not want your money, Michael."

Hands fisted at his side, he finally met her stare. "What is it then?"

She approached him and touched his arm.

He flinched, but she refused to back away.

"I want to know why? I need to know if you ever loved me. I demand to know if everything you told me was a lie." There, she'd said it. She dropped her hand away.

He was pale and thin. Little of his robust figure shone through the robe. "I never lied to you."

"Then why?"

He turned away again. "I would have thought your parents explained that to you already."

She kicked at the rug, unsure of how to continue.

"Didn't your mother explain?" Anger rolled through his words like an army.

In all the time they'd courted, she had never seen any signs of temper from Michael. He'd always been kind and loving. Through her fear, her own anger pushed her on. She stood toe-to-toe with a clearly dangerous man. "I was told that our engagement was dissolved because you cannot father a child. I will admit it took my mother quite a long time to get around to explaining that much, and I do not actually think she knew any more. What I want to know is what that has to do with you crying off?"

Then he turned. "I did not cry off. You did."

"I did no such thing." She stomped her foot.

"Then your father did." His tone had gone flat.

"He had no right. If you did not end our engagement, then

why were we not married today?" She tried to sound sophisticated, but tears pushed to the surface. His attitude was so changed. She didn't know him. Maybe she never had.

"Your mother explained that." He lumbered across the room and poured himself a rather large brandy. The smooth glide that she always admired was gone from his step.

"So if we had married, then we found that I was barren, you would have tossed me over?" She was rather proud of how rational she sounded in spite of her sorrow and raging temper.

"Don't be ridiculous." He swallowed half his brandy. His shoulders slumped.

"Then why would you think that I would care?"

"You do not understand." The second half went down in one swallow.

"Clearly. Perhaps you can explain it to me."

He was pouring a second glass and laughed rather madly.

Perhaps she should not have come. This Michael was a stranger, and there was no telling what he was capable of. "I assume it has something to do with your injury. I know you think I am stupid, Michael, and perhaps I am naïve, but I did grow up on a farm. I know something of reproduction. What I do not understand is—could I have one of those?"

He turned and looked at her.

She nodded toward the brandy.

His eyes grew wide before he shrugged, poured another, and handed it to her, making sure his fingers never touched hers. "I did not know you drank, Elinor."

"I do not, but I thought this might be a good time to begin." She winced at the harsh taste, but enjoyed the warmth seeping into her chest.

"Indeed." He jerked away so quickly that he nearly toppled.

It was a struggle not to run to his aid. She took another sip, and it didn't taste so bad. "What was I saying?"

"What you do not understand." He downed his drink and slapped the glass down on the table.

"Yes. What I do not understand is why you would think that I would stop loving you or why you have stopped loving me. It occurred to me that perhaps you did not love me to begin with. That would explain your ease in abandoning me." She wasn't really talking to him, more to herself.

"I did love you, Elinor. I did not lie."

"But no longer."

He wouldn't meet her gaze. He stared at every item in the room but her. "How did you get here?"

"I came in a hack." She squared her shoulders and drank more brandy.

"Really, Elinor, what were you thinking? I shall have my carriage brought round to take you home." He ambled toward the cord to call a servant.

"No!"

"No?"

"I am not leaving until I have an explanation. I waited over a year for you. Then tonight I risked my reputation, came all the way over here in a hack, and I will not leave until you explain to me how you could do this." She put down her empty glass. She was warm and exceedingly bold.

He limped across the room and grabbed her by the arms.

She squeaked in pain as his fingers bit into her flesh. She had always known that he could hurt her, but until that moment she never thought he would. It made no difference. She had loved him faithfully, but he obviously hadn't loved her enough. She stood straighter and met his angry stare. "I assume you are going to strike me now. You may as well get it over with. I am not leaving, Michael, no matter what you do to me. I was supposed to be in this house today as your wife, and I will remain until I have what I came for."

He released her, but did not move away. He cocked his head and narrowed his eyes. "It's an act. You act the fool, but it's not who you really are."

"I would not call it an act." She crossed her arms over her chest.

"Wouldn't you?"

"No. I behave exactly as my mother and father wished me to behave. In this, I am no different than the rest of the husband-seeking women of the ton." She forced herself to keep her gaze locked with his.

He shook his head. "No. I suppose not."

She touched his arm. "Michael, tell me what happened."

He flinched and moved away. "I am no longer the man I was, Elinor. I am sorry. Now I see that you are not who I thought you were either, so perhaps this is all for the best."

"You are saying that you do not love me anymore because I am not as stupid and vapid as you believed?" The horror sunk in, and she wanted to strike him.

"I am saying that neither of us are who we were."

"Perhaps the difference is that I would have honored our agreement, Sir Michael Rollins." She was so angry now, that her voice shook. "You are no gentleman. You have no honor. If we could not have children of our own, then we could have found some that needed a home and raised them. Your brother's children could have inherited, but we would have been happy. I would not have cared, that is how great my love for you was."

"Was?" His shoulder slumped.

She laughed, but without humor. Pent-up tears rolled down her face. "I shall love you for the rest of my life, Sir Michael, but now I shall also hate you in equal measure."

"Elinor, please."

"Please what? Please forgive you for ruining both of our lives. No, that I shall never do."

"I am sorry."

"Yes, it would seem so. Please, if you have an unmarked carriage that can carry me home, I would like to go now." She grabbed her cape from the chair. It had been a mistake to come, but at least she knew now that he wasn't the man for her.

"Don't you understand? I am only half a man. I cannot marry you. I can never marry anyone."

"Have you had an amputation then?" Sympathy seeped into her voice. It was too horrible to think about.

His face colored. "Elinor! My God!"

Horrified, she touched his arm. "I am sorry, Michael. I didn't realize the injury was so severe. Should you be out of bed?"

He jerked his arm away. "Really, Elinor, I have no idea who you are. The woman I was engaged to would never even have known about such things."

Her cheeks were on fire, but the brandy made her bold. "As I said, the country estate is a farm. It's not as if I haven't any idea how babies come about." She cleared her throat. "I think perhaps you should take yourself to bed. It must be too soon for you to be out of bed with an injury of this kind."

"Nothing has been amputated, Elinor." His shout should have brought the staff running, but no one came.

Tempted to run for the door, she scooted a few feet away. "If what you say is true, then why are we not to marry?"

"Elinor, cannot your mother explain this to you?" He rubbed his temple and ran his hand through his hair.

"Evidently not. She tried, but got no further then you could not father children."

"Well. I am not obligated to explain the male anatomy to a

silly little girl." He punched the wall, causing the sconces to flicker.

It was he who acted like a child. She'd risked everything to see him, and he had the nerve to call her names and dismiss her like a bothersome whelp. "I do not believe you. I do not believe there is anything wrong with you. You were just looking for a way out of a marriage you never wanted. It is all a lie. And even if it is not, the doctors cannot know in such a short time what will happen with your injuries. It makes no difference now. The carriage, if you please."

He crossed the room, tore the mantle from her hand and pushed her against the wall. Where there had once been passion, now his eyes burned with rage.

She screamed his name, then held her tongue.

He pressed his groin into her and smirked horribly. "Do you feel that?"

"I feel nothing but the pain from where your hands are bruising me."

"Exactly. You feel nothing, because I am no longer a man, Lady Elinor. I will not marry you or anyone else because that part of me that once raged with desire is dead, and now all that is left is the rage." He pounded the wall beside her head.

She cringed, but when his hands fell away from her, she did not move. Instead, she kissed his cheek. "I am sorry that you are suffering so."

He pulled away, but she grabbed his arm. She wanted to sob, to hit him, to hug him, to tell him what he'd put her through. Part of her wanted to walk away and never see him again. "Don't, Michael. Don't pull away from me. None of this matters to me. Marry me."

He straightened and looked into her eyes. "I cannot." All emotion left his voice. He was an empty shell of the man he'd been, and he no longer wanted her.

It was over.

He rang the bell, and Dolan appeared a few seconds later.

Once the carriage was ordered, Elinor put her mantle on and walked to the foyer.

Her mind reeled. He had been so angry, then cold. There had been a moment of passion but then only anger and resignation.

When the carriage was ready, Michael followed her and handed her up. She wanted the door to close so that she could cry. She had been holding back and now she desperately needed release.

Michael stepped up into the carriage and sat opposite her. He'd changed his robe for a long coat, but wore no neckcloth and wasn't properly dressed for a London evening.

"What are you doing?"

"I am seeing you home. I am a gentleman, in spite of what you might think." He crossed his arms and watched her.

She crossed her own and looked out the window. The carriage jerked forward, and the street lined with townhouses rolled by. A barouche sped past, and then a cart pulled by a sturdy workhorse. Elinor needed the distractions to help her swallow her emotions.

"Elinor, I am sorry. Regardless of what you think of me, it is because I have so much regard for you that I will not marry you. You deserve to have a whole husband and children of your own. I cannot give you what you need. You would come to regret our marriage, and in time you would have hated me for trapping you."

"How convenient. Now I hate you, and we didn't have to waste all that time." It was liberating to speak her mind instead of playing the dope all the time.

He cringed, and his knuckles turned white where he gripped the window frame. "I suppose that is true. I do not want you to think what we had was unimportant to me. It was everything. I wanted to be your husband more than anything in the world."

"Evidently, it was not enough."

He moved to the other side of the carriage and took her hand. "Please, Elinor, do not do this to me. Tell me that you understand, and you do not hate me. I could not bear that too."

Loving him was impossible and hating him just as hard. A single tear escaped and rolled down her cheek.

He leaned forward and kissed it away. Then he straightened. "I am sorry. I had no right."

She held her words. It would do no good to rail at him. Another tear followed the first. When the carriage stopped in front of her home, she turned to him, and let her voice grow cold. "I regret this unpleasantness. I cannot forgive you. Good evening."

The footman opened the door and let down the step. He handed her out, and she rushed toward the front door of the townhouse.

She hadn't yet reached the door when tears fell in earnest.

"Back home now, my lord?" Teddy, his footman, asked.

"Yes." Michael stared at the closed door of the Burkenstock townhouse. He wished he'd thought to bring brandy for the ride home. He longed for something to kill his pain.

With a nod, the footman closed the door, and a moment later, the carriage moved again.

At first, he thought it would be better if she hated him, but hearing her say those words was too much. He prayed that God would make his heart stop so that this horrible agony would end.

God's answer was, "No."

Michael lived and breathed. London rolled past in a blur of houses and humanity until the carriage door opened at his front step.

He made it halfway up the steps before the pain in his groin and leg overcame him. Rather than topple, he held tight to the stone rail and pulled himself through the front door. He clung to the foyer wall and Dolan's arm to get to his study.

"Should I call the doctor, sir?"

Michael was sick of doctors and their terrible predictions. "Just bring me that decanter of brandy and a glass, Dolan."

Dolan placed the decanter on the table beside Michael. After a quick bow, he left the study, closing the door behind him.

Michael poured the brandy to the brim and gulped it down. It warmed his chest to his belly. He poured another and drank.

Elinor had every right to be furious with him. The things he'd said and done were not gentlemanly and should not be forgiven. He'd only meant to frighten her off, but his temper had gotten the best of him.

Taking the decanter and glass with him, he went to the couch. Sleep wouldn't come, so he sat up and poured more brandy.

After midnight, the study door opened.

"Dolan, I do not require anything but to be left alone."

"That's too bad." Thomas Wheel sat across from him on the wingback chair. He ran a hand through his red hair.

"What are you doing here, Tom?"

He stood and took the decanter out of Michael's reach. "I had a very odd note from your butler and thought it best if I stopped by before going home tonight." Tom poured himself a brandy and sipped.

"Meddling servants."

Thomas raised an eyebrow. "Servants who worry about their master's wellbeing are to be cherished. Your domestic affairs aside, why are you drunk?"

"Who says I am drunk? I am entitled to a bit of my own brandy when I'm in pain." The brandy was too far away, and his leg throbbed.

Tom poured Michael a glass. "Perhaps you might sip that, Mike. I am sure your father had the same thought at some point. He would just have one to dull some pain of injustice. I am sure at the start he thought he deserved to drink his own brandy and act like an ass. He then justified his behavior with his level of drunkenness."

Michael put down the glass. His father's legacy had ruined his family. The best thing he'd ever done for them was die. It wouldn't do to leave that same horror for his brothers to deal with when he turned up toes.

Tom put his down as well. "Why are you drunk?"

Michael sat up. The room spun. "Elinor was here."

"Here. When?"

"Tonight. She put herself in a hack and showed up at my door."

"Courageous girl. I didn't realize she had that kind of meddle." Thomas leaned back.

Michael closed his eyes, but the spinning didn't stop. His Elinor had been a delicate flower, but tonight she'd shone like a warrior queen. "Nor I. She was nothing like the girl I fell in love with."

"So you no longer love her. Is that why you've put yourself in this condition?"

His heart hurt worse than his wound. "I think I love her more."

"Did you tell her that? Did you renew your engagement?" Thomas stretched his legs out and crossed his feet.

"She was so beautiful and I tossed her from the house."

Tom jerked to the edge of the chair and spread his arms wide. "Why?"

"I have nothing to offer."

"Then why are you drunk?"

Michael leaned back and stared at the ceiling. "Tom, can we just sit here and not talk of Elinor Burkenstock? I will speak of anything else, but when I think of her, I just want to lose myself in that decanter."

"I am happy to sit and speak of the trouncing I gave Daniel during our fencing match on Monday."

Michael took a deep breath, ready to lose himself in one of Thomas's amusing stories. "Start at the beginning and leave nothing out."

Chapter Three

"Lord and Lady Marlton, accompanied by Mr. Thomas Wheel," the housekeeper announced.

Elinor put aside the list she'd been jotting into her journal and stood as they entered. As the men bowed, she and Sophia made their curtsies.

Sophia called on her from time to time, but never with his lordship, and she'd certainly never had a call from Mr. Wheel before. "Good afternoon. I was not expecting guests. I will call for tea."

Sophia sat, and the gentlemen waited for Elinor to finish ordering tea. Once she sat next to Sophia, they also sat.

"How are you, Elinor?" Sophia asked.

"Fine." There was a hollow tone to her voice she didn't like, but couldn't seem to alter.

"Will your dear mother be back soon?" Thomas's voice sounded too sweet.

Elinor didn't like it. There was something suspicious about this visit. "Not for several hours. She rides in the park at this time of day."

He nodded.

"Mr. Wheel, it is a particular surprise to see you today. I do not believe you have ever paid me a call before, or were you calling on my 'dear mother'?" Hard as Elinor tried, the viper's tongue that emerged the night she visited Michael couldn't be tamed.

Thomas studied her for a long moment. He then looked at Sophia, who nodded and shrugged.

"I shall not toy with you, Lady Elinor," he said.

The silent conversation between him and Sophia annoyed her. "Oh no, please don't."

He almost smiled. "I have come because Sir Michael is in trouble and you are the only person who can save him."

"Then he shall perish." She never took her gaze from his.

Lord Marlton cleared his throat. "Elinor, will you not even hear him out?"

"Why should I?" Betrayed again, but this time by Sophia. "Are you party to this as well? You call yourself my friend." She stood, forcing the men to stand.

"Elinor, I only said I would bring Tom here. I will support whatever you wish to do." Sophia plucked at the fringe on the yellow settee.

"You are just like all the rest. The three of you may leave now." Elinor turned her back on her company. It was the height of rudeness.

"That will do, Lady Elinor," Thomas said.

She faced him.

"You will apologize this minute to Lady Marlton, or I swear I will take you over my knee. How dare you be so discourteous to your closest friend? She had only your welfare in mind, and it took much convincing to get her to agree to this visit. You have been hurt, and for that I am sorry. You blame Michael, and perhaps you are correct. I am only privy to part of the story. What I do know is that you are behaving as badly as the horrible gossips that nearly ruined you last year. What is worse is you are behaving that way toward the person who saved you. If not for Sophia, you would no longer be welcomed in society. Now apologize." Frowning, he propped one fist on his hip.

Elinor's heart pounded. She wanted to close her ears to him and blind herself to what he said. He'd sapped the anger out of her, and she looked at Sophia, who cried quietly. Elinor burst into hysterical sobbing.

Sophia rushed to Elinor and took her in her arms.

Between sobs, Elinor said, "I am so sorry, Sophia. I never meant... Forgive me..."

"Of course I forgive you. It is nothing. You were distraught." Sophia gave Thomas a harsh look, to which he merely shrugged.

When she had calmed enough and was sitting on the settee next to Sophia, she looked up at Mr. Wheel. "What has happened now?"

"A comment was made about you at a gaming hell, and Michael has challenged the man to a duel." Thomas sat and folded his arms.

Dueling was idiotic and illegal. "What does that have to do with me? I understand that it is foolish, but Sir Michael is said to be a superior swordsman as well as a superior shot with a pistol, is he not? I am sure he shall emerge victorious."

"That is not all, Elinor." Daniel exchanged a look and nod with Thomas. "Thomas and I do not believe that Michael intends to win the duel."

"I do not understand." She tugged at a loose thread on the yellow cushion. When it gave, it left a run in the fabric.

Daniel cleared his throat and walked to the fire. He poked at the flame, forcing it to catch.

Thomas brushed his breeches for the second time and tugged on his waistcoat.

Elinor hoped a hole would open in the floor and suck her out of the room and its uncomfortable silence. Unfortunately, the townhouse was solid. "Where is this duel to take place?"

Thomas stood rigid and crossed his arms. "On a wooded property just outside of town."

"When?" Her voice was strong, but still, she did not allow emotion to cloud her judgment.

"Just after dawn tomorrow," Thomas said.

She nodded. "Come and collect me early enough to stop this madness. I shall be ready."

"You are doing the right thing." Thomas relaxed.

Elinor hated everything about this plan. "I will not have his blood on my hands. That is the only reason that I am doing this. If he means to kill himself, he will have to find some other excuse."

Thomas pointed at her and drew in a long breath.

Waving her hand about, Sophia said, "Very well then, we shall leave you to the rest of your day, Elinor. Daniel and I will, of course, be joining you in the morning. No need to give the gossips more to flap about."

They made a hasty exit.

Tears rolled down Elinor's face. She'd cried a river since her meeting with Michael a month earlier. She was sick of crying.

~

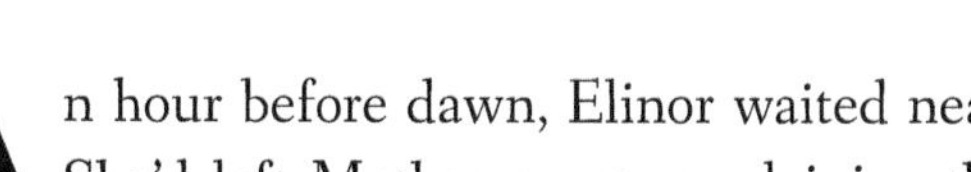

An hour before dawn, Elinor waited near the front door. She'd left Mother a note explaining that she had gone out early for a walk. She would think it outrageous, but since Virginia never rose before ten, she would assume early was perhaps nine o'clock. If things went as planned, she would be home before Mother had much time to think about the matter.

The servants would only answer direct questions, and Mother wasn't likely to ask the time of her departure.

When the carriage stopped in front of the stoop, Elinor rushed from the house. Her heart pounded, and the temptation to run back upstairs was strong.

The footman hadn't dismounted before she stood waiting to be handed up.

"Good morning." Elinor climbed in and sat next to Thomas Wheel. Sophia and Daniel faced them.

They muttered good morning before falling silent for the winding route out of the city. At the early hour, only servants and workers occupied the streets.

She should demand they take her home and let Michael take care of himself. That would be the prudent thing to do. Never having done the prudent thing where Michael was concerned, Elinor remained silent as she toyed with the seam of her glove.

Sophia cleared her throat. "What will you say to him, Elinor?"

Elinor shrugged. She had no idea what she would say when she confronted him again. She might strangle him for the trouble he'd caused. Maybe she'd slap his face. There would be some satisfaction in that.

Thomas ran his hand through his hair, causing the dark red locks to stand straight up, "Have you no idea? Perhaps you could tell him how much he has to live for."

Elinor met his gaze. "Is that what you told him?"

"Yes."

"And yet he still insisted on the duel?" Elinor wished she could jump out of the carriage and get as far away from Michael and all the things that reminded her of him. Yet, they barreled forward toward the very man who had ruined any hope of her happiness. Idiot.

Thomas straitened his white cravat and fidgeted in his seat. "I see your point. You could tell him how much it would hurt you if he were dead."

"Mr. Wheel, I appreciate your concern, but you asked me to do this, and I will. Do not presume to tell me what to say."

He held up a hand, palm out, as if asking for peace. "I apologize. I am sure you will handle the situation to the best of your ability."

They arrived in an empty field surrounded by trees. The mist hadn't yet lifted as the sun breached the horizon. Without a soul in sight, panic rose in Elinor's stomach. Might they be at the wrong field? The idea of Michael lying dead somewhere made her dizzy. She couldn't bear the thought.

Searching for some sign of life, Elinor saw only leaves swaying in the light breeze.

"To the left." Daniel pointed to a smudge of something dark moving in the fog.

The driver crossed the field, stopping several yards from the armed men.

As soon as the steps were down, Elinor alighted. She couldn't make out the faces from twenty feet due to the heavy fog, so she closed the gap.

Four men turned toward her. Two were armed. The others she assumed were their seconds.

Michael stood to her left holding a sword. He rushed toward her. "What do you think you're doing?"

"I—what am I doing? I am keeping you from making a complete ass of yourself, not to mention saving your family from certain ruin. The more interesting question, Michael, is what are you doing?"

"I am protecting your honor." He stomped his foot.

Could he really believe that? No, she was just his excuse for bad behavior. "My honor is well protected without your interference. You are no longer charged with its protection. You willingly gave up that right."

"I was not willing." He spoke softly enough that she could pretend she hadn't heard him.

She spun and faced the other duelist. "Rosferd Nash, you should be ashamed of yourself."

"Lady Elinor. Sir Michael issued the challenge." Nash was as petulant as he had been when they were children. He was a fool who thought more of frippery than anything else in life. He preferred a good neckcloth to good conversation and never spoke of anything of any interest to anyone. Not even a good gossip, he only insulted those who were already suffering and therefore surprised no one with anything he said.

Elinor raised her hand for silence. "You have been insulting me since we were children and still, you do not tire of it. Now you have nearly gotten yourself killed for your foolishness. Had I known it was you who had insulted me, I would have let Sir Michael run you through. Now get in your carriage and get out of my sight before I do the job for him."

Rosferd Nash left the dueling field at a full run. He couldn't have run faster if there were a mad dog chasing him rather than the words of a young woman.

The seconds bowed and removed themselves. "Damned inconvenient," one man said as he climbed into his phaeton.

"Well done, Elinor," Sophia whispered from behind.

Michael and Elinor stared at each other. The temperature warmed, and the fog lifted as the sun rose.

Daniel, Sophia, and Thomas backed away and waited by the carriage.

Michael swept the top of the grass with his sword. "You are not at all the woman that I thought you were."

"No. I suppose I am not." She pulled her shoulders back, ready to withstand anything he might say.

"You had no right to come here and interfere with my plans." He wouldn't meet her gaze.

"You will not kill yourself on my account, Michael. If that is truly what you want, then you shall have to find another excuse. I will not be made to live with that guilt."

He looked over her shoulder. "Is that why you came?"

"Must you have reasons?" She wanted to slap his stupid face, then kiss away the pain.

"I admit I am curious about this new Elinor. I have no idea why she does or says anything, and it intrigues me."

"A moment ago you were willing to die, and now you find something intriguing. I should think a suicidal person would find little in the world of interest. Maybe you just long for attention."

He looked away. "No, it's not that. I am nothing, Elinor. Don't you see? I am not even a man."

"No. You are a fool." She walked up behind him.

"I suppose I am, but my life is such that I have nothing to live for," he whispered.

She had to lean in to hear him. "You have a family who loves you, Michael. Your brothers would be shamed if their hero brother died in such a dishonorable way. Did you think of anyone besides yourself?"

"I thought of you." He looked up.

She met his stare. "You thought what of me. You thought that my life would be better if you killed yourself? Is that what you thought? Perhaps you thought I would find a husband if society knew that you had died rather than marry me. Do you think I would be happier if you were dead? You are the most selfish man I have ever met."

"Selfish!" He towered over her.

She held her ground, the Elinor who cowered long gone. "Yes, selfish."

"I gave up all my hopes and dreams so that you could go and have a normal life with a whole man. I wanted you more than anything in the world and worked myself ragged to give you a life you could be proud of. I took that damned last mission because I was promised a title if I succeeded. Everything I've done was for you, and yet you stand there and call me selfish."

"Did you notice how many times you said 'I' in that little speech of yours, Michael?" She was angry, but determined to keep her composure. He had abandoned her, and she couldn't forgive him for that. Their noses were practically touching as they argued. "It made no difference to me if you had money or title. I loved you. You wanted to go off for one last exciting mission. Somehow, you thought that our life together would not be entertaining enough for you. Everything you did, you did for yourself, even ending our future together. I am just glad that I learned of this flaw in your character before I made the mistake of marrying you." She turned and strode back to the carriage.

Michael resisted the urge to run after her.

The angrier she became, the more vibrant the blue of her eyes. Her eyes flashed, and her hair came loose from the chignon. Still his sweet Elinor, that lovely naïve girl, but more exciting and more intelligent than he realized. Magnificent.

He was excited by this new Elinor he hadn't known existed, stirred in a way he hadn't been in a long time. Perhaps the doctors had been wrong about the severity of his injuries and their permanence. He wouldn't be fathering any children immediately, but there was sensation, which he had not experienced in the ten weeks since his injury.

Pain shot through his neck. Searing pain that he tried to ignore as it crept up his skull and into his forehead, where it skewered him. The joy from his revelation was gone as he struggled not to collapse from the pain in his head.

Thomas walked over, allowing the carriage to leave without him. "Are you all right?"

"Perhaps I am. I do not really know yet." Michael held his head. It might split in two. As the pain ebbed, he grabbed Thomas's shoulder to keep from succumbing to a bout of vertigo.

Thomas grinned like an idiot. "That is a far cry better than you have been, Mike."

Her carriage disappeared into the mist.

"I have a bit of a headache and need to rest." Michael knelt on one knee. With his elbow resting on his thigh, he put his head in his hand.

"You are unwell." Thomas crouched next to him. "Daniel is sending the carriage back for us. I think it is unwise for you to ride your horse in your condition."

"You may be right, Tom."

They waited in silence. By the time the carriage returned, the pain had eased to a dull ache.

Chapter Four

Michael ducked behind a group of trees but kept his eye on the road, where many carriages passed. Hyde Park had become his daily stop.

"What are we doing here, Mike?" Thomas asked.

Michael had dragged Thomas out for a ride in the park under the guise of needing the exercise.

"Waiting. She and her mother always ride through the park when the weather is fine." Michael's heart pounded.

Shaking his head, Thomas whacked at the bushes with his walking stick. "Do you mean that we are waiting here to spy on Lady Elinor and her mother?"

Not sparing him a glance, Michael kept his eyes fixed so as not to miss her carriage. "It sounds quite tawdry when you put it that way."

"I believe it is disturbing without regard to my phrasing." Thomas tugged on his gloves.

"I must see her."

"Why don't you just go to her and beg her forgiveness?"

He shook his head. "It won't work. And besides, I am not

yet ready to make that commitment. I am not quite the man I used to be, Thomas."

Despite their longstanding friendship, they hadn't discussed Michael's injuries in detail. His potency was a topic he found uncomfortable. He imagined it would be the same for whomever he shared his troubles with.

Thomas cleared his throat. "I have heard the rumors, Mike. Is it certain you shall not recover?"

"I thought the damage was permanent, but lately I am not so sure the doctors are correct." No amount of circling the facts would make the topic easier to discuss.

"I realize this is a prickly subject, but I am at your disposal if you need to speak to someone." Another bruising hit on the bushes, and Thomas leaned on the stick.

Michael had no idea how to respond. Luckily, the Burkenstocks' open carriage, carrying two lovely blonde women, saved him from having to. He pointed. "There."

The carriage stopped, and Virginia spoke to a red-haired woman in an adjacent carriage. Elinor stared out the other side of the carriage, seeming to ignore the conversation, leaning her chin against her hand.

She looked sad, and his stomach twisted with shame that he had caused her pain. Then, realizing his arrogance for assuming her malaise related to him, he shook his head. She was right about him. He was selfish and arrogant, and it was a character flaw. If luck was with him, he would get an opportunity to prove to her that he could change.

When the carriage moved off, he turned to Thomas. "Thank you, Tom. That is generous, but talking will not solve this problem. I am hopeful that time really does heal all wounds. In the meantime, I must pray that Lady Elinor does not fall in love with someone else. Though if she did, I would be inclined to wish her joy. She has endured enough at my hand."

Thomas fidgeted in his saddle. "I am no gossip, Mike. However, I do have the ear of Lady Elinor's dear friend, Lady Marlton. From what I have been told, Lady Burkenstock has been working night and day to find a husband for her daughter."

Rage flashed through Michael, but he quelled it. "I should have guessed as much. The sooner she marries, the more the gossip will be controlled. Her father hates scandal of any kind."

Thomas said, "My understanding is that Lady Elinor refuses to entertain any suitors at this time. The Earl is furious with his daughter, and her mother is in tears nearly all the time since father and daughter are at odds."

"Will his lordship travel soon?" A plot tickled the back of Michael's mind.

Thomas smiled. "I do not know if Lord Malmsbury's diplomatic work will take him out of the country any time soon. Perhaps you could make some inquiries. You certainly have enough friends in high places and low ones."

"I will give it some thought. If my health does not improve, there is really no point in pursuing this." His emotions were a jumble.

The two of them walked their horses along a seldom-used path.

Thomas fidgeted with his reins, starting to speak twice and stopping. "Do you think your... 'condition'... would matter to the young lady? I don't mean to pry into your personal affairs, Mike, but I should think if she loved you, it would make little difference to her. She is innocent. She might not even notice."

She had said as much. Her father might have ended the engagement, but it was Michael who drove Elinor away. "She should have children."

"Perhaps that is not important to her. Have you discussed the matter?"

Michael pushed a hallow laugh through his sorrow. "She has informed me that she would have been happy to raise any child, and it would not need to be her own."

Thomas clapped his hands together. "See there. There are plenty of children in England who need a good home. She is a capital girl, Mike."

"Yes, she is, but I will not relegate her to a life with a man who is not whole. I am certain that eventually she would come to hate me and find her pleasure elsewhere."

"Nonsense. She doesn't seem the type."

Michael petted his horse. "Three months ago, I would not have thought she was the type of girl who would stand toe-to-toe with a man holding a sword and tell him what a fool he is. I feel I hardly know her at this point. Who is to say that in five years, when she has tired of me, she won't find pleasure with a real man?"

Fists on his hips, Thomas stared him down. "You do her a disservice speaking this way about her. She is a fine woman who loves you. It is true, she has changed since you ended your engagement. However, she has shown caring and honor. I have seen no duplicity in her character. Of course, she has been angry, but who could blame her?

"And Michael, it is none of my business, and I would not presume to tell you how to conduct your intimate affairs, but there are many ways to pleasure a woman."

Anger flared in Michael. He jerked the reins, and the horse sidestepped. "Don't you think I know that? But until I am whole and can be a real husband, I will not pursue Elinor Burkenstock. Not until I can consummate the marriage. She has been through enough at my hands. I want her to be happy. I know that in my current state, I can give her only misery."

When Elinor arrived at the Skivingtons' ball, all eyes were on her. It was the first public event she had attended since the demise of her engagement. Some staring at her looked sympathetic. After all, the match with Sir Michael had been a love match, and all of London knew that fact. Others, mostly women with daughters of marrying age, looked triumphant, as if the failure of her impending marriage somehow gave them a leg up. Those small-minded people thought of the marriage mart as a winnable competition.

Elinor did her best to ignore them all, though with little success.

"My word, Elinor," Lady Dorothea Flammel said. "I hardly recognized you."

Mother had insisted she attend, and so she was there. She held her head up. She had taken special care to look her best in a daring blue gown. Mother had wanted her to return to wearing the pale pink and white dresses of a young girl trying to catch a husband. Elinor refused and insisted on dressing in the gowns that she had purchased for after her marriage. The darker blue wasn't appropriate for an unmarried woman, but she didn't care. "Hello, Dory. You look beautiful."

Dory looked down at her pale blue dress. It was flattering, showing off her ample bosom. The fabric fell straight down from just under her breasts in the newest style from Paris. "I am outdone by far, dear Elinor. You are stunning. That dress makes me think that I should go back to wearing a corset."

Elinor appreciated Dory's attempt to amuse. "Your mother would be pleased."

Dory cocked her head and winked. "In that case, I will continue with my current fashion choices."

They laughed.

The crowd stared, and some commented in hushed tones, making the room drone.

Dory linked her arm through Elinor's. "Shall we take a turn around the room?"

Once they were away from the entry, they blended into the crowd.

"How are you, Elinor?"

"Fine," she said.

"Have you heard from Sir Michael?"

Her heart jumped as it always did at the mention of Michael. She quashed the unwanted emotions. "Not since the day of that ridiculous duel. I don't wish to hear from him. He is not the man I thought he was. He has no honor."

Dory's eyes widened. "Perhaps we should speak of something else."

Shaking away her reaction, Elinor forced a smile. "I am sorry. I'm afraid the subject of Michael Rollins puts me in a foul mood."

"Then we shall definitely talk of other things."

Virginia Burkenstock burst through the crush, dragging a man behind her. The well-dressed gentleman might have been a sack of flour the way she pulled him along.

"Mother." Elinor had never seen her in such a state of joy.

Virginia had to catch her breath before she could speak. "Oh, Elinor, thank goodness. I want you to meet the Duke of Middleton."

Elinor was mortified. Not only had Mother obviously dragged this man across a crowded ballroom, but she neglected to introduce him to Dory, who stood beside her.

She dropped into the appropriate curtsy, and the duke bowed politely.

"Lady Elinor." His eyes wrinkled at the corners, lit with

amusement, and he covered a chuckle with the clearing of his throat.

She smiled. "It is a pleasure to make your acquaintance, your grace. May I introduce you to my dear friend, Lady Dorothea Flammel."

He bowed again. "A pleasure, my lady."

Silence fell over the foursome.

Lady Burkenstock grinned and stared from one to the other.

Middleton broke the awkward silence. "Lady Elinor, may I have the honor of this dance?"

She nodded. "Thank you, your grace."

Once the dance began, he moved with smooth confidence. "Your mother is charming."

How she would hold in her mortification, she didn't know. Mother had clearly lost her mind. "Thank you. You are most kind."

Brown eyes simmering with laughter, he asked, "Has she always been so exuberant, or is this a recent development?"

Bubbling with hysteria, Elinor bit the inside of her cheek to keep control. "I suppose having an unmarried daughter who is at the center of scandal almost all the time has made her more, as you say, exuberant."

He frowned and leaned in so that only she would hear him. "I was quite sorry to hear of your misfortune, Lady Elinor. Sir Michael is a fine man."

She should have thanked him politely and changed the subject, but any mention of Michael stirred her anger. "Oh, do you know Michael Rollins?"

"Sir Michael and I were at Eton together. I was a year ahead, but we did know each other. He was a fine boy at school, and history will record him well also."

She longed to have a day where Michael did not foul her

enjoyment. Of course, it was her own fault. She should be stronger and push her emotions aside. "I apologize, your grace. I am afraid those wounds are not quite healed."

He shook his head and smoothly moved them around the dance floor. "I would not expect they could be so quickly."

"Perhaps you could explain that to my mother. She seems to think that three months is ample time to have moved on to a new fiancé."

"She is worried about you."

"I know." Elinor should be kinder about her mother.

The dance ended, and he walked her back to Dory. "Thank you, Lady Elinor, that was the most delightful dance I have had in a long time."

She curtsied. "Thank you, your grace."

"Perhaps you could save me another for later in the evening?" he asked.

"It would be my pleasure." A jolt of surprise hit her. She'd actually meant what she said.

Once he left them, Dory raised an inquiring eyebrow.

Elinor shrugged.

Michael stood on the veranda while Elinor danced with Middleton. It was a struggle to keep from rushing into the ballroom and beating Preston to a pulp. The problem was, he had no right to do anything. He didn't have any right to be watching. She should find someone else. She should be happy. Preston Knowles was a good man, and it was only a dance.

After the dance, Elinor spoke to Marcus's sister, Lady Dorothea, their heads bent together. Watching people was what Michael had been best at. Spying for the crown had made people think of him as a hero.

The blue of her gown was rich and sensuous. The gown was several shades darker than her eyes and made them seem darker and more mysterious as well. The form-fitting bodice showed every curve and was cut so low, it was a miracle her bosom was contained. Her hair shimmered in the candlelight, its golden color accentuated by tiny crystals woven throughout.

A tap on his shoulder spun him around.

Thomas shook his head. "Since when do you allow a man to sneak up behind you? I swear the entire time I was approaching, I thought you knew I was there." Thomas grinned.

"I am afraid my concentration was elsewhere." Michael looked back through the windows.

Thomas followed his gaze. "I see."

"Yes, well, I cannot seem to help myself. She occupies a good deal of my thoughts these days."

"Then why don't you go and ask her for a dance?" Thomas straightened his jacket.

"She would say no." He couldn't blame her.

Nodding, Thomas said, "It is a risk. But you have taken bigger risks, Mike."

"I really have made a muck of this, haven't I, Tom?"

"Perhaps, but I do not think it is irreversible." Thomas crossed his arms.

Michael's gut tightened. "I am not ready to take that step."

Lady Elinor looked divine in a blue gown that showed her exquisite figure. Young men surrounded her and the crowd grew to at least ten men.

Thomas pointed to them. "You may not have the luxury of time, Mike."

"I am aware of that, but I require more time to know if I can be the kind of husband she deserves." Michael couldn't have had the conversation with anyone else.

"I will repeat myself and say, I do not think the lady will

care one way or the other. I believe her feelings for you were true. She would not have obeyed her father's decree to cry off if you had been more...affectionate."

"I practically threw her out of my house. And when I succeeded, I felt so terrible I begged her forgiveness. Why would she ever want to be in my presence again? I have behaved like a coward."

"And now your plan is to stand outside ballrooms and spy on her?" Thomas adjusted his perfectly fitted jacket and picked a piece of lint from the sleeve.

Michael shook his head. "It is rather pathetic, but I cannot go in. Not yet."

Thomas slapped him on the back. "Let's get out of here. I think a stiff drink and a good game of cards is what you need."

"Whites?"

"Indeed."

"You're a good friend, Tom." Torches lit the garden, and several couples hid in the shadows. Michael looked the other way, trying not to allow longing for Elinor to ruin the remainder of the night.

They walked around the house where the carriages waited.

Once again, the conversation had been all about him. "Was there a lady in the ball that you had come to see?"

Running his fingers through his hair, Thomas took a long breath. "Not really. I always come to Skivingtons' because they have that exquisite pianoforte, and I am hopeful that someone equal to the instrument will play."

Michael laughed. "You and your fascination with music. Why don't you just play the thing yourself? You play well enough."

Thomas waved to his driver, signaling their departure. "I am an adequate musician. I practice diligently to be merely adequate. I have heard myself play for years. I truly love to hear someone with talent. I cannot help but be drawn to a really fine musician."

"When you find her, will you marry her?"

He stopped halfway into the carriage and cocked his head.

Michael understood marrying for love or money, but for music was absurd. He laughed. "I cannot believe it. You actually would marry some chit just because she could play."

"I did not say that." Tom sat. "However, it would be nice to spend my time with a wife who has the same interests. That is not so strange a notion."

Michael tugged on his cravat, happy to relax for the ride to their gentleman's club. "I suppose not, but try to see beyond the music and make sure you can actually look at the woman as well as listen to her."

They both laughed.

~

Elinor braced her hands on the stone wall and leaned out over the garden, letting the cool air clear away the strain of the crushing hot ballroom.

"Is it inappropriate for me to tell you that I find you quite charming?" Middleton asked.

"Of course it is, your grace." Elinor hated to admit that after only two dances, she liked him.

He was handsome—of that there was no doubt—tall and broad with straight, white teeth and kind eyes. He was charming and quick-witted. "Would it also be inappropriate for you to call me 'Preston'?"

"You are quite familiar with the rules that govern our society, your grace. Therefore, I can only assume that you are trying to shock me."

"And are you shocked?" He leaned in and brought the scent of warm spices with him.

"Absolutely."

A comfortable silence fell between them. She hadn't planned on liking anyone Mother introduced her to.

"What is it that troubles you, Lady Elinor?" he asked.

"Why do you think I am troubled?" She looked over the gardens, away from his analysis.

"You were one moment enjoying a lively conversation with me and in the next, the expression on your face told me that you were thinking of something unpleasant. I apologize, but it was obvious." He touched her chin, bringing her face around to look at him. "It is all right there, in your eyes."

She stepped away from his touch. "I could lie to you and tell you that you are mistaken."

"I believe that would be out of character for you." His voice grew soft and intimate.

Her all-too-familiar anger returned. "You know nothing about me, your grace. Two dances and you think you know something of my character. That is the most arrogant thing I have ever heard."

Taking a breath, he tugged on his waistcoat, then let out a long sigh. "Forgive me. You are correct, of course. I do not know you. But I do like you, Lady Elinor. That much I can tell in the first moments after meeting a person. I wish to get to know you better, and I hope you will honor me by telling me what troubles you."

It was impossible. Liking anyone wasn't in her plan, and she was tired of letting men or her parents run her life. They had made a mess of it so far. "I am in love with Sir Michael Rollins. I cannot like you or anyone else."

He nodded. "I see."

"Do you, or do you just think I am a silly girl with childish ideas about love and marriage?" Her voice was more accusatorial than she would have liked. She tried so hard to be sophisticated, when all she really wanted was to cry until no more tears would come, then cry some more.

"Let's sit for a moment, shall we?" He led her to a long bench. "I do not think that love is either silly or childish. I am certain you have been deeply hurt, and those types of wounds take time to heal. I can only ask your forgiveness if you have felt that I was dismissing your feelings for Sir Michael."

She stood, walked a step away, and slapped the stone wall enclosing the veranda. "Oh, why do you have to be so nice?"

Standing, he followed but didn't crowd. "I feel like I should apologize again, but that seems redundant at this time."

Damn, but he was funny, too. She turned toward him. "Your grace, thank you for a lovely evening. You have made this ball tolerable when it should have been excruciating, and for that, I am grateful. Good evening."

He kissed her gloved hand and bowed deeply. "Good evening, Lady Elinor."

She curtsied and walked back into the ballroom, where she found Mother and Father, and demanded to go home.

An hour later, Elinor was safely ensconced in her bedroom, waiting for the torrent of tears to come. But by some miracle, they did not. Pulling out her notebook, she went over the evening.

A nice visit with Dory
Anger over Michael
Mother's terrible behavior
Meeting the Charming Duke of Middleton
Accepting she still loved Michael
Not one single tear

She didn't love Preston Knowles, The Duke of Middleton, but to her surprise, she liked him. It would delight her mother and father if she became a duchess. Being married to a man with whom she could laugh wasn't such a bad future.

He was not Michael.

Chapter Five

Michael stepped into James Hardwig's new office. It was quite a step up from the one he'd occupied as a detective. His new title of inspector gave him prestige. His promotion was in no small part due to his quick action a year earlier when Daniel Fallon, the Earl of Marlton, had been kidnapped. Hardwig's assistance made it possible to rescue Daniel and capture his assailant.

Naturally Daniel had spoken favorably to people within politics, so much so that the director himself had offered Hardwig the position of inspector. It was a huge leap up.

"Sir Michael." Hardwig rushed across the office and shook his hand. "Thank you for accepting my invitation. I cannot tell you how much it means to me to have another opportunity to meet with you."

He liked the man well enough, but people who thought his actions during the war made him special and worthy of worship always made him uncomfortable. "Thank you, Inspector. The pleasure is mine."

"When the director told me, I was persistent about being

the one to tell you. He was stubborn, but as you can see, I won out." He rubbed his pot belly.

Michael had no clue what Harwig was on about, and the man just sat there staring at him with a ridiculously pleased look on his chubby face.

Finally, Michael had no choice but to ask. "And what was it you have the good fortune to tell me, Inspector?"

Sitting up straighter, James pushed back his thinning hair. "Right well." He picked up a piece of paper and studied it for a moment, then cleared his throat. "The Prince Regent made a promise to you, Sir Michael, which it would be a shame to renege on. You set out on a mission, and you were successful in spite of your injuries. Therefore, it is with great honor that I tell you, you shall be elevated to the rank of Duke of Kerburghe. This is a Scottish title and comes with the English title of Marques of Innis."

He must have heard wrong. Blood rushed through his ears.

Hardwig fidgeted with the paper. "Of course the prince will make it all formal, but I wanted to be the one to tell you. Did you hear me, your grace?"

The joy of earning a title wasn't what he had hoped when he'd taken the assignment. Still, he had his brothers and mother to consider. "Thank you, Inspector. I assume that there are lands attached to the title."

James's eyes narrowed. "Kerburghe is a fine piece of property in the borderlands. The Innis title is not landed."

If Elinor were still his, she would have been his duchess.

"Is something wrong, your grace? Frankly, I thought you would be more pleased. After all, you risked your life for your country and nearly lost it this last time. From what I've heard, you lost quite a lot in the past few months. I would have thought this would be some compensation. You should be happy."

"It's 'James,' isn't it?" Michael ached like a man much older than his twenty-seven years. It was too late, and the fact sent a shot to his heart far more painful than the pain from his wounds.

James came around the desk and sat in the chair next to Michael. He met his gaze with clear, honest eyes.

Michael could see why Thomas liked him so much. "Unfortunately, James, what I have lost is so much greater than anything the crown could replace, that I am a bit underwhelmed. I thought the title and lands would make me happy, but that was only possible with her in my life. Now it just seems like baggage I will happily leave to my brother or his son someday."

"Is there no possibility for reconciliation?" James leaned his elbows on his knees. The wear on his breeches showed that he took this pose often.

Michael let a modicum of hope seep into his heart. "Perhaps, if luck is on my side, I can repair the damage I have done."

James shook his head. The hair combed across his bald spot flapped to one side.

His words had apparently upset James, but Michael couldn't fathom why. "What is it?"

James looked up with sorrowful eyes. "I am a little embarrassed, your grace."

"Would you honor me by calling me Michael?"

"The honor is mine, Michael." He replaced the wayward strands of hair.

"Now what do you have to be embarrassed about?"

With a few stops and starts, James finally said, "I thought you were above all of that. But you are only human."

It was the first good laugh Michael had enjoyed in months. "I am afraid so. Sorry to disappoint you, James."

"Actually, I am rather pleased. If one's heroes are only human, then there is hope for any of us."

"You are too modest. Thomas Wheel has told me many stories of your work on the continent. You have done more than your share for this country."

James puffed up his chest and sat up straighter. "Well then, we'll make a formal notice of your elevation shortly, your grace."

Both men stood.

"Thank you, Inspector."

They shook. "It was my pleasure."

It was clear why Thomas liked James Hardwig so much. The man had a way about him. Michael bowed and left the office.

"Sorry to inconvenience you, Daniel." The light from the sconce danced along the dark woods of Daniel's study. Michael sipped fine brandy.

"Not at all." Daniel passed a glass to Thomas and Markus, who had been summoned an hour early to Fallon house. Lady Marlton was giving a dinner party, but Michael had requested the four men meet early.

"What's this all about, Mike?" Markus Flammel asked.

Thomas was the last to arrive.

It was important to him to tell them all together. He detested the idea of them hearing from the papers or through gossip. He wanted to tell them of his good fortune. Perhaps that would make him feel more joy about his prospects. The dinner party was a convenient moment, since they were all meeting at Daniel's townhouse anyway.

"I hope Lady Marlton was not too put out by my request." Michael eased his grip on the crystal glass.

"She is as curious as I, but she is American so less patient. I am afraid, unless you swear us all to secrecy, I will have to tell her what this is about no more than twelve seconds after we open those doors." Daniel grinned.

They all laughed.

"Out with it, Mike," Markus said.

Michael turned to Thomas. "I met with your friend Hardwig yesterday."

"He didn't dare to ask you to go on another mission. I'll break his neck." Thomas stood, downed his brandy, and slammed the glass down.

Markus stood as well, pointed at Michael, and paced the dark red rug. "They wouldn't dare ask you to go over to France again. That mission was to be the last. It was agreed. They can't possibly go back on their word now. And Hardwig of all people, after all we did for his career."

Daniel watched Michael with one brow raised.

It was good to have friends who cared so much. "Sit down, both of you. I am not going to France."

"What did you meet with James about, then?" Tugging on his jacket, Thomas returned to his seat.

Heart pounding, he had to draw a deep breath to steady his nerves. "I want you all to be the first to meet the Fourth Duke of Kerburghe."

"W-what?" Markus stuttered.

"It seems the third duke died without anyone to inherit. The title and that of Marques of Innis remitted to the crown. For my efforts, I was presented these titles." He surprised himself with the calm tone of his voice, because his heart pounded out of his chest.

"You're a duke?" Wide-eyed, Thomas leaned forward.

"I am afraid so," Michael said.

Thomas leaped up and grabbed him in a bear hug that staggered him. Then he laughed. "Daniel, get more brandy. We need a toast."

There was a great deal of laughter, back-slapping, and toasting. They each must have called him "your grace" a dozen times. When it was time for the rest of the guests to arrive, Michael was feeling much better and more comfortable with his new title.

A knock brought all four heads around like boys caught stealing sweets.

Finally, Daniel said, "Come in."

Smiling, Lady Marlton glided into the room. Crystals stitched into her bodice caught the light exquisitely. She looked at the brandy decanter and shook her head. "Will you all be competent this evening? If not, I certainly hope the reason for your indulgence is extraordinary."

Daniel strode to his wife and kissed her cheek. "You mean you will forgive us if we tell you what this is all about."

"Of course." She slapped his shoulder.

Daniel looked at Michael for permission. Once he had a nod, he said, "Michael is no longer a knight."

Wide-eyed, she transformed into a threatening viper. No one would want to get on the wrong side of the Countess of Marlton. "What?" Hands clenched into fists, she propped them on her hips. "How can this be?"

Michael stepped forward. These were his closest friends. On the first day of school, Thomas Wheel had been fun and outgoing. He had been the one to bring them all together with his quick wit and easy manner. It was thanks to Markus and Daniel that he and Thomas had passed all their classes. They shared a rare friendship, each one willing to risk their life for the others. "Your husband is teasing you. I am not a knight because I have been elevated."

Her dark hair hung loose around her shoulders. "Elevated to what, Michael?"

Thomas and the countess were great friends. Before Daniel proposed, Thomas had offered for her. "You can no longer call him Michael. He is too grand now. You must call him your grace."

She gasped. "A duke." She rushed forward and hugged him, then backed away a step. "They've made you a duke. Oh, Michael, that's wonderful news."

Filled with joy, he kissed her hand. "Thank you, Sophia. It is comforting when one's friends are happy with your good fortune. I suspect many will not be so generous."

"Why should anyone complain about this? You have served your country well. If you do not deserve a dukedom, then I do not know who does." She huffed.

Daniel kissed her forehead. "There are many in England who think when a title is not inherited, it should revert to the crown and that should be the end of it. Plus, if I remember correctly, there was a distant cousin who made a claim on the title of Duke of Kerburghe, but his claim was flimsy and he was a criminal of some kind. The Prince denied his claim. There will be those who will be difficult, but really, who cares? We are happy for you, Mike."

"That is all a man can hope for," Michael said, with a short bow.

~

"The Earl of Malmesbury, Lady Malmesbury, and Lady Elinor," Fenton, the Marlton butler, intoned from the Parlor door.

Sophia rushed over to greet Elinor and her parents.

"Lord and Lady Malmesbury, it is so good of you to come." Sophia was the perfect hostess. Everyone in their circle adored her and had gotten used to her American accent.

"Happy to be here, Lady Marlton." Father rubbed his bulging belly, keen that dinner party meant food would be the first indulgence.

"There are some nice canopies near the pianoforte, my lord, and I am certain Marlton will fix you a drink should you require one." Sophia knew what Malmesbury was after.

Elinor rolled her eyes so only Sophia could see.

"Capital idea." Father bounded toward the refreshments.

Mother drifted over to where Lady Daphne Collington sat. Sophia's great aunt was on the gruff side, but she was a mainstay in London society, and even those who did not like her would never admit such a thing. Those who knew her, like the Burkenstocks, admired the dowager greatly.

Lady Collington had recently started carrying a cane, which she often wielded like a sword. She pointed it at Mother. "You have not come to call in far too long, Virginia."

From across the room, Elinor couldn't hear Mother's response, but the two women sat close talking.

Elinor smiled at Sophia. "They will be occupied for hours gossiping."

"Leaving you free of your mother's matchmaking." Sophia leaned in conspiratorially.

Elinor nodded. She was in another daring gown of green. It curved around her body like a second skin, showing off more than it hid. "Mother is crazed over the interest the Duke of Middleton has taken in me. I do not know what to do with her. She is now convinced that I shall be a duchess, and she will hear nothing else."

"Do you like Middleton?" Sophia asked.

The idea made her tired. "I do."

"And that is the end of the world?" Sophia said sympathetically.

"He is kind and funny. He seems to like me a great deal, and he does not even seem to mind that I am in love with someone else."

Sophia looked up to see Michael across the room, watching them. She pulled Elinor into a corner. "You didn't tell him that."

"I did, but he seemed to understand. He sent me a note today thanking me for the dance at Skivingtons'."

"Amazing." Sophia shook her head.

"What is amazing?" Dory asked as she joined the pair.

Dory waited for the full explanation. "Perhaps this is not the place to discuss this." She too glanced over to where Michael sat with her brother Markus. "Why don't we meet at my house tomorrow for tea? Then we can have a frank discussion and see if Middleton is a possibility. Do you think you can come without your mother?"

Elinor longed for time with her friends and time away from Mother. "I shall manage. I would like a talk. I feel alone these days."

Dory took one hand and Sophia took her other. Sophia said, "You are never alone, Elinor. You shall always have the two of us, and we will all three have each other no matter what life brings."

A tear slid down Elinor's cheek. "Thank you."

Dory said, "No tears tonight. Go and calm yourself in the sitting room upstairs. We shall make your excuses."

"Good idea." She took a step toward the door.

"Don't take too long," Dory called after her.

They all three smiled, and Elinor left the room.

She pulled herself together and rejoined the party. Then she spent the rest of the evening avoiding Michael. It was easier than she would have thought. He seemed to be avoiding her as well. They were seated at opposite ends of the table during dinner. Afterwards he joined the men having brandy and smoking cigars while she sat with the ladies waiting for the cake to be served.

"I think I shall go out on the terrace for some fresh air." Elinor put down her lemonade and stood.

She let herself out, closing the door behind her. August had come, and the weather was warm, but the evening afforded a nice breeze. She walked to the low stone wall, leaned forward, closed her eyes, and breathed in the scent of roses and other assorted greenery.

With her eyes closed, she could pretend her life was as it had been four months earlier. She could imagine she was soon to be married to a man she loved and trusted, and all would be well.

She opened her eyes.

Michael stood a few feet away, watching her.

"Your grace," she said, "I did not realize I was being watched."

"I am sorry. I came out to get away from the cigar smoke. When I saw you, I didn't know what to do. You looked so peaceful, I hated to disturb you, and yet I didn't want to run away." He shrugged and winced.

"I am glad that I have a moment to congratulate you, your grace."

"Please don't call me that, Elinor." He closed the gap between them.

She couldn't bear his sorrowful tone, but she insisted on keeping her head. "Whatever would you have me call you?"

"Michael, if you please."

"I cannot." Her heart pounded. She wanted to feel nothing, but it was impossible.

Frowning, he stepped closer still. "I heard that Preston Knowles is courting you."

"We danced at a ball." London gossip was appalling.

He put his hands behind his back. "Preston and I went to school together."

"Yes, he said as much."

"You talked to Preston about me?"

"Briefly."

An awkward silence fell between them. She longed to run to him and hold him in her arms. Longed for the days when there was no awkwardness between them. They could talk or be silent for hours without feeling odd.

Michael combed his fingers through his hair. "He is a good man. I wish you every felicity."

"It was only a dance. His grace has not proposed, nor do I expect him to."

"Then he is a fool." He clenched his hand into a fist as his jaw twitched. "But he is no fool, so I am sure he will ask for your hand in no time."

"Is that what you want?" Her heart was near exploding. As hard as she tried not to care about Michael, she still loved him.

He opened his eyes wide. "What I want?"

It was all she could do to keep her temper from erupting. "Yes. It occurs to me that it would be much easier for you if I were married and no longer causing you guilt."

"Guilt?"

"You are the sort to feel guilty for our situation. I am sure you would like it if I were off of your conscience." Not the nicest thing she had ever said, but he brought it out of her.

He watched her. "May I speak frankly, Lady Elinor?" Taking her silence as consent, he continued. "I do feel guilty for what became of us. I feel guilty for going to France and risking our life together. I feel guilty for the way we fought when you came to my house on our wedding date. What I do not feel guilty for is wishing you happy. I shall love you to the end of my days, and I feel no guilt over that, either. I want you to be happy. I ruined our life together, but I sincerely hope that you will find joy in your life, Elinor."

"Michael, I—"

He held up a hand to silence her. "I hope my being here this evening was not too uncomfortable for you. Good night, Elinor." He stepped forward, took her hand, and kissed it.

She was so stunned that she couldn't say anything. Having forgotten her gloves in the parlor, she watched him kiss her hand. His lips were warm and moist on her skin. She trembled at his touch, and still she couldn't find her voice. Their eyes met and, in that moment, everything might have been fine between them. If only they could stay on this veranda, then all would be well.

But the moment passed, and he straightened, turned, and left through the garden gate.

She wanted to call out to him, to tell him she loved him still and would marry no other. But she couldn't. He hadn't renewed his wishes to marry her. He had merely released her of her own guilt. It was quite a noble thing he had done, but she kept it to herself.

In a daze, she walked back into the parlor and rejoined the ladies.

When the men arrived, Michael wasn't with them.

Chapter Six

When Elinor entered the Flammel townhouse, music from heaven filled the front hall. Elinor's heart warmed, and she told the butler she would show herself into the music room.

In spite of the fact that Dorothea's mother, the Countess Castlereagh, did not approve of her daughter's over-exuberance toward music, she did set aside a parlor for all the instruments. Dory excelled at more than six instruments, but at the pianoforte she was a miracle.

The strains drifting out of the music room filled Elinor with joy and sorrow. It touched her in ways music rarely had. When they were small and lived in the country, she would often listen without announcing herself. Often the games would have to wait until Dory was finished practicing. Many times the entire day would be spent on music. Elinor tried to accompany Dory on the harp, but by the time they were twelve years old, Dory had far exceeded Elinor in talent and was composing her own music.

Eyes closed, Elinor let the final notes wash over her.

"How long have you been standing there?" Dory asked.

"Not long enough." Sorry the music ended, Elinor walked inside.

Dory smiled. "You always were my biggest admirer."

"What was that piece you were playing?"

"I wrote it last week and have not named it yet. It's a bit sad. I am not exactly sure why I was feeling so down last week, but the music is nice." She shrugged and plucked one key before closing the pianoforte.

"I love it. If you would allow more people to hear you play your own music, you would attract many more admirers." Elinor strolled to the pianoforte and ran her hand along the golden oak inlaid. A darker wood formed a delicate vine along the edge.

Dory shrugged again and gestured for Elinor to sit. "How are you?"

"Frankly, I do not know." She flopped into the Queen Ann chair set in a small conversation group around a low table.

Sitting on the settee across from her, Dory smoothed her pale blue skirt.

Sophia rushed into the music room. Her dark hair was coming loose from its chignon, the bottom of her dress was covered in mud, and her cheeks were bright red. "I'm late!"

"Sophia, whatever happened to your dress?" Concerned that Sophia had an accident, Elinor stood.

"Is it raining?" Dory rose as well.

Sophia gave them both a look that she might use on her son, Charles if he was being particularly willful. She tossed her reticule down on the settee "No, it is not raining. I was already late because Charles fell from the third step in the main hall."

"No!" Elinor's heart leapt in her throat. "Is he hurt, poor dear?"

"He's fine. He received a small bump on his forehead for

his trouble. The nanny, and I thank the lord for her daily, is taking care of him. I believe a cooled cup of chocolate was the medicine she prescribed, and little Charlie seemed quite pleased with the prospect. I believe he is, even now, looking for other ways of injuring himself in order to receive more of the same treatment." Sophia flopped down on the settee and took a deep breath.

"Though I am pleased to hear that little Charles is recovering, that does not explain your dress, Sophia." Dory pointed to the mud.

She muttered something in Italian, her mother's native language, as she looked down at the hem of her dress. "That happened as I rushed from the house. I was not three steps from the door when I found the only puddle in all of London today and promptly splashed into it. I suppose I should have gone back inside and changed like any good Englishwoman, but as an American, I thought it better to be somewhat on schedule than fashionable. Besides, it's only the three of us."

The day Sophia Braighton came to London was a lucky day for them all. Elinor and Dory had been friends since childhood, but with Sophia their trio was complete. "Oh, Sophia. You really are a treat. I would have rushed back in and taken an additional hour in dressing all the while crying over my lost garment."

Sophia and Dory exchanged glances.

Dory said, "I think you might have done that six months ago. Now I am not at all sure what you would do. Honestly, Elinor, I have known you since I was two months old, and I am surprised by you every day."

Would she have changed today? Elinor wasn't sure. "I supposed that is true."

"I know we have not been friends as long as you and Dory.

But Elinor, I must know, were you pretending all those years?" Sophia asked.

In the essentials she was the same, at least in private she was. "Pretending? No. I behaved exactly the way that my mother wanted me to be. I thought that was what I was supposed to do. Mother always told me that smart girls don't find a husband. She said that girls who appear too intelligent are left to be old maids. She said that I must hide my wit in favor of charm. A simple girl will make the best match, she would say all the time."

"So what happened?" Sophia leaned forward and plucked a biscuit from the tray.

"I stopped caring." It was good to let some of her thoughts out. She'd kept them to herself so long, it was as if a shroud lifted off her.

Dory sat in the chair next to Elinor. "Stopped caring about what, dearest?"

A tear welled up, and she looked from Sophia to Dory and dashed it away. "I stopped caring if I married, I stopped caring about being an old maid, and I definitely stopped caring about anything my mother or father said."

"Are you happier not caring?" Dory's voice was gentle, and she took Elinor's hand.

Happy? She hadn't even had a happy thought in months. "No, but at least my anger gives me some relief."

"But you can never go back," Sophia said.

"No. I know that." It would be impossible to play the fool again.

Sophia smiled and took her other hand. "Well, Elinor Burkenstock, I liked you when you appeared foolish and cried all the time, and I like you now that you are witty and the toast of the town. Now, if you will tell us what it is you want from life, we shall set about helping you achieve it."

Elinor squeezed the hands of her two best friends and drew a deep breath. "That's the problem. I don't know."

Dory said, "Last night you said you liked Middleton."

"I do, but then I saw Michael."

Sophia cocked her head. "You mean other than at dinner?"

"He and I spoke on the veranda."

"Start at the beginning and tell us every word," Dory commanded. "No. Wait. First, tell us all about Middleton. What did you and he talk about, and what did he say in the note? Then we shall get to the new Duke of Kerburghe."

When she finished telling her friends all they wanted to know, Elinor was no more certain of herself than when she'd arrived. She wished Dory would play the pianoforte, and she could close her eyes and forget about everything.

"Mother is completely smitten with Middleton. Last night on the way home, Father said he wished he had allowed the wedding to Michael. Now that he is a duke, all Father can say is that he should have made him marry me. He even went so far as to say he could have bought us a child from some beggar on the street. The entire thing is unflattering. My father buying children and having to force someone to marry me. It's not as if I am without admirers. And it was Father who begged off, not Michael."

Dory stood and paced. "I am sorry, Elinor, but your father must be losing his mind."

"Would you be opposed to adopting a child, Elinor?" Sophia brushed out her wrinkled skirts.

"Of course not. I would love any child. I could never lie about the baby's origins, though. I could not cheat Michael's brothers out of their inheritance. You are right, Dory, my father has gone mad and my mother is not far behind. I love Michael, and while I realize I may have to marry Middleton, I shall always wish for a different life. Is that fair to Middleton?" The entire situation left her cold and alone, but wishing she could go back would not make it happen.

Dory leaned on her pianoforte. "It seems to me that if you don't wish to marry Middleton, then you don't have to. No one can force you to marry."

Elinor traced the light pink damask roses on the couch arm. "That's just it, I do not really mind the idea. It's just..."

"Michael." Dory finished her sentence.

Elinor nodded.

"Well, then that's the answer." Sophia brightened and stood.

"What do you mean?" Elinor stared from one smiling friend to the other. She felt more the fool now than before her ended engagement.

Dory clapped her hands. "You will marry The Duke of Kerburghe. We shall just have to figure out a way so that it is his idea."

"How do you propose to do that?" Sophia asked.

Elinor took a biscuit and nibbled the corner. "I am once again sounding rather desperate for a husband, and it is very degrading."

"Nonsense." Dory's enthusiasm soared, and she gestured wildly. "You are not desperate, but we shall help you marry the correct man. If, in the process, you decide that you prefer Middleton, then we can change tactics, as they say in war. And ladies, this is war. We shall have our victory." She thrust her fist in the air.

"Dorothea." Sophia giggled.

"Sorry. I got carried away."

"Indeed." It was the most fun Elinor had enjoyed in a long time. "I was beginning to think of the two men as countries rather than dukes."

Sophia cleared her throat. "I hate to put a damper on your

war-waging, but you still haven't told us how you intend to get Michael to marry Elinor."

Dory shrugged. "First we must have them meet accidentally a few times in London. But the real battle will be fought in the country, when we all go to your annual house party, Sophia."

Sophia smiled. "Shall I invite Middleton then?"

"Of course."

Both were pleased with the plan, but Elinor hated the sound of this. She walked to the window seat. "I do not like the idea of trapping Michael or any other man into marrying me. I am also not sure I like the idea of using Middleton for our purposes."

Dory crossed to her and took her hands. "He loves you, Elinor. You know he does. In fact, he told you so last night. He just needs to be reminded of what is important and what is not. Once he realizes he has made a mistake, then you can refuse him if you wish. The point is to give you the option you were not given before."

"Refuse Michael." The notion was ridiculous.

"Works wonders." When Marlton first asked for her hand, Sophia had refused.

Dory was determined, and Elinor was a tad excited to be part of one of her plots. They were always so interesting. "How will we make sure Michael sees me in London, and what of Middleton?"

Dory perched next to her in the window and lay her long finger on her chin. "Last night was a boon for us. We know he still cares for you. I will talk to my brother and see if he knows of any of his grace's engagements. As for Middleton, I am afraid he is a casualty of war."

"Dorothea, that is not kind." Elinor liked him too much to hurt him.

Dory shrugged, took a biscuit, and ate it. "You told him you were in love with someone else. He knows what he is getting into. I think we have been more than fair. And if his infatuation with you pushes our plan with Michael forward, all the better."

"You are ruthless." Excitement bubbled in Elinor's belly.

"I will check with Thomas. He may know where to find Michael and may wish to help. I'll feel him out before asking his assistance." Narrowing her eyes, Sophia fussed with her gloves.

"You will not tell Marlton?" Dory asked.

Sophia shook her head. "My husband is too honest. He would go to Michael immediately. We may need that if all else fails, but it is my experience that men prefer to think things are their own idea or that fate played a hand. They do not like to be manipulated by the women in their lives."

"Agreed." Dory clapped again before agreeing to play another of her original pieces, this time on the harp.

Chapter Seven

Elinor was ready for the theatre a full thirty minutes ahead of time. She paced her room for ten minutes, then forced herself to sit at her vanity and looked in the mirror for a full minute searching for something to fix. She stared so long, her image faded and blurred.

She daydreamed about a ball one year earlier. Michael had promised to marry her that night. He had begged her to wait for him. He had kissed her until she lost all sense, and she'd begged for more. Thinking back on that night made her sorry for her loss, but also she was ashamed of all the liberties she had allowed a man whom she thought would marry her.

Father cleared his throat.

Surprised that she hadn't heard him enter, she looked up at his reflection in the mirror. Turning, she stood and said, "Good evening, Father."

He cleared his throat again. "You are going out?"

She forced a smile. "I am to go to the theatre with Lord and Lady Marlton."

He nodded his head copiously. It was a sign that he knew of

her plans but had forgotten, and now he was overcompensating. "Yes. Fine. Marlton is an earl, after all. Don't know why he married that American, but shows good judgment on your part that you befriended her. American or not, she is a countess now."

There was no point in reminding him that she had befriended Sophia long before she married the Earl of Marlton. It was a shame that he had become so obsessed with the peerage, but it wasn't her place to comment on his faults. She planted a smile on her face and waited to find out what he wanted.

Perhaps he had forgotten why he had come. He shifted from foot to foot.

"Was there something you wanted of me, Father?"

He began the nodding again. "I have to go to Spain."

Mother must be beside herself. "When? I thought you were to remain home from now on, since you are an earl."

When she mentioned his title, he puffed up. "I have a duty to this country, Elinor. I must leave at first light. I just wanted to tell you that I think you are doing a fine job with Middleton. I am quite proud of you."

"Thank you, Father." What else could she say? Her father understood nothing, and there was no sense in enlightening him. Why waste her breath?

"I know you cared for that Rollins fellow, but this will be better. You will see." He rubbed his belly and pulled his shoulders back.

Every time she was in his company, she had to hide her annoyance with him. It was tiresome. "I am sure you are correct, Father, and that Rollins fellow is now the Duke of Kerburghe."

"Right you are. Two dukes after you." He laughed and stepped forward. The hug was awkward, and now she knew that Mother had sent him in to show his affection, something she had been doing since Elinor was a child. He hated it, and she had always known it was her mother's doing and held no genuine feeling.

When she was only three or four, the nanny foisted her into his reluctant arms. It was one of her earliest memories, a quick image, really. He had been horrified by the idea of holding his daughter. Rolf Burkenstock wanted a son. It was no secret. He wanted a boy to make into a man, not a silly girl to cost him money and give little back.

She believed he really was proud of her for attracting a duke. It would look good to have a daughter who was a duchess.

"You're a good girl, Elinor." He patted her shoulder and moved back several steps.

"Thank you. I am glad you are pleased."

"Indeed. I will return in a few weeks, and perhaps by then we can sew the whole thing up. You could be married by Christmas." He clapped his hands. Grinning and nodding, he reminded her of the apes she has seen at the carnival in the country as a child.

What a relief that her father would be out of London. Not her kindest thought, but her entire body relaxed with the knowledge that no marriage contracts would be signed during that time. It meant she might actually have the time to work on Michael, if that's what she wanted.

A burst of anger consumed her whenever she thought of her former fiancé. He had broken his promise. He couldn't be trusted. How could she ever be sure that he wouldn't betray her again?

Her friends' enthusiasm for the plot was far greater than her belief it would work.

The Marlton carriage pulled up in front of the house, and she was handed up by the footman.

Mother had opted to remain home since as a married woman and a countess, Sophia was a suitable chaperone. Virginia liked drama, and her husband's sudden departure gave her an excuse to remain above stairs for a few days.

"Are you all right, Elinor?" Sophia asked once the carriage was moving.

"Yes, fine." She looked from Sophia to the earl, then put on her best smile and reminded herself to look happy. Internally, she wasn't at all happy and would like to change her mind, if only she could make up her mind to begin with. Deciding that now wasn't the time to think of these matters, she resolved to give it a good deal of thought tomorrow.

"You look very distracted." Sophia reached across the carriage and patted Elinor's hand.

"My father just informed me that he will travel in the morning." At least it was mostly the truth.

Marlton adjusted the rose in the vase near the window. "How odd for him to take an assignment now that he is titled."

It was likely her father was tired of his life in London and ready for whatever life he had in Spain.

The theatre was crowded. Crushes of people met in the lobby. Marlton pushed through and the two ladies followed closely behind. Once they reached the Marlton box, Elinor let out the breath she'd been holding.

Dory arrived with her mother a few minutes later, but Lady Castlereagh did not remain for more than three minutes, claiming a prior engagement. It was more likely that she still hadn't gotten over the fact that a member of the peerage had stooped to marry an American of no birth.

Elinor watched the crowd roll in like a wave. She loved the theatre. It was always lively. It didn't even matter if the play was good or bad. If it was good, people would be animated and talk of the brilliance of the actor or the story. They would say how it was a triumph for the director or playwright. There would be talk of whose salon the playwright was spending time in, and that would start an entire discussion about the salons. If terrible, people would go on about how the lead man couldn't carry it off. Or they might say that the script was inadequate for the talent of the actors. In any case, there would be high emotions in the theatre, and she loved to watch as they developed.

"Sorry, what was that?" Elinor only caught the tail end of whatever Dory said.

Dory gave Elinor a sympathetic look. "I was just asking if you are nervous."

Elinor looked back at the throng of people. "No. I do not feel nervous at all."

"That's good."

"Do you know what the play is about?" Elinor asked.

"No. But word is that there will be scandal." Dory smiled with glee at the prospect.

"Oh good. There's nothing like a good scandal."

Dory looked out over the bustling theatre. "You do love all the drama, don't you?"

Elinor nodded. The heavy curtains were drawn, but she imagined elaborate sets lay behind and actors rushed around preparing for the night. Her heart beat wildly.

"Good evening, ladies," a deep voice said from behind them.

They turned to find Middleton had joined them in the box.

Making a pretty curtsy, Dory said, "How do you do, your grace?"

He was staring at Elinor, then turned to Dory. "It is a pleasure to see you again, Lady Dorothea."

Excusing herself, Dory went and sat with Sophia.

"How are you tonight, Lady Elinor?" He stepped closer.

She looked up at his handsome face, his features chiseled to perfection. Looking very fine in his crisp black evening coat and white cravat, he was perfect by London standards. He obviously liked her a great deal. For him to come and greet her publicly was a great boon to her, and all she could think was how happy Mother would be when she heard about it tomorrow. It was strange that when Middleton was near, her first thoughts were of her mother.

"I am very well, your grace. I hope you are the same."

His smile revealed those straight white teeth and made his eyes sparkle. "I am. I trust you will enjoy the play. It is getting some good reviews."

"I love the theatre. It is of little consequence if the play is good or bad. It's so distracting."

"Do you require a great deal of distraction?"

Did she? She certainly appreciated distraction. She loved to make her lists, which was a distraction of a kind. "No more than I deserve."

He laughed. "I never know what to make of you, Lady Elinor."

"Must you make something of me, your grace?"

"I think I would be foolish not to try to figure out how your mind works."

"Oh my." It was an absurd notion that anyone would care to figure her out. "That might take you some time to work out."

His smile was intoxicating, and she wasn't immune. "I shall enjoy the challenge. You are charming and beautiful."

She couldn't help the blush that crept up her neck and to her cheeks. Her pale skin made it impossible to hide. Suddenly the low-cut peach gown revealed too much, and she wished for her wrap. "You are too kind."

Out of the corner of her eye, she spied a flash of white against crisp black. Instinctively, she knew that Michael was in the theatre. His family had a box several over from the Marlton box, and even without turning her head, she could tell that he was there watching her.

The idea of using Middleton was no longer a theory, and it made her skin crawl. It was one thing to speak in conjecture about accepting a man's affection while hoping another will notice. It was quite another to actually do so. She liked Middleton. That was the problem.

He sat next to her. "Is something wrong? Did I say something that offended you?"

She forced a smile. "Of course not, your grace. It is not you."

He looked around and almost immediately spotted Kerburghe in his family's box. "I see," he said more sternly than she expected.

"I apologize, your grace." She was a terrible person, and Middleton was too good for her. There had to be a better way to find happiness.

He sighed and stood. "None needed. I shall return to my own box. I hope you enjoy the play, Lady Elinor."

"Thank you, your grace." She met his gaze.

Michael gave her a half-smile that might have held some apology in it. The lights dimmed, making it hard to be sure the expression had been real and not her imagination. What did Michael have to be sorry about?

Dory and Sophia took their places on either side of her and Daniel sat behind. The theatre darkened and the curtain opened.

Chapter Eight

Elinor let the play consume her, escaping all the men in her life.

Several houses of Mediterranean design surrounded a courtyard on the stage. A large fountain and statues dotted the courtyard. Flowers filled every available space in rapturous colors. And most impressively, every surface was draped in white gauze.

It took Elinor's breath away.

The entire audience gave a collective gasp.

Loud and raucous performers took the stage. It was a celebration. There was to be a wedding. The bride and groom were both splendidly attired in all white, their dark hair glistening in the stage lights. The families laughed and sang, showing support for the marriage.

Elinor brushed away a tear as the lovers kissed under a shimmering canopy. A great "hooray" went up from the crowd on the stage.

The orchestra played light strings, and a single flute trilled throughout the wedding.

As a sinister figure took the stage, the music changed to an oboe and clarinet, and the piano played in a flat key, darkening the mood. The man was older and the baron of the nearby lands. His anger at being thwarted by the girl was evident. He lamented over how her entire family had disrespected him and that they would pay. He sneered at the groom, who only smiled in victory.

Once he left the stage, the wedding party continued, and Elinor let out the breath she'd held.

In the next scene, the baron paid a wizard handsomely to kill the groom before the wedding night.

Elinor leaned forward, her knuckles white against the balustrade. It was not at all ladylike to show so much emotion, but she couldn't help it.

The lights came halfway up on the stage, revealing the bedroom of a small home.

The audience gasped at the audacity of the playwright to show a bed on stage.

There would be a scandal. Elinor had to sit on her hands to keep from clapping.

The wizard appeared in the doorway, and seeing the beauty of the lovers, couldn't kill the groom. Instead, he transformed the young man into a horse.

Trapped in the small house, the horse went mad and chased the wizard away. The bride collapsed in tears on the floor, and seeing her distress, the horse calmed and put his large head on her shoulder.

Married but still a maiden, she insisted on remaining with her husband regardless of his form. Together, they rode all over the country in hopes of finding the wizard who cursed them and forcing him to reverse the deed.

Tears rolled freely down Elinor's cheeks. From over her shoulder, Daniel handed her a handkerchief. She assumed

Marlton would sleep through the play, but he was riveted on the strange theatrical.

The maiden and the horse walked off the stage crying out for the wizard as the lights went down, and the theatre was one again illuminated.

Sophia and Dory used the intermission to freshen up, but Elinor remained. She didn't want to risk bumping into Michael. She laughed at herself. The entire point of coming to the theatre had been to see him, but now she wished she had stayed at home. She really needed to spend some time thinking about what it was she really wanted.

Male laughter and voices filtered from outside the box before Michael stepped through the curtain. Dressed in all black, save for the crisp white of his cravat, he had not one hair out of place. He watched her, but said nothing.

In the entrance, Thomas Wheel laughed and talked with Marlton.

She stood and curtsied.

Bowing, he took a long breath, then shuffled his feet. "I see you are well, Lady Elinor."

"Tolerably so, thank you."

"How is your mother?" he asked.

"She is lamenting my father's departure tomorrow for the continent, but otherwise she is well, thank you. Is your family well?" The more she thought of her father leaving, the better she liked the idea.

His eyes lit up. "Mother is in the country and the boys are at school. They are all thriving. I am looking forward to school break when Everett and Sheldon will come home, and I can spend some time with them."

"Good." Not a single clever remark came to mind. She looked to the other gentlemen for help, but they were engrossed in their conversation.

She sighed. "I can think of nothing more to say."

Studying her, he tipped his head. "We could comment on the weather."

Oh lord, the entire evening was a disaster. "I suppose that is an option. I could giggle and simper and you could tell me how lovely I am."

He frowned. "I meant all the things I ever said to you, Elinor. I was not merely wooing you. You are lovely and..."

She turned away. The crowd below milled about, and many watched them. "I know you did, Michael. I apologize. That was unkind of me. I do not wish to be bitter or unpleasant, but it is not easy to meet you in social events."

He took a step closer, keeping enough distance for propriety's sake, and lowered his voice. It was intimate. "You have nothing to be sorry for, Elinor. You have done nothing to deserve what I have put you through. I shall never forgive myself for taking that last assignment, so why should you? I regret that my presence gives you discomfort. I will attempt to stay out of your way, though our common friends make that difficult." He left the box.

When Dory and Sophia returned, they questioned her about the meeting, but she kept the content of the conversation to herself. Her answer was so short that neither inquired further.

The lights in the theatre dimmed. In the box Michael and Thomas shared, Michael sat forlornly staring at her.

Why couldn't she be nice? A pleasant conversation with the man she loved was all that had been required of her. She silently berated herself until the lights on the stage came up, and she could lose herself in the performance.

The maiden and the horse traveled the countryside for months. Both were worn and weary when her family found them and forced the girl to go home. She tried to explain that the horse was her love and begged to be allowed to stay with him. However, her angry father did not believe her and dragged her back home.

Her father assumed the young husband was dead and arranged a wedding between his daughter and the baron.

Thrilled because he got everything he wanted, the baron paid for an enormous wedding celebration, far fancier than the one the maiden had before.

The ceremony began with the maiden crying. The further the priest got into the ceremony, the louder the girl cried.

Hearing her wailing, the horse burst into the wedding and reared. He trampled the baron. The crowd attacked the mad horse, stabbing him repeatedly with swords and knives.

All the while, the maiden screamed in protest and tried to help her love. But all was lost as the horse crumbled onto the stage. She rushed to him and dragged the horse's head off, revealing her husband within. Declaring his love for her with his last breath, he died in her arms.

The maiden held him, vowing to never marry another.

Michael waited in the atrium to get one more glimpse of Elinor before the night was over.

Sophia and Daniel rushed her out of the theatre and into the carriage. Tears ran down her face.

Wishing he could comfort her, his gut clenched.

Many of the women shed tears over the silly play. He hadn't even wanted to attend the performance. Now he was torn between being happy that Elinor had been there and distraught over the effect his presence had on her. He didn't believe such an insipid theatrical could have caused her so much distress. He had upset her, and a wave of guilt washed over him.

"What did you think of the play?" Thomas stood next to him, avoiding the crush of humanity trying to escape the theatre.

"Terrible, of course." If he rushed for the door, he could be in his carriage and to her family townhouse in less than an hour.

"Indeed. I believe I could do with a drink after that torture. Shall we go to the club?"

It was better to leave her alone. She deserved a new life that didn't include him. She should find someone who would make her happy.

The ride to the club filled his head with a series of questions. What if he hadn't taken that last assignment? What if he had fought her father on the dissolution of their engagement? What if he had been kind to her when she risked everything to come to him on their thwarted wedding day? So many questions and all impossible to answer, because he had chased her away at every turn.

Once inside White's Gentlemen's club, Thomas ordered brandies and found a quiet corner where they could enjoy them in peace.

It wasn't to be.

A man whom Michael had never seen before approached them. The drunk and furious red-faced man stumbled to a stop and pointed a bony finger at Michael. "You are a pretender."

Michael had been in battles where men dropped at his feet. He'd seen men's limbs cleaved off. As a spy for the crown, he'd borne terrible atrocities. This man was no threat, but he gave him a thorough and leisurely looking over.

The man listed to one side before straightening. He was perhaps five feet eight or nine with thin red hair. Probably in his early thirties, but looked older because he was at least two stones overweight. His sparse hair was uncombed, his face freckled and his eyes ringed red. The jowls under his chin warbled, and he huffed and puffed in place.

"Who are you?" Michael asked.

Washed-out blue eyes bugged out their sockets and sweat trickled from his temple in spite of the fact that the temperature in the club was quite comfortable. "Who am I?"

Michael raised his eyebrow and waited for an answer.

He puffed up like a pigeon in the park. "I am Carter Roxton. I am the rightful heir to the Kerburghe Dukedom."

Now it fell into place for Michael. "Did you petition the crown?"

The man advanced a step and wobbled drunkenly. His face turned almost purple. "Do you think me a dunce? Of course I did. Months ago I went to the prince and explained my close relation to the past duke."

"And what was that relationship exactly?" Thomas grinned and sipped his drink.

It really wasn't funny.

"The Duke of Kerburghe was my father's brother's wife's cousin's uncle." There was a practiced cadence to his announcement.

Barely managing to contain his mirth, Thomas slapped his knee.

"I see," Michael said. "And the crown denied your claim?"

"I have appealed." Mr. Roxton stomped his foot and clung to the chair.

There was humor in the situation, though it was more like a bad farce. This man was rather ridiculous, but he was also drunk, so he took pity on the poor sod. "Your uncle's wife's cousin's uncle, you say."

Thomas burst into laughter.

Roxton turned his head sharply toward the laughter. The effort sent him off balance, and he toppled to the floor in an unceremonious heap.

Thomas's hysteria was not helping the awkward situation.

Michael sighed, put down his brandy glass, lifted the unconscious Roxton from the floor, and put him into a large chair. Giving Thomas an annoyed look, he once again took his seat and picked up his brandy.

The three men sat quietly. Thomas and Michael enjoyed their brandies and ordered more while Roxton was comfortably insensible throughout.

Roxton opened his eyes and shouted, "Pretender!" It took him a moment to gain focus on the two gentlemen sitting with him.

"Welcome back," Thomas said.

"I have petitioned the crown." His words slurred into one long one.

Michael placed his empty glass on the table and stood. "Then we shall see if your appeal stands up, Roxton. Good evening."

Thomas stood as well. "A pleasure to have met you, Roxton. Do stop by again." Then he followed the Duke of Kerburghe from the club.

Chapter Nine

At her writing desk, Elinor listed all Michael's attributes and all of his failings. She included reasons she should not consider Dory's quest to reunite them and also her own feelings for her ex-fiancé. She wrote how angry she was when he was near and how sad after he walked away.

"Darling, do you think the yellow or the blue for Castlereagh's ball?" Virginia stood in the doorway with a small writing book similar to Elinor's. Holding it in front of her face, she did not even look at her daughter.

Elinor closed her book of lists. "Has Father left already?"

Waving a hand, Virginia sighed. "Before dawn. I said my goodbyes last night. I will never understand why these trips he makes must always begin at such inconvenient times. It is not at all gentlemanly to rise so early."

Elinor gave a small smile. "I believe it lends to the mystery and import of the trip."

"I suppose." A tear spilled down Virginia's cheek. "What are you doing, dear?"

Elinor kept the little book closed. "Making some lists."

"Excellent. I always say it is the best way to be certain you have not forgotten anything."

"I know, Mother."

"Is there anything I can help you with?"

"No, thank you. I am just sorting through a few things."

Virginia smiled and patted her own book. "Then making lists is just the thing. I can never sort through anything without my lists."

"The blue would be lovely," Elinor said.

Virginia examined her own list with narrowed eyes. "Yes, the blue would be perfect. Thank you, dear." She swirled out of the room.

Relieved her mother hadn't asked further questions about her list-making, Elinor sighed. They both had an obsession with lists. Many people would think it silly to make so many lists about so many things, but the lists always put her frantic mind in order and gave her focus. Most days her lists were about what she needed to accomplish or buy. Then she might make a list of requests from the household staff or trimmings for her next gown. She almost always had a list of people she needed to call on.

Elinor returned to her book. There wasn't enough on either the positive side or the negative side to make a decision.

How she wished she could consult Mother about the whole messy subject. She couldn't, however. Virginia was enamored with Middleton, and nothing would sway her. She told all of her friends that her daughter was to be the next Duchess of Middleton.

Elinor rubbed her temple and tore the list out of the book. She put it next to her other list detailing Middleton's attributes and failings. She picked up the Middleton list. Most of her comments had been favorable. He was smart, kind, and exceedingly rich. He obviously did not like that she was pining for

Michael, but he had been patient thus far. He was handsome and elegant, and she liked him. Mother was thrilled with him, and Elinor liked to make her parents happy. In fact, she only had one negative comment.

I do not love Middleton, and I never will.

She put both lists together and tucked them away inside her desk.

"I am not ready to make a decision. I need to see Michael and talk to him without losing my temper, and I must spend more time getting to know Middleton." No one was there to argue, so she opened a new page and wrote those two objectives down before placing it with the other two.

Throughout the day, she would return to her room and pull out the three lists. She added to them and scratched notes in the corners.

She was to go to the park the next day with Dory and Sophia. Somehow, Sophia had knowledge of Michael being there. Her stomach fluttered. She took a deep breath. It was what she needed, more time with both men.

Summer hadn't been particularly hot, but it had been quite rainy. A sunny day was unusual and brought most of London to the park.

Michael scrutinized every vehicle, afraid with all the additional carriages he might miss seeing hers. It was undignified, but he waited behind a grouping of trees anyway.

"Are you looking for me, or do you just enjoy watching the carriages, Michael?" Elinor asked.

He was so shocked he might have lost his mind. It couldn't

be her, but he turned, and there she was a few feet away. He must have fallen from his horse, hit his head, and started dreaming.

Her pale green dress swayed in the breeze, and the sun behind her cast her in a golden glow. He held his breath, expecting her to disappear at any moment.

Thomas stood with Sophia and Dorothea Flammel. The trio pretended not to watch them.

Not a dream.

"Will you stand silent, then?" She fussed with the cord of her reticule.

"In all honesty, I thought you a vision, and if I moved, you might disappear."

She blushed and trailed her hand along the bushes. "I am no dream, Michael."

There was nothing more stunning than Elinor when embarrassed, except maybe her glorious anger. He rather liked her passion as well. "What are you doing here? Where is your mother?"

Shifting her weight, she continued to torture the fabric of her little bag. "Mother is home. I came to see you."

"Why?" He should just say something nice.

Huffing, she shook her head. "Honestly, I am not sure. I wanted to see you, to speak to you, but now that I am here, I have no idea what to say."

"I see." The awkwardness between them was his fault. He could blame no one else.

"I made a list," she said.

At least one thing hadn't changed about his sweet girl. "You and your lists, Elinor."

She frowned, plucked a leaf, and crushed it in her gloved hand. "I know you think them silly, but they help me figure things out."

"Not silly, adorable." He stepped closer, her flowery scent bringing back a hundred memories of holding her close.

She dipped her head shyly.

"What was on the list?"

"Nothing, really. I listed all the reasons I should stay away from you, and all the reasons I should not."

It was an odd place to have a rather personal conversation. Their friends stood several yards off, pretending to watch the ducks in the pond.

Michael stepped closer, and Elinor was inches away. If he reached out, he could touch her cheek, then push back the errant curl that tickled her neck. He longed to touch her, but held back. "What were the reasons why you would not wish to see me?"

Her gaze captured his. "I do not think I should tell you."

It would be so easy to get lost in the depth of her blue eyes. "Why not?"

"You will be angry with me. I do not wish to make a scene here in the park," she said.

"What if I were to promise not to lose my temper?" He loved the way tendrils of her hair escaped and flew in the breeze.

"Can you do that?" She tucked a wayward strand behind her ear.

"I will make my best effort."

Crossing her arms, she bore holes into him with her bright blue eyes.

Kissing that expression off her face was out of the question. He wanted to win her, not vex her. "I promise I will not be angry with you, Elinor, no matter what was on your list."

She turned her back to him. "I do not think you were at all fair to me when you decided to end our engagement. I was given no say in the matter. You have not been honest from the start, when I came to you on what was to be our wedding night, you were quite cruel."

"I am sorry." It wasn't enough, but what more could he say?

"You betrayed me." She turned to him.

His heart ached. "I was trying to protect you."

"Pft..." She waved her hand.

It was time for some honesty. "And I was angry."

She stared at him with one hand on her chest. "Angry with me?"

"Never." How was he going to make her understand? "I was angry over my situation. I had lost everything I ever wanted. Not to mention that my personal business was all over London, and not at all flattering."

"I don't know if I can forgive what you've done. Whenever I see you, I am filled with rage." Eyes like daggers, fists clenched at her sides, and her back as stiff as an oak, her ferocity left no doubt of the truth in her statement.

"I never meant to hurt you, Elinor. In fact, it was the one thing I swore never to do. I want you to be happy. I can accept if that happiness may be with another man, but please don't say you will never forgive me. I do not think I could bear that."

"I shall try to forgive you. That is all I can promise."

"I am grateful." He bowed. Moving closer again, he stroked her cheek with the back of his knuckles.

She leaned into his touch, and he couldn't help pulling her into his arms and breathing in her sweet scent. "My God, Elinor, you are so perfect."

He kissed her head and her ear, and when his lips touched hers, she whimpered. He released her and backed away. "I am sorry. I lost my head. I had no right."

She stared at him, her blue eyes wide.

Clearing his throat, he searched for words to keep her from running away. "May I ask what was on the list in my favor?"

She blinked a few times, and her expression blanked. Her eyes misted over. "I love you." She turned and ran back to her friends.

Still giddy from Elinor's declaration, Michael arrived home. He had heard her say that she loved him many times before and during their engagement, but in the park her words gave him hope. If only he could be sure he would be able to make her happy. A foolish notion, since no one received those kinds of assurances.

His butler opened the front door. "Mr. Rollins awaits you in your study, your grace." Dalton's gray eyes were far too serious for his age, though appropriate for his station.

"Sheldon was sent home from school?" Michael handed over his hat and gloves. His youngest brother was often in some kind of minor trouble. He was fourteen and, much like Michael, had trouble focusing on school. Father had given him a particularly severe whipping the last time he'd been sent home after playing a prank on the headmaster.

Dalton said, "It is Master Everett who has arrived in your absence, your grace."

"Everett?" He had never had any problems from Everett. Quiet and shy, he'd been a fine student who would take a first upon graduation.

Dalton confirmed with a nod and removed himself from the foyer.

In the study, Everett stood at the window, reading a book. Tall and lean, Everett was the image of Michael, albeit a far more studious version.

Everett turned and closed the book. "Your grace." He bowed.

That wouldn't do at all. "Everett, you need not call me by a title. I am still your brother before I am a duke."

Everett nodded and placed the book back on the shelf. Squirming, he pushed dark hair back from his brown eyes.

Michael sat on the couch and gestured for Everett to sit. "You were not expected for two more weeks, Everett. Then I supposed you would join Mother in the country."

"I have run into some issues that I thought might be best to discuss with you rather than with Mother." Everett ignored Michael's invitation and crossed to the chair.

"I see. Then you had best tell me about it, and we shall see what can be done."

Everett stared wide-eyed. "You are not angry?"

"Not yet. I have always found you to have a very rational countenance. I regret that our age difference has not allowed us to have the time to become closer, but I always thought that once you had grown and we were both men, that would change. You are nearly a man. Whatever has happened must be grave, but you did not run and hide from whatever the trouble is. You came home to confront me, which could not have been easy for you. I respect that. I cannot guarantee that once you enlighten me, I won't be furious, but I am not Father, Everett. I do not lose my temper without due cause."

"Yes, well, Father was drunk most of the time." Everett sounded like a man far beyond his seventeen years.

Michael should have stepped between his brothers and father long ago. He'd been too occupied with his career, and let them suffer for it. "I am quite sober, so why don't you start at the beginning and tell me what happened?"

"I need one hundred pounds," he stated flatly.

Michael raised an eyebrow. "That sounds more like the end of the story than the beginning, Everett."

"Perhaps it is." He stood and paced. Then he stopped and

faced Michael. "You should have written when you were raised to duke."

It should have occurred to him that it was big news in England, and his brothers should have heard it firsthand. "I assumed Mother would inform you and Sheldon. But perhaps you are correct. I apologize."

Arms akimbo, Everett frowned at the floor.

Michael tried to be direct but kind. "Everett, I find it is best to start at the beginning of the tale. If fear of my wrath is holding you back, I promise not to interrupt until you have said your piece. You can be assured I do not have our father's temper. I have never struck you, nor do I intend to alter that fact today."

Straightening to his full height, Everett met his gaze. "I am not afraid of you, Michael."

"I am glad to hear it."

"I just don't want you to think I am a fool."

"I could never think that. I am quite proud of you, Everett, and always have been."

"You are not making this easier." He kicked at the carpet, took a deep breath, and sat facing Michael. "I have a classmate by the name of Lemmy. His real name is Lamont Roxton."

Not another Roxton to deal with. Michael groaned.

"I have never really liked Lemmy, and I admit it was mostly because I have always thought that anyone who allowed people to call him such a foolish name must be an idiot. So I have avoided any friendship over the years."

"That seems wise." Michael was both amused and impressed by his brother's reasoning.

Everett nodded. "When you became a duke, Mother did write, and I was quite pleased for you, as was Sheldon. We spoke of it, and I think Sheldon even boasted to his friends. However, the rumors of your injury rather overwhelmed your promotion. It was all either of us could do to fend off slurs against you, and Sheldon was reprimanded twice for fighting."

"I was not aware of that." Michael's gut twisted.

"Mother was notified, but she probably didn't want to trouble you with such things."

He would make a note to speak to Mother about sharing the burdens of raising the boys. "What does any of this have to do with Roxton?"

"Lemmy began to badger me about your title. I didn't know why you had been given the dukedom, Michael. Frankly, I still don't, but I assumed you deserved it. I never once thought you might have paid for the title of duke. That is what Lemmy kept saying. He would approach me daily to say that you were a pretender. I ignored him at first, but then he started to say such things in public and this I could not tolerate. I would not have our family name disparaged. I was sure you would never buy a title."

"I appreciate your loyalty, Everett. You are correct. It was my sacrifices for the crown that earned me the title. I am not certain I deserved such a large prize, but His Highness determined it is my due. I am pleased the lands and income from them will allow you, Mother, and Sheldon to live comfortably for the rest of your lives."

Everett scoffed and fiddled with the rope trim on the edge of the seat cushion. "You had already assured that by paying off Father's debts and making the Rollins lands profitable again. I think we can allow that you deserved what you got for your trouble.

"Lemmy would not let it alone, though. He continued to badger me, and one night I was tired and we had been drinking some brandy that Ralph Skivington had pinched from his father. Lemmy pushed and pushed until I agreed to a wager." Putting the pillow aside, Everett looked at his hands.

"What was the wager?" Michael asked.

Everett's eyes shone with regret. "I bet him that I could beat him at chess, and that the Rollins' intellect was such that we could not be defeated by such a slug as him. I was angry, and I lost my head. I said you would marry Lady Elinor, proving that the rumors about you were not true and that I could beat him at chess."

Relief flooded Michael's heart that the wager hadn't been something more personal. "Can I assume that you did not win the chess match?"

"I lost miserably. I never stood a chance. Lemmy is a master at chess."

It was likely an exaggeration. "You will have to practice for next term. When you come home for the summer break, we shall play every day, and you will improve. In the meantime, I will pay your debt, Everett. I am flattered by your loyalty and proud to call you 'brother.' It could not have been easy to live with all that was happening here in London while you were cloistered away at school, never hearing from me. I promise I shall write more often to both you and Sheldon. I have been remiss, and I apologize."

"I am sorry, Michael. I should have been smarter. I should not have let Lemmy get under my skin."

"I have met young Roxton's brother, and he was quite annoying. If Lemmy is anything like him, I understand."

"Are you going to marry Lady Elinor?"

Nearly every moment of the past few months, he'd spent wondering that same thing. "I love her, but it is complicated. If she will have me, then I will marry her. Currently, the Duke of Middleton is giving me some competition, and I have made some grave mistakes with regard to her feelings. I am trying to rectify the situation."

Everett opened his mouth as if to speak, then closed it and wordlessly nodded.

Michael sat next to Everett and clapped him on the back. "Stay the night and have dinner with me. We can have a game of chess, and in the morning, I will see you back to school. Perhaps I will have a chance to see Sheldon as well. You will be home in a couple of weeks, and we will spend some time together. We can all go to the Marlton house party together. Mother will be pleased."

Everett smiled brightly and looked more boy than man. "I am really sorry, Michael, but I appreciate your understanding."

"Come, let's pester Dalton for something to eat, then we can take a ride in the park before supper."

Chapter Ten

The ride to Eton was delightful. It was warm for June, and another sunny day kept the roads fine and dry. Michael and Everett spoke of sport and classes. He hadn't spent this much time with Everett since he was home from his own school breaks.

When he was ten years old, his father had announced that he would have a sibling in a few months. Even at that young age, Michael thought it odd that Mother would give birth to another child at twenty-nine, which he considered quite old at the time. When Everett was born, he had been fascinated by the baby. When home for breaks, he would stare with amazement at how the child grew with every visit. Three years later, Tabitha brought Sheldon into the world. She was then two and thirty, and most of London was gossiping about having children at her advancing age.

He had gone to Tabitha one Christmas break after an older student had informed him that his mother would die if she continued to have more children. She cried and hugged him, but they never spoke about it again, and she did not have any more children. Michael had no idea if his plea had anything to do with the result.

By this time, he was almost fourteen. He was at Eton and doing well. Sheldon was just an infant and he'd seen one of those before. He was busy with studies and friends, and by the time his brothers were old enough to be interesting, he was grown and starting his own life. Then their father died, and there was no time for anything but cleaning up the mess left behind.

Perhaps he would have more time to get to know the boys. After Everett's confession of his debt, the two had spent the afternoon together, and in the evening played two rounds of chess. Everett was smart and easy to speak to. He was far too serious for his age, but perhaps that would work out with time and the security Michael intended to give him.

Michael vowed to make more time for his brothers, and while they were home, they would spend time with Mother as a family. With their father gone, there was no need to be cautious. No drunken rages were likely.

Eton College came into view. Its majestic halls and tall spires had stood since the 1400s, daunting and magnificent. Michael cherished his memories of his time there.

They stepped down from the carriage, and he turned to Everett. "You had best get your robe and go to class. You are likely to get some trouble for running off, but I will try to smooth it over with the headmaster."

"Thank you, Michael. See you in two weeks." He smiled and held out his hand.

Michael took it and pulled Everett in for a hug. "Now off with you."

Everett's smile brightened, and he ran toward his rooms.

~

Directed to the main hall, Michael found Sheldon confined to a small room.

At fourteen, Sheldon was tall, gangly, and in trouble again. Sheldon looked up, his bright blue eyes filled with contempt. One of them was ringed with a dark bruise. His chin was also bruised, though that one was older and greenish-yellow.

When Michael walked in, Sheldon's expression changed to something between horror and joy. He stood. "Have I been sacked?"

Michael couldn't believe how much Sheldon had grown in a few months. "No. Not yet."

"You've never been called before. I must have really done it this time." His voice trembled.

"Why don't we take a walk together, Sheldon?"

Sheldon backed up to the wall. "I am not to leave here until supper."

Michael remembered the small punishment room with only a chair and a desk. He'd hated being confined there. "I've made arrangements for your early release."

"That was nice of you." Sheldon narrowed his eyes.

"That is what brothers do for one another. I understand you have been taking a bit of guff for me lately."

He shrugged his thin shoulders and looked at the floor.

They walked out on the greens between tall buildings with arched doorways.

"You should have told me you were having some trouble, Shel."

He shrugged again. "I can take care of myself."

Michael adored Sheldon's toughness, though he regretted the reasons for it. Their father had been particularly tough on his youngest son. "I would prefer if you would stop fighting. I am a duke now. There is no need to defend me. Everything will be fine. Ignore those boys if you can."

"I do not know if I can do that, Michael. They have been saying terrible things about you. I do not even know what half of it means, but I can tell it's not right. I won't have them making a mockery of my family."

Patting Sheldon's back, Michael had to hold back a wave of emotion. "I am a lucky man to have such loyal brothers. Try not to fight. Get through the next two weeks, then you'll come home, and the four of us will have a fine summer together. Okay, Shel?"

Sheldon's face lit with pure joy. "Really? You will spend the summer with us?"

"I thought you and Mother and Everett might like to come to the Marlton house party with me, then we can go to the country house for a few weeks."

"Can we go to London as well?" He bubbled with excitement.

"I think that could be arranged for a week or two. Now, I've cleared up the mess you've been in, as well as Everett's little troubles. I have to get back to London, but I expect you to enjoy school and not show up with a shiner. You do not want to upset Mother, do you?" He pointed to his brother's black eye.

"No. I suppose not." Sheldon kicked the dirt.

"Good. I'll see you in a couple of weeks." He hugged Sheldon and ruffled his dark hair. "Go to class."

"Yes, sir." Sheldon grinned and ran off.

Late in the afternoon, Michael arrived in London.

"Your grace, Mr. Wheel awaits you in your study." Dalton took Michael's outerwear with a bow.

"My word, can't a man arrive home to an empty house now and then?"

"Apparently not, your grace." Dalton bowed again.

Michael went to his study. "Hello, Tom. I do not know whether to call you out or thank you for that little stunt yesterday."

"If I have a choice, then I choose for you to thank an old friend who was only looking out for your best interest." At least Thomas's smile was weak with apology. He plopped on the couch and crossed his feet in front of him.

"The choice is not yours." Michael sat.

Thomas fiddled with his pocket watch, replaced it, then brushed off his breeches. "How did it go with Lady Elinor?"

Seeing Elinor had been wonderful and painful. He longed for her, yet didn't deserve her. "I am not sure. She said she loves me. That's one good thing."

Thomas clapped his hands and laughed. "That's great news. Do you think she will marry you?"

"One step at a time. Let's see if I can get her to dance with me at Markus's mother's ball before I begin to speak to her about marriage." Michael refused to get worked up about his small success.

"I supposed you're right. But I heard that Middleton intends to offer for her. You may not have that much time." Thomas plucked lint from the overstuffed chair.

Michael rubbed his face. It had been a long few days, and this was not the news he wanted to hear. "I cannot do anything about that. If Elinor accepts Middleton, then I will wish her well, but I think she will stall and make sure she has satisfied her lists."

"Her lists?"

Michael waved. "It's a long story. Shall we go for dinner, Tom? If you'll wait for me to dress, we can go to the club."

"I'll wait if you'll allow me to try out that harpsichord you hide away in the library."

"Help yourself." Michael trudged up to his rooms.

Forty-five minutes later, Michael stood in the library doorway listening to Thomas play some piece of music that he should have recognized but didn't. He liked music, but admitted he was sadly uneducated. Thomas, on the other hand, was an aficionado about music in all forms and was constantly hunting for the best and brightest musicians or the perfect composition.

He could have stood there another hour listening, but Dalton interrupted. "Pardon the intrusion, your grace. A Mr. Hardwig is calling. He comes from Scotland Yard and says his business is urgent."

Thomas stopping playing. "James is here."

Michael lamented the end of the music. "Evidently."

In the study, James Hardwig stood, rocking heel-to-toe with his hands behind his back.

"Hello, James," Thomas said. "Good to see you."

Looking from Michael to Thomas, James's jaw dropped before recovering and shaking Thomas's hand. "Wasn't expecting to find you here, Wheel, but it's good to see you, too. Been too long."

"Good evening, Inspector. It's a pleasure to see you again." Michael shook James's hand.

"Your grace, I am sorry to disturb you. I thought to catch you before you went out for the evening. I have some important news, and I didn't think it should wait." He brushed the hair meant to cover his bald spot into place.

"We were just going to dinner, but we are not on a schedule. What is your news?" Michael sat and offered James a seat.

James cleared his throat. "I do not mean to be rude, Wheel, but this is personal news for his grace."

"You may feel free to speak in front of Thomas. He and I have been friends so long that secrets seem a waste of time. He always knows what I am thinking, anyway." Thomas knew everything about Michael's life. Nothing the inspector could say would be hidden from his true friends.

James nodded. "I noticed that when I first met you. You four have a rather odd way of communicating."

"We've been together since we were in short pants, James," Thomas said. "It's a bit hard to get out of the habit. Marlton, Flammel, Kerburghe, and I have been through quite a lot together."

"What was your news?" Michael asked politely.

James sat on a brown wingback chair facing Michael. "The crown has asked me to do a thorough investigation of Roxton's claims on your title."

"And what did you discover?" Michael wished he was indifferent, but he liked the idea of leaving more for his brothers and maybe even children one day. He quashed the notion.

"The claim is complete bunk as you might have guessed."

"I hear a 'but' in your tone, James," Thomas said.

James Hardwig stared at the carpet and rubbed his forehead. He ruffled his thinning hair and breathed long and steady.

Maybe he didn't know what to say. Michael looked at Thomas, who had known the inspector a long time.

Thomas waved dismissively. "Give him a moment, if you will, your grace? He is usually worth the wait."

Michael went behind the desk and adjusted a stack of papers on the corner.

Thomas flopped on the couch and crossed his feet.

Finally, Hardwig raised his head. "During my investigation,

I found some rather strange anomalies in the estate of Kerburghe."

"The title goes back several hundred years, Inspector. What kind of anomalies did you find?" Michael didn't like the sound of this. It was one thing if someone else had a prior legitimate claim on the title. He would have to live with that. He had never expected to be titled, let alone a duke, but if this was the crown backing out of their promise, he would seek justice.

"Relax, your grace. You are the Duke of Kerburghe. No one will dispute that. That is not what I meant. What I found was that someone has been playing the part since the last duke's demise. At least that's what I think."

A sinking feeling settled in Michael's gut. "What do you mean, 'playing duke?' How can that be?"

"At first I thought I must be crazy. The last Duke of Kerburghe died over a year ago. His name was Willoghby Roxton. He was ninety-four years old at his death and had never married. He left no sons and no brother who had sons who are living, and so the title returned to the crown. It's a fine holding, even though it is in Scotland. Just before this Roxton passed, his very distant nephew, one Carter Smyth, convinced the old duke to allow him to change his name to Roxton. In fact, he changed the name of his entire family: two brothers, a sister, and even his mother. I am not certain if the documents are legal. He may have forged the old man's signature. In any case, he then proceeded to Kerburghe lands and took over, saying he was the heir apparent when the duke died. He named himself as successor, taking the profits from a coal mine and good farmland and living quite well for himself."

Michael didn't know what to say. It was absurd. He laughed.

Open-mouthed, James watched him. "You think it's funny,

your grace? This cur has been stealing from you. At least, that's my supposition. I haven't any hard proof yet."

"No, it is not really funny. But we've met Roxton and frankly, he did not seem smart enough to pull this off. You have to admit it's rather clever."

"As I said, I do not have hard proof."

Thomas said, "I know you, James. If you've come up with all of this, then your evidence must be compelling. You just need proof that will stand up in court."

"What do you plan to do now?" Michael asked.

"With your permission and your help, your grace, I'd like to catch him in the act, so to speak. He's been living in Scotland, but I heard recently he took up residence in London. Bought himself a townhouse and seems very comfortable."

"With my money, I presume." Michael liked this Roxton or Smyth less and less. He'd gone from annoyance to problem in only a few hours.

"I would surmise as much." James stood and buttoned his jacket.

"What's the plan?" Thomas stood as well, looking ready to fight the next battle.

James shook his head. "My original plan won't work now. I didn't realize that you had met Roxton, umm, Smyth. Thought you could go to Scotland and surprise him. Then I could arrest him with the help of a few of my men. Now I'll have to think this through for a day or two. Do I have your permission to go to your lands, your grace?"

If Thomas trusted James, he could, too. "I trust you, Inspector. You saved the life of two of my closest friends over the years."

James blushed.

"You may act on my authority. I would appreciate being

kept apprised of what is happening, and if you need my assistance, I shall be available."

"I will let you know when I have a plan in place, your grace. I appreciate your faith in me."

"Why don't you join us for dinner, James?" Thomas plucked his gloves from the top of the desk.

James puffed up and grinned. "I would not want to intrude."

"Not at all," Michael assured him. "You would be most welcome."

Smiling, the inspector accepted, and the three left for dinner.

Chapter Eleven

Elinor entered Flammel house just as Dory glided down the stairs toward the foyer.

Lord and Lady Castlereagh greeted their guests under the elegant crystal chandelier. Maids and footmen bustled in crisp gold livery.

Elinor curtsied before her hosts. "Good evening, my lord and lady. Thank you for inviting me."

"So glad you could come, Lady Elinor. I know Dorothea will be happy you are here to hear her play." Lady Castlereagh grinned like a cat who'd caught her mouse.

Lord Castlereagh turned to Dory. "You look truly lovely, my dear." Tall and handsome, he was still a favorite among the ladies.

"Thank you, Father." She smiled, but it did not light her eyes.

"I understand you are to play for us tonight." He kissed her cheek.

"Yes, Father. Mother has made a special request." Dory dipped into a small curtsy for both her parents.

"I look forward to it, Dorothea."

Dory took Elinor's hand, and they escaped into the ballroom.

"Are you all right?" Dory asked.

"I am glad you and your mother came to an understanding about your playing."

Dory shrugged. "She made me feel guilty, so I agreed to play for twenty minutes and not a minute longer. But I was asking how *you* are, not about my family squabble."

Elinor had hoped to escape more conversation about her situation. "Fine. I was nervous earlier, but now I feel quite well."

"Why is that?"

"I took a taste of Father's brandy." She made a face. "Tasted like the devil, but it did take the edge off of my nerves."

Dory shook her head. "Don't get drunk. You must keep your wits about you. Both Michael and Middleton will be here tonight."

"Are you sure?"

Nodding, Dory patted Elinor's hand. "Middleton is already here, and he is heading this way. I wonder where Sophia is."

"They are always late," Elinor said.

As elegant as the prince himself, Middleton arrived and bowed. "Good evening, ladies. Lady Elinor, may I request the first dance?"

Her cheeks heated. Damn her fair skin. "Thank you, your grace. I would be delighted."

The music had not yet started.

He kissed her hand. "Until then."

Several other young men came by and asked for dances from both ladies.

"Kerburghe had better get here soon if he wishes to have a

dance with you. Your card is almost full already," Dorothea said.

There would always be space on her card for a dance with Michael.

When the music began, Middleton came to claim his partner. "You look beautiful, Lady Elinor."

It was a moment before the dance brought them together again. "Thank you, your grace."

On the next pass, he gazed into her eyes. "Did you enjoy the play the other night?"

"I love the theatre, and while the play itself was foolish, I think the message was quite good."

Middleton cut a fine figure, in black with a crisp white shirt and perfectly tied cravat. He cocked his head and took the hand of the next woman before coming back to Elinor. "What message are you referring to?"

"Love."

He laughed. "I am afraid I will require more instruction than that, my lady."

She accepted the next gentleman's hand and they promenaded. Would Michael have understood her? No, he'd probably hated the play. Men never understood such things. They came together for the final turn and Middleton walked her off the floor. "People should be willing to give up everything for true love."

"Do you really believe that?" His handsome face was expressionless, but his tone made her think that he found her ideas on love foolish.

"I do."

"And would you?" he asked.

Her heart skipped a beat. She was saved by the music as her next partner claimed his turn on the floor.

The night continued on and on this way. She danced with almost a dozen young men.

Eventually Lord and Lady Marlton arrived. Sophia looked flushed, so the reason for their delay must have been a pleasant one.

Still, she couldn't shake the question of whether she'd risk everything for true love. She'd thought she would, but he had rejected her, and she hadn't risked everything. She had complained but taken no real risk other than going to see him that one night. Would she give up everything for love?

Sophia's husband approached. "You look like a woman with a lot on her mind, Lady Elinor. Would you care to dance with an old married man?"

She smiled. "I would be delighted. Your advancing years are a concern, but I shall make the sacrifice."

"I am exceedingly grateful." He offered his arm and led her onto the floor.

Daniel was a fine dancer. "I have become aware that my wife has been meddling into your life lately."

Elinor smiled. "Sophia and Dory are trying to help."

"And are they helping?" he asked.

She laughed. Speaking to a man about one's love life was strange and unfamiliar. He was one of Michael's closest friends and had always been kind to her. "I don't know. I am still sad and confused. I really don't know what to do. I love Michael but I am so angry with him. I do not know if I can forgive him and even if I did, would he have me? Really it would be a disaster if I chose him and he rejected me again."

"It is a risk," Daniel admitted.

There it was. She wasn't the woman she thought she was. She'd been so afraid of embarrassment, that she hadn't followed her heart. She looked at Daniel. "Thank you, my lord."

As the music ended, he bowed. "You are flushed. Can I do anything?"

"I will just go and get some air." She turned toward the veranda.

"Shall I accompany you?"

"No. I need a moment alone."

"The veranda is likely filled with people, Lady Elinor."

The heat in the ballroom would have sent half the crowd out of doors. "I practically grew up here. I know all the best hiding places, my lord."

He nodded, and she walked away.

Elinor snuck through the library to a small private veranda. She breathed in the night air. Her situation was ridiculous. Middleton hadn't offered for her, but it seemed he was likely to. He was kind and stable. She ran over her list in her head.

"Forgive me, my lady." Middleton startled her.

"Your grace." She searched behind him through the darkened library, but he was alone.

He joined her outside. "No one saw me enter. I apologize for following you. I wonder if I might have a word?"

"It's unseemly for us to be here alone together." She said what was expected, but in truth she was too curious to know what he wanted to care about propriety. Besides, she'd been ruined before.

He nodded and stepped to the low stone wall. "I know, and I won't risk your reputation for long. I just wanted to know if my attention is a delight or a bother. Normally I can read a person, but I find myself stumped by you. Rather than cause either or both of us distress, I thought it best to just ask."

"You are not a bother, your grace. You have been wonderful company on the occasions we have met."

"Are you still in love with Kerburghe?"

Her heartbeat tripled, and she gripped the stone to steady herself.

"Don't answer. I can see that you are. However, Elinor, if you do not mind my company too terribly, I still enjoy your company very much. Who knows what the future will bring. Perhaps I can sway you in my favor."

"Why must you be so kind?"

He smiled, took her hand, and kissed it.

The crowd in the ballroom hushed as the music stopped.

Elinor pulled her hand back and left Middleton in the library as she rejoined the party.

The Countess of Castlereagh announced that her talented daughter would treat them to a rare and excellent performance on the pianoforte.

From her mother's side, Dorothea smiled dutifully, then turned into the music room, which was lined with chairs.

Everyone filed into the long hall with cream wall coverings and two fine chandeliers.

Dory sat at the pianoforte.

Middleton strode in and sat on the left side of the room.

Elinor needed space from all the men in her life. She sat in the corner, obscured by the harp.

When Dorothea Flammel put her fingers to the keys, there was a kind of magic. It was genius. She played Chopin first, and dulcet tones rang through the room, bounded, and reached a crescendo before Dory brought them back down to earth.

Each composition she played was better than the one before. The crowd applauded wildly between each. The last started softly. It was light and funny, but in the middle, a sad story found its way into the music. By the time Dory let her hands rest on her lap, half of the crowd was in tears.

Everyone applauded vigorously. Even those who knew nothing of good music could understand that they had heard something extraordinary. Many stopped to congratulate her on her accomplishments. Some people congratulated her mother, which Elinor would never understand.

The guests returned to the ballroom, where the orchestra readied to play again.

Intent on sitting with Dory for a few minutes, Elinor stayed in her fine hiding place.

Thomas Wheel waited at the far wall until everyone had gone.

Dory sat at the instrument again, but she did not play. With her head bowed, she caressed the keys. A tear fell and she wiped it off the precious ivory.

"You are magnificent," he said.

"Thank you," she replied, without looking up.

"Are you sad because they don't understand?" Thomas placed a hand on her shoulder.

Elinor should have made her presence known, but she wasn't ready to give up her solitude.

"I am sad because it was wasted." Dory looked at him and brushed her tears away.

He knelt facing her. "Not so, Lady Flammel. I heard every note. I reveled in your glory and sorrow. Your music was not wasted on me. I am humbled by your gift."

A wisp of a smile lit her face. "Thank you, Mr. Wheel. You are very kind. But if we were to be seen now with you kneeling before me, I am afraid you would have to marry me, since the gossips will insist you are proposing."

He stared at her for a long minute.

"Please get up, Mr. Wheel," she whispered.

He complied but did not move away. "The last piece was your own composition?"

"I only finished it last week. It really was not ready to be played, but I didn't think it would make a difference tonight." She stood and smoothed her skirts.

"You are too hard on yourself. It was beautiful and touching. Half the crowd was in tears when you finished." He offered his arm, and they walked toward the ballroom together.

She smiled. "Thank you."

"Thank you, Lady Dorothea. I feel I have been given a gift this evening."

"You have made this evening tolerable, Mr. Wheel. I hate performing in public."

He inclined his head, and they left.

Elinor remained in her hiding place long after they'd gone but eventually had to rejoin the party.

Feet aching, Elinor was sick of dancing with men Mother threw at her. She stepped off the veranda and walked into the garden. Eventually, she found a quiet, secluded area near the orangery.

Having been friends with Dory since they were children, she knew her way around the gardens quite well. No one ever came to the large glass building where the Earl of Castlereagh had decided to keep orange and lemon trees as if his home were Versailles. She stepped into the warm humid air. It reminded her of when she and Dorothea played in the greenhouse. If the season was right, they would eat oranges and get sticky with the juices. Sometimes they would dare each other to eat a lemon and laugh at the faces the sour taste produced.

"I cannot tell if you are happy or sad." Michael stood a few feet away, watching her.

Heart in her throat, she opened her eyes. "You scared me."

He closed the gap between them. "I am sorry. I saw you come in here, and I followed."

"I didn't even know you had arrived yet."

That guilty smile charmed her as it always did. "I admit I have been keeping out of sight, hoping to catch you alone. I really do not wish to be the focus of gossip."

"If people know you followed me into the orangery, then we shall both be the center of attention, and not at all good."

"It is worth the risk to see you."

"Was there something you wanted to say, Michael?" More curious than afraid, she stood her ground, even though he was close enough that the warm scent of him weakened her knees. It was like being a lamb stalked by a wolf.

"There are many things that I should tell you, my Elinor. But for now, I would just like to look at you. I cannot describe how beautiful you are to me." His tone was humble. "The way your lips curve and how you lick them when you're nervous."

Elinor jerked her tongue back into her mouth.

"I love your hands. They are strong, yet delicate. I always thought so. It is strange that I only noticed the rest of your strength after I'd lost you."

She folded her hands in front of her. Then, not knowing what to do with them, she pulled them behind her back and clasped them there. This motion thrust her chest forward.

Michael's eyes traveled from her arms to her breasts. "I long to touch you, to feel your perfect breasts in my hands and caress you until you cry out for more." Tears glistened in his eyes.

"Michael." She rushed into his arms.

"Oh, Elinor." He crushed her to him. "I miss you so. You should have been my wife by now. Every day I should be touching you, and every day I regret everything I have done in the past few months."

She knew she should run from him before she made another mistake that would ruin her life. Desire too great to ignore kept her in his arms. "Just hold me and be quiet."

Laughter sounded from outside.

The greenhouse butted up against the stone wall around the Castlereagh property. Potting tables and some stools had been stored in the corner. Lemon trees hid the storage. Once Michael and Elinor were behind them, they were secluded in the obscured garden light.

Michael pulled her into his arms and kissed her cheek. Then he licked her earlobe, sending a bolt through her. Trailing light kisses along her jaw to her chin, he traced alluring paths with his fingers, up and down her arms and back.

"Michael." His name came out on a sigh. Longing to express her feelings, the words wouldn't come. Desire swamped her.

His mouth covered hers, gently at first, then on a moan, his tongue touched hers. The rhythm he set intoxicated her into following his lead.

Nothing was as wonderful as wrapping her arms around Michael's shoulders and playing with the curls at his neck. Nor was any felicity as grand as his kisses or what they did to her.

Grabbing her bottom, he pulled her into him.

"Oh, Michael, I want..."

"Yes, my love, what do you want?" He was hard against her.

Since the termination of their engagement, she had formed an idea about what his malady actually was. Perhaps she had been wrong, but if not, he seemed much better. Curiosity and desire well overrode her shyness, making her bold. She rubbed him through his breeches.

Growing harder, he pressed against her hand, his breeches near bursting. He moaned. "Elinor, please."

Afraid of hurting him, she yanked her hand away. "But, I thought..."

Shadows hid his face, but his voice filled with joy. "Yes, well, it seems the doctors were wrong. I appear to be healing."

"I do not know what to say." Gasping, she caught her breath.

He scooped her up and placed her lightly on one of the tables. "Do not say anything, my love." Standing between her legs, he caressed the edge of her bodice. "Shall I stop?"

Everywhere he touched burned for more and left her moaning in answer.

Tugging the fabric, he exposed her nipple, which he covered with his mouth.

Gripping his head, she pressed him tighter to her and a squeak of surprise and delight escaped her lips. Something tightened in her stomach, and sensations flurried between her legs. Michael caressed her calf, but she was distracted by the delights of his mouth.

He paid the same attention to her other breast, and his fingers crept higher on her leg.

Only the rhythm of their tongues touching and lips melding mattered. The good-girl voice in her head tried to warn her, but she shushed the pesky droning.

He traced up her inner thigh and touched her most intimate spot.

Wanting to call for more, all she managed was an unintelligible cry as she wrapped her legs around him. "Oh. What—"

"Shhh. It's all right, Elinor. Trust me. You are so wet. I would make you mine, but it's too soon."

As he slipped a finger inside her, she clutched him tighter. Wanting something she couldn't describe, she pressed into his hand.

Rubbing her bud, he thrust quicker until the straining

ruptured into pure delight. With a demanding kiss, he muffled her cries.

Sensations rolled over and through her, and she couldn't speak. Rapture swelled and broke, and she clutched him tighter with each wave.

"My God, Elinor. I cannot wait until you are mine." He kissed her forehead.

Finally, everything settled. "You mean there is more?"

"Yes, sweet, so much more." On the sharp angles of his features, joy turned to agony and he gripped his head. Staggering, he clutched the table.

Jumping off the table, Elinor's heart raced. She wrapped her arm around his back. "What's wrong, Michael? What is it?"

"I am okay." His knees buckled, forcing him to kneel.

"You are in pain. What can I do?" Exposed and awkward, she righted her gown.

Sweat beaded on his brow, and his skin was like parchment. Vital moments earlier, he now looked near death, panting for breath. "I am afraid I am not quite healed. Would you see if you can find Thomas? I believe I shall need some help getting home."

"I will go at once." Before she could take a step, he grabbed her hand.

A few labored breaths later, he said, "Elinor."

Their eyes met, and she touched his cheek. In that moment, in that gaze, they shared their feelings. This kind of love could survive anything, even a London scandal.

Chapter Twelve

Elinor rushed from the Orangery in search of Thomas Wheel. She hoped she wouldn't have to go into the ballroom. Certain she looked thoroughly ravished, she shouldn't be seen by too many guests.

Luck was on her side. Not a hundred yards from where she left Michael, she found Sophia and Daniel strolling in the garden.

Elinor rushed to intercept them, then grabbed Daniel's jacket. "Daniel, it's Michael."

"What about him?" Frowning, Daniel kept his voice steady.

"He has collapsed in the orangery." Without waiting for reaction, she ran toward the greenhouse.

Daniel and Sophia followed close behind.

Michael perched on the edge of a chair, with his head in both hands.

"Mike, what is it?"

"I need to get home, Dan." The low tone and grating in his voice broke her heart.

She had done this to him. Somehow, their passion had caused him injury.

Nodding, Daniel helped him to his feet. "We'll go out the garden gate and take my carriage. Lady Marlton will see that your driver returns home. Lady Elinor, will you see that my wife gets home safely? I would like to remain with his grace until he is well."

"Of course," Elinor said. She longed to go with the men and take care of Michael, but it was neither appropriate nor possible.

Sophia and Elinor followed them to the garden gate.

As he turned, Michael's hair shone in the moonlight, out of sorts with his sickly pallor. "I am fine, Elinor. I just need to rest."

"Come, Elinor." Sophia tugged her elbow. "We cannot remain here." She led her toward the garden.

Elinor stopped, straightened her gown, and brushed out her skirts. "Do I look all right?"

Sophia put Elinor's curls back in place and fixed the lace at her collar. "Your color is high, but the heat of the ball can be used as an excuse."

"Then I suppose we had better return." She took a deep breath and swallowed a lump of emotion building in her chest.

"Is there anything you'd like to talk about before we return?" Sophia cocked her head.

"Perhaps at another time, Sophia. Right now my head is spinning with too many things."

With a nod, Sophia took her arm and they walked back to the house.

The moment they entered the ballroom, Tabitha Rollins appeared before them. "Lady Elinor, what a pleasure to see you again." Michael's mother smiled warmly.

Elinor dipped into a curtsy. "The pleasure is mine, my lady."

Behind her, a quadrille played and dancers clomped around the dance floor.

"Countess Marlton, you are looking as lovely as ever. Is your husband nearby? I hoped he might know where my son is."

Sophia stepped close and lowered her voice. "I am afraid that his grace, your son, was not feeling well. Marlton is seeing him home."

Eyes wide, Tabitha leaned forward. "Was it something serious?"

"I believe he had a rather bad headache. I do not think it's anything for you to worry about. Daniel just wanted to make sure Michael was well and home." Sophia had managed the account better than Elinor could have.

"I see. I will call on him tomorrow." She stepped away, then turned and touched Elinor's arm. "It was nice to see you again, my dear. I am staying with my friend, Lady Cheltingham. I would be pleased if you would call on me. It has been a long time since we had a chat."

Since it was impossible to visit Michael, perhaps she could glean his condition from his mother. Emotions brimming, Elinor couldn't take much more from an already staggering evening. "I shall call the day after tomorrow, since you will see your son tomorrow, if that would suit you, my lady."

"Lovely, I'll look forward to it." In a rustle of lavender fabric, Tabitha disappeared into the crowd.

"Come on, let's see if we can locate Dory," Sophia said.

At the edge of the ballroom, Dory and Thomas Wheel stood too close, deep in conversation. Talking about music, they were so engrossed neither noticed they were no longer alone.

"Are you enjoying the ball?" Sophia said.

Thomas stepped back. "It is quite distracting."

Sophia raised an eyebrow. "Your concert was magnificent, Dory. Don't you think so, Tom?"

"We were just discussing it."

"I am glad you enjoyed it, Sophia." Dory smiled.

"I will leave you ladies to your privacy." Thomas turned to Dory. "Thank you, Lady Dorothea, it has been a pleasure." He winked at his good friend Sophia before leaving.

"What was that all about?" Sophia asked.

Dory shrugged. "He liked my music. That is all."

"Hmmm," Sophia said.

As soon as he arrived home, Michael removed his jacket and cravat and tossed them on the chair in the corner of his study. He sprawled on the soft couch and closed his eyes.

Daniel closed the door. "Shall I pour you a drink, Mike?"

"You do not have to stay and nurse me, Dan. I only have a headache." He put his arm over his eyes. The pressure helped ease the pain.

Daniel rang for a servant and the butler appeared a moment later. "Would you get his grace a cold cloth please?"

Nodding, the butler retreated.

"I am not nursing you. I am seeing an old friend home when he is under the weather. I only thought you might need a drink of brandy. I know I do." Daniel's jacket was crisp and his cravat tied to perfection. Not one hair was out of place.

"Help yourself. None for me, though."

Ignoring him, Daniel poured two drinks, then sat in the large wingback chair across from the couch. "Drink. It might help."

Michael drank it in one swallow, then rested his head on the arm of the couch.

The door opened, and a maid arrived with a cold cloth on a silver platter.

Placing it over his eyes, he sighed with the slightest relief.

Daniel refilled both glasses. "Better?"

"A bit."

"Good. Have another drink, then tell me what has been going on." Daniel spoke softly, but it was a demand nevertheless.

The pain in his head dulled to a bearable throb, and Michael sat up. He tossed the cloth on the tray and picked up the brandy glass. "What are you talking about?"

"We have been friends a long time, Mike. I know you are exalted to the title of duke now and far outrank your lowly friend, The Earl of Marlton. However, I feel privileged."

"How so?"

"I am glad you asked." Daniel sipped his brandy, leaned back, and crossed one leg over his knee. "I know all your secrets. So, duke or not, I would like to know what is going on. Are you still pursuing Lady Elinor and, if so, why did you toss her aside to begin with?"

"I did not toss her aside!" Shouting had been a mistake. He gripped his head.

Daniel wagged his finger and tutted. "Best not to lose your temper."

After several moments, Daniel still waited for an explanation.

"Relentless." Everything that had happened to him since returning from France defied all honor. "I did not think I could be a true husband to her on account of my wounds. The indications were that I would never recover fully. All the doctors were certain the effects were permanent. I thought it only fair to release her from our contract, and her father was most adamant about it."

Putting his glass on the table, Daniel leaned forward. "What did the lady think?"

Michael drank the remainder of his brandy, reveling in the slow burn. "She said she did not care about my injury. She still wished for the marriage. Of course, she is innocent and had no idea what she was talking about. I had to release her. It was the right thing to do."

"Hmmm." Daniel had been both serene yet intense since they were boys. "What changed?"

"The doctors appear to have been wrong about my...capabilities returning."

Daniel clapped, but apologized immediately for the sharp noise that went right to Michael's head. "And the headaches?"

"A new phenomenon. When I become excited, the pain is quite leveling." Michael took the brandy decanter from the shelf, refilled both glasses, and sat back down.

With a shrug, Daniel accepted the drink and leaned back. "The pain may also be temporary."

"I hope so."

Tugging on his cravat, Daniel pulled the knot free. "What were you doing in the orangery to bring on this headache tonight?"

Every moment of his life was public domain. Elinor would be mortified, but luckily only their true friends would ever know anything. Their secrets were safe. "I have not ruined her, if that is what you are asking."

"Good. Middleton would not appreciate his wife being sullied before his wedding night."

"Middleton will never have her!" Pain shot through his skull. He gripped his throbbing head. "I will somehow repair all of this. Elinor Burkenstock will be my wife. Hell, she should already be mine. If I hadn't been such an ass and allowed myself to be talked into that damned last trip, I would be happily making love to my sweet wife every night."

Daniel lifted his glass, then cocked his head. "Then you might never have known who she really was. The events of the last few months have brought out a lot of intriguing characteristics in Miss Burkenstock. She is much more interesting now, and she has lost none of her sweetness. I rather like her more."

"She is different," Michael said. "I think of her night and day, Daniel. I can barely manage my estates. My mind is constantly preoccupied with her and how I will win her back."

"What are you going to do about these headaches?"

It was a fair question, and he wished he knew the answer. As it was, there was little to be done. "I am going to hope they are as temporary as my original malady."

"Perhaps you should discuss the matter with your physician."

Michael loathed every doctor and nurse as if they were the cause rather than the cure. "No. If not for that idiot, I might have begged Elinor to wait a few months. We could have postponed the wedding. That damned doctor acted so certain that all was lost. What a fool I was to believe him."

A wide smile spread across Daniel's face as he downed another brandy. "Do you remember the time we caught all those frogs?"

All the troubles of his adulthood fell away with the memory. "I cannot even remember why we started that."

"I do not recall either, but when Thomas found us we were covered in mud and had corralled at least two dozen creatures in a rather large bucket."

The joy of the long-ago day flooded back as if it were yesterday. "It was Thomas who decided to catch a hundred and release them into the kitchens.

"Markus was aghast when he was recruited to help us."

"He did it though. Complained the entire time, but I know he thought it was funny."

The two laughed and reminisced for hours. At dawn, Daniel left an inebriated Michael asleep and feeling no pain.

~

The Cheltingham townhouse was well-appointed, though small. Michael's mother's reasons for staying with her friend rather than her son were a mystery to Elinor, as was the reason for her invitation to tea.

"Lady Elinor Burkenstock to see you, my lady," A maid announced as she showed Elinor into the parlor.

Tabitha sat near the window with a book and a cup of tea. She looked up at the maid's announcement and smiled warmly. "Lady Elinor, please come and sit with me. Would you care for some tea? I was just about to pour myself a cup."

Elinor walked into the parlor of pink, rose, and lace and sat on the plump love seat across from Michael's mother. "Tea would be lovely."

Tabitha Rollins gracefully poured the tea.

Elinor had no idea why the older woman had invited her to visit, and she had no idea what to say. After all, it had been Elinor's father who had ended the engagement to Tabitha's son. In most cases, the mother of the groom would be furious with the bride's entire family.

Lady Rollins smiled warmly and passed a steaming cup of tea across to Elinor.

Hesitating only a moment, Elinor had a passing thought that Michael's mother might poison her in an act of revenge. She took the cup, laughing inside and thinking that she must stop reading those novels by Mrs. Radcliff. She'd become far too dramatic in her thinking.

"How have you been, my dear?"

Elinor took a sip of tea to cover her distraction. "I am well, my lady."

"I saw you a few weeks ago in the park. It was at a distance, but you were with The Countess of Marlton, and you looked put out."

After marching out on the dueling field and stopping Michael from behaving like an idiot, she had asked Sophia and Daniel to take her to the park so she could calm herself before returning home. She had stomped around Hyde Park for over an hour, soiling the bottom of her dress to the point that her maid had taken umbrage over the cleaning required to save the garment. "I did not see you, my lady. I apologize that you had to see me at such a weak moment. I am afraid I was having rather a bad morning."

Smiling, Tabitha shook her head. "Don't trouble yourself. I was merely concerned about you, my dear."

"I am well." Impossible to say more about that day, Elinor turned her attention to her tea.

"I heard Middleton has made an offer for your hand."

"I have not had the honor of such an offer from that gentleman." Lord, she hated London and its merry-go-round of rumors and gossip. *Why couldn't everyone mind their own business and leave her alone?*

"Oh. I apologize. I had heard that you were on the verge of accepting. I admit I had hoped to talk you out of such a contract."

Elinor didn't know whether to jump up in excitement or outrage. It was lovely that Tabitha liked her so much for Michael, but an offer from a duke would give her a good life. "Why should I not accept Middleton should he offer, my lady?

He seems a nice man. Is there something you would have me know about his character?"

"No. No, it's not that. Middleton is a good match for any girl. He is rich, handsome, and by all accounts, a fine gentleman."

Elinor looked questioningly at Tabitha and waited to hear more. If there was something off about Preston, she wanted to know.

"I had just hoped..."

The maid arrived and announced, "The Duke of Kerburghe to see you, my lady."

Michael's arrival put an end to any conversation about Middleton, or whatever Tabitha was about to reveal.

Michael bowed as he entered. His lungs might have burst, as he'd forgotten to exhale at the sight of Elinor visiting with Mother. She was perhaps the last person he expected to see during the social call. However, she stood before him making a curtsy and looking as shocked as he.

"Good morning, Mother. Lady Elinor."

"Michael, I had not expected you this morning." Mother's lie was accompanied by a blush.

"No?"

"I thought we had arranged for a later visit."

Michael checked his pocket watch and raised an eyebrow at Mother.

She ignored him. "You are here now, so come and have some tea. Lady Elinor and I were just having some, and a lovely chat."

"I would not wish to intrude, Mother." He teased, as they

both knew he had arrived at precisely the hour Tabitha had requested.

"Not at all," she said, and indicated the seat he should take.

"Perhaps it is time for me to take my leave," Elinor said.

"No," Tabitha shouted. "You must stay and keep Michael company. You see, I have forgotten to speak to the cook, and I must settle that now. It would be such a favor to me if you could stay and keep my son company for just a few minutes, Lady Elinor." Tabitha babbled as she retreated.

"Of course." What else could Elinor say?

"That is so good of you." Tabitha was already out the door by the time she completed the sentence.

Michael had to hold back a laugh. "I believe we have been maneuvered."

Elinor smoothed her skirts and retrieved her tea. "It would appear so. Shall I pour you some tea?"

"If you really must go, please do not feel obligated to entertain me, Elinor."

She poured him a cup of tea and handed it across the table. "Are you feeling better, your grace?" Her cheeks pinked.

It was so charming, he almost forgot to answer. "I am well, thank you."

"I was concerned."

He smiled. "You honor me."

"At the ball..."

"I wanted to apologize for my behavior in the orangery."

She put down her tea. "Apologize?"

"Yes. I took liberties I had no right to and regret causing you any discomfort."

"Discomfort?" Her eyes were wide and her back stiff.

Obviously he had said something wrong. Not sure where he had misspoken, he added, "I only meant to steal a kiss, and I am afraid I lost control of myself in my desire to give you pleasure."

She cocked her head. "So it was an accident?"

"Yes," he said in relief.

"I see." She stood and brushed out her skirts. "I think it is far past time for me to leave. I would appreciate it if you would give your mother my regrets for not saying farewell. As for you, your grace, please make an effort to stay as far away from me as possible in the future, so there shall be no more *accidents*."

Elinor strode to the door.

Michael jumped up and blocked her exit. "Elinor, I am an idiot. I have obviously led you to believe that I was not pleased with our encounter in the orangery, when just the opposite is the case. I only wanted to assure you that your feelings and wants are my main concern."

Eyes a mixture of anger and mirth, she looked up at him. She shook her head and rolled her eyes. "Oh, Michael, you are correct about only one thing today. You are an idiot."

She left the parlor, then the house.

A few minutes later, Tabitha found him sitting alone in the parlor looking confused. "Where is Lady Elinor?"

He looked up, trying to give an air of disinterest. "She had to leave. She regretted not bidding you goodbye."

Tabitha threw up her arms. "What did you say, Michael? Here I gave you the perfect opportunity to make amends with the one woman who can make you happy, and you chased her off."

"I tried to apologize."

"It obviously didn't go very well if she left." Tabitha paced the gray and blue Persian rug. "What did she say?"

He sighed. "She said that I was an idiot."

"Yes, well of course you are. Now we shall have to find

another opportunity. And quickly, before Middleton makes an offer."

Damn, why was he always chasing after Middleton? He'd made a complete mess of his life. "What have you heard? Will he offer?"

Stopping her trudge, she turned to Michael. "I had heard that he had already made one, but the young lady informed me today that such an offer is not yet on the table. You still have time. Perhaps you will do better at the Marlton house party."

"I had a thought about skipping Marltons' this year. Give Lady Elinor a break from all the gossip." Perhaps get some rest and hope his remaining maladies sorted themselves out as well.

She put her fists on her hips and stared him down. "You will do no such thing. I forbid it. I have it on good authority that Middleton is invited to the country. If you are not there to remind Elinor with whom she is in love, then he will surely propose and be accepted. He would be a fool not to, and Middleton is no fool."

"No, he is not," Michael confirmed. "Perhaps she would be better off with Preston. He's a good man. He has not hurt her in the ways that I have. He would be a good husband to Elinor."

"Oh, Michael." She touched his cheek. "You really are an idiot."

Chapter Thirteen

The front door opened before Elinor reached the top step. That never boded well. It meant the butler had been waiting on her. She sighed, stripped off her gloves, and handed them to Kendall.

"Lady Elinor, his grace, The Duke of Middleton awaits you in the blue parlor," Kendall said with a bow.

Elinor slumped, and all the air rushed out of her lungs. "Thank you, Kendall. Is my mother with his grace now?"

Kendall shook his head, causing his heavy jowls to bobble. "Her ladyship is not at home. She is expected shortly."

"I see. I shall go immediately." Her desire to rush to her room and make a new list of Michael's flaws would have to wait.

She checked her hair in the hallway mirror. Spring had given way to summer in London, and the ride home had left her patting perspiration from her cheeks. Squaring her shoulders, she entered the blue parlor. "Good afternoon, your grace."

Preston Knowles stood across the room looking out into the

garden. He was impeccably dressed in a dark blue morning coat and fawn trousers.

He turned, smiled warmly, and straightened his broad shoulders. "Good day to you, my lady. I have a very important question to ask you."

Elinor's heart leapt in her throat. Instinct told her to run, but there was no way to manage such a maneuver without being cuttingly rude. With her back plastered to the door and her hand on the doorknob, she forced a polite smile. "Oh? What question is that, your grace?"

With the sun shining in through the window highlighting his impressive form, he was breathtaking. "Why is this called the blue parlor? I have discovered only one blue chair. Everything else in the room is brown or yellow."

The air rushed back into Elinor's lungs. Her relief at not being proposed to eased every muscle. "My mother does not enjoy change, your grace."

He watched her and tipped his head to one side. "I am not sure I understand."

Releasing the door and her breath, she forced herself further into the room and sat on the large brown couch. "Of course you cannot understand. I do not understand, either. However, when my mother is asked that particular question, her response is always that she does not care for change."

He chuckled. Strangely, the sound made her feel more at ease. He had a warm smile and his eyes laughed before the sound made its way into the world. He would make a fine husband. Perhaps she shouldn't be dreading his proposal.

He had a long jaw, which she didn't particularly like, but his eyes were kind and his nose straight. All in all, he was nice to look at. "Do I have dirt on my face?"

"No, your grace. Why would you ask such a thing?"

He sat beside her. "Because you are staring at me as if I've been wrestling in the mud."

"I apologize." Heat infused her cheeks, and crept up to her hair and down her chest.

"I would be honored if you would call me 'Preston.'" He leaned in close, bringing the faint smell of vanilla and mint.

Oh, why couldn't he be horrible?

When she looked into his eyes, he smiled. There was no flutter in her stomach, which always accompanied such gazes from Michael.

The air simmered around them. He was going to kiss her.

Mother burst into the room. "Your grace, how wonderful to see you again. We are so honored by your visit. I must apologize for not being available to you when you arrived. I trust my lovely daughter has acted the lady of the house in my absence."

He stood. "She has been a delightful companion."

Virginia beamed at her daughter. "I am so glad. You know she has been raised to take care of such things. She can run a household of any size, more than one household. I expect you have several houses, your grace."

"Mother," Elinor gasped, unable to believe Mother's attempt at selling her like a prime cow to the highest bidder. She knew that her face must be nearing purple with embarrassment.

"Indeed, Lady Malmsbury."

Unhindered and oblivious to her daughter's mortification, Virginia continued, "You should never have to worry about their care, should you make my Elinor your duchess."

Elinor scurried to the other side of the room. She pretended to examine a small glass bauble on a table. She even considered pouring herself a large glass of brandy. Mother had lost control of her mouth and all sense of proper behavior. Elinor was at a loss for what to do. She couldn't scold her in front of Middleton, and so she just pretended to not hear the insane dialogue coming from the other side of the room.

But she did hear Preston. "I am fortunate to have several competent stewards who manage the bulk of my properties."

"Excellent. Still, you can never be too careful. A well-educated wife will keep the servants from robbing you blind."

Elinor couldn't help herself. She turned to get a glimpse of him and his reaction. He must be eager to rush from the house.

Her mother's back was to her, so she had a good view of his handsome profile.

Maybe he sensed her stare.

He looked at her, holding back a grin. He did not look like he was about to bolt from the room. He smiled wider. "Indeed."

Elinor couldn't take another moment of it. She crossed back to the grouping of chairs where Mother sat. "Your grace, you mentioned another appointment you are required to keep."

It was rude. She knew that, but she suspected he would be grateful for the excuse to escape her mother and likely overlook her bad manners.

The smile in his eyes made her stomach flip.

Virginia jumped up. "I didn't know we were keeping you from important business. I must apologize."

"Not at all, my lady. However, your charming daughter is correct. I must go. Thank you so much for a delightful visit." He bowed over her hand and kissed her knuckles.

Taking her hand back, she pushed down a bout of giggles. The entire scene was like something out of a novel. That is what her life had become. "Good day, your grace."

He strode out, and Elinor collapsed onto the chair.

"Elinor, I am so proud of you. You are going to be a duchess." Virginia clapped her hands, as giddy as a small girl.

Elinor put her face in her hand and laughed. "Oh Mother, you've gone mad. You really have."

"What are you talking about, Elinor? And why are you laughing? I think I should call the doctor. You seem unwell."

Pulling herself together, Elinor stopped laughing and looked at her mother.

Virginia picked up a sewing ring and hummed while she pulled her needle through the fabric.

"I am sorry, Mother. I do not know what came over me. I do not require a doctor. Perhaps I will just go and have a nap until we dine." Elinor rushed from the parlor and ran up the steps to her room. No amount of reason would make her situation less comical. Only one short year earlier she had been ruined, and now two dukes vied for her attention. Ridiculous.

She pulled out a scrap of paper. At the top she wrote:

Reasons I should love Middleton.

He is kind
He is rich
He has a good sense of humor
He has put up with her mother's antics
He seems to like me

Elinor's eyes blurred, or she could have written ten more reasons why she should love Preston Knowles. A tear smudged the word "love" at the top. Before she could stop them, a dozen tears marred the page. Liking a man who was good and kind was one thing; loving him was something else entirely. But perhaps fondness could evolve into more.

Chapter Fourteen

Since guests were arriving at different times the following day, Sophia had arranged a buffet luncheon to be served throughout the afternoon.

Michael entered the small parlor as Lady Daphne Collington exited. "Good afternoon, Lady Collington."

"Kerburghe, I am glad to see you have made a recovery."

He wasn't sure what to say. "Thank you, my lady. I am honored by your concern."

She nodded, as if his honor was to be expected. "I must go and find my friend, Virginia. She and I have much to talk about."

He bowed and watched her go.

Sophia sat at a small desk in the corner and stood as he entered. Several papers were spread across the desk and a quill and ink sat out.

He could see why Daniel was so taken with the young American. She was lovely. Her dark hair fell around her shoulders in dark ringlets. Her skin was nothing like that of an

Englishwoman. Her mother's Italian heritage gave Sophia creamy olive complexion.

"Shall I come back at a more convenient time, Lady Marlton?"

Without a proper curtsy, Sophia rushed across the room, took Michael's hands, and kissed his cheek. "My aunt interrupted my letter-writing to my brother, Anthony. Why are you so formal? I hope to always be 'Sophia' to our closest friends."

He smiled. "I thought under the circumstances, I should resort to formality."

Sophia's smile wavered. She maneuvered him over to the couch and sat. "What circumstances, Michael? Is everything all right?"

"I am afraid I have imposed on our friendship and brought my family along with me. I meant to write to make the request but my timing was poor, and I think my note shall not arrive for another day or two."

Her face brightened and she clapped her hands. "Your mother is here?"

"And my two young brothers." He should have left the boys home, but he had promised them they would attend and couldn't bear to go back on his word. Selfishly, he wanted to spend time with them and not miss out on time with Elinor in the country.

She stood. "Wonderful. I cannot wait to meet them, Michael. Have you informed the butler?"

Michael stood as she did. "Rooms have already been arranged. Your staff is quite efficient."

"Excellent. Have you had something to eat?"

"I arranged to meet my mother and brothers in thirty minutes. They are settling in. Is Anthony in London? I thought he had returned to America," he asked.

Joy bloomed on her face. "He arrived in London a few days

ago and joined my mother at my uncle's estate in Sussex. I hope they will all join us here in a few days."

"I look forward to seeing your family again. I will let you get back to your letter."

"Never mind that. Come and sit with me a while. My aunt and I were just talking about you."

How odd to imagine Lady Collington speaking of him. "Really?"

"Indeed. She was saying how happy she is that the crown has recognized your sacrifice."

The notoriety of his exploits as a soldier had been bad enough. Now all of London knew his situation, and it was extremely uncomfortable. "I appreciate her notice, Sophia."

"You know my Aunt Daphne is a particular friend of Lady Malmsbury's. She and Virginia Burkenstock have been friends a very long time."

"I was not aware of that." His stomach did a flip.

"Oh, yes."

"What are you up to, Sophia?"

"Nothing." Her cheeks pinked, and she smoothed her skirts. It was a good thing Sophia didn't take up gambling. She had more tells than anyone he'd ever seen. Her every thought was written across her pretty face.

"Something."

Cocking her head, she sat up straighter. "She just might tell her friend you would be an excellent choice for her daughter."

The butterflies in his stomach turned into snakes. "I do not think that is necessary."

She waved her hand. "My aunt always arrives a day early so she can ensure the best room, in spite of the fact that she has her own suite of rooms here at Marlton. She and I have had hours to talk, and you came up a few times. She's been impressed with the way you have handled things over the last few months. I am sure her endorsement will help sway Lady Malmsbury in your favor, or have no effect at all. There is no harm in it."

There was no hope for that, but no point in saying so. "I suppose not. I'll let you get back to your letter. I have to find my room and meet my family for the meal."

"Cook has put together a marvelous spread of food. Enjoy."

He bowed and left the room. He closed the door and turned to face Elinor's clear blue eyes. "Elinor, you've arrived."

She curtsied. "I have, your grace."

He bowed out of habit. His heart leapt into his throat, and it took him several swallows to find his voice. "I hope the journey was pleasant."

"The roads were dry." It did not light her eyes, but her smile was polite.

His palms were damp, and sweat trickled down his back. Nerves? He had traveled the continent and faced death for his country a dozen or more times, but this small blonde bundle of woman caused his stomach to churn and his tongue to tie. He laughed at himself.

"You find something funny, your grace?" She stared at him.

He bowed again. "I find it funny that I cannot speak to you without making an ass of myself. Forgive me, my lady. I shall endeavor to be more gracious in the future."

After a quick curtsy, she held up her hands and shrugged. "I am sure I have no idea what you are talking about."

He should walk away, but he wanted another moment in the dim corridor with her. He'd ruined everything, and this was all he could expect. "My family accompanied me for the house party."

She transformed from wary to delighted in an instant. She smiled and looked around the hallway as if they were going to appear at any second. "The boys are here?"

At least something he did brought her joy. "They are, and they are quite anxious to see you again."

She immediately straightened and forced her face into a calm smile of mild interest. "I look forward to it as well, your grace."

"I wish you would not use my title, Elinor."

She narrowed her eyes and opened her mouth.

From behind them, Mother bellowed her name.

She turned and, noting Mother wasn't in sight of them, she turned back. She leaned in close to him. "I do not wish this house party to be uncomfortable for either of us."

"Nor do I, Elinor." He refused to use the formal address and emphasized her name.

She frowned, curtsied, and rushed toward the sound of her mother's voice.

By the time Elinor descended from her room, other guests had arrived. Dory had traveled with Elinor and her mother, Dory's mother having refused the invitation. She claimed her schedule was already full. However, they all knew Lady Flammel had never approved of the "American who had married above her station."

Elinor cringed at what Dory must have endured to attend the house party.

Dory played the pianoforte in the conservatory. The strains filtered through the hall, and Elinor walked in that direction. The room was empty save for Dory and Thomas Wheel, who skulked in the shadows. In the dim lighting, she made him out by the light reflecting in his eyes. His focus on Dory and the music was so intense, he did not notice Elinor's arrival.

She drifted toward Dory, who was still playing with wild abandon.

Dory's eyes were closed, and the candelabra on the instrument created a glimmer in her hair and on her skin. Enraptured by the music, she swayed from side to side.

A poet could make a fine rhyme of such an expression. Elinor glanced at Thomas watching from the back of the room. *Was he such a poet?* As quiet as her approach, she was only halfway across the room when Dory's eyes popped open and she stopped playing.

"Don't stop. It was so beautiful." Elinor rushed forward.

"Handel." Dory looked at the keys and sighed.

Elinor smiled. "Yes. Something about water, isn't it?"

"*Water Music*," Dory said. "I am impressed you remembered."

"You drilled music into me for years. Something had to stick in my dunderheaded mind."

Dory shook her head and smiled. "You can save the simple talk for the masses, Elinor. I know better." She stood and trailed her hand along the keys. "Shall we join the others? They must be in the parlor by now."

Elinor nodded and the two of them walked arm-in-arm toward the door. Just before exiting, Elinor called to the corner of the room, "Would you like to escort us in, Mr. Wheel?"

Thomas moved out of the shadows and away from the wall.

Dory's eyes grew wide, and she blushed, which was unusual. Clearly, the gentleman hadn't made his presence known to her whilst she played.

"It would be my honor, ladies." He moved to join them.

Each took an arm, and the three strolled into the front parlor where the party gathered.

Thomas brought the two ladies over to their hostess and bowed deeply before leaving them.

Elinor watched him cross to the other side of the room before turning back to her friends. "Mr. Wheel seems quite taken with you, Dory."

Dory straightened, scoffing. "Nonsense, he just likes music. I assure you, that is his only interest in me."

Elinor and Sophia exchanged glances.

Elinor wasn't so sure. "If you say so, Dory."

Middleton sat next to Elinor at dinner, while Michael had been seated across the table and several places to the left.

The room was blistering and while the conversation was lively, Elinor couldn't seem to follow what was being said. Her dress pulled and pinched with perspiration.

Middleton spoke of the weather, riding, and plans to go for a ride the following day.

Her gaze wandered toward Michael.

He was engrossed in whatever his brother, Everett, told their host about life at school. It was unusual for boys of Everett and Sheldon's age to join an adult party for dinner. Sophia's American sensibilities differed, and she insisted the boys were quite old enough for such a gathering.

Elinor smiled down the table at Michael's youngest brother, Sheldon. He sat across from Daniel's sister, Cecelia, and gazed longingly at her. Obviously, he was enamored with the slightly older woman. The young lady spoke to her dinner partner, oblivious to the adoration from the other side of the table.

Sheldon looked down the table and spotted Elinor watching him. He colored deep red, then smiled brightly and waved.

"Lady Elinor," Middleton said.

"Yes, your grace?"

He lowered his voice for her ears only. "Might I have a few moments of your time tomorrow afternoon?"

She had to stifle a sigh. If he was going to propose, what would she say? "I believe we shall have a picnic on the lawn tomorrow, your grace. You shall certainly see me."

He smiled and leaned forward. His warm scent followed. "I thought to have a private moment."

In spite of the fact that it meant more complications, she liked his company and could think of no reason to deny him. *Damn.* "I see. Then I shall meet you in the gazebo before the gathering. Will that suit, your grace?"

"That would be delightful." He smiled brightly while nodding.

When the last course was served, Elinor was grateful. She put down her fork and breathed a sigh of relief. The heat was beyond bearable. "Would you excuse me, your grace?"

He rose as she did. "Are you unwell, Lady Elinor?"

"Not at all," she assured him. "It's just that I am quite warm. I shall return shortly."

"Shall I accompany you?"

She touched his sleeve, hoping the gesture would keep him in place. "No. I just need a moment for..." She trailed off, leaving him to believe nature called.

The heat of the day still lingered in the garden, but a breeze blew and it was extremely pleasant to be alone and quiet. She knew she should return to the table. The gentlemen would adjourn to the library soon, and the ladies would begin to wonder where she was. But as she stood with her eyes closed, the breeze against her skin was so delicious that she couldn't force herself to return to that heat-box.

"You look like a goddess standing there."

Her eyes snapped open. "Michael."

"I didn't mean to frighten you."

"No. I had thought I was alone. I should go." She stepped back.

He closed the distance between them and rested one hand on her shoulder. "I wish you would stay a moment. We have had little time to talk since the orangery, and what conversation we did have did not go as I'd planned."

Being near him made her want to cry but it also made her want to fall into his arms and never leave. It was ridiculous. "Do we need to talk?"

"I think we do."

She wasn't sure what to say, but she wouldn't cower like a school girl when the topic became intimate. Silence and miscommunication had gotten them to this point. "Are you still suffering from head pain?"

Wide-eyed, he cocked his head. "I don't know."

"You don't?"

A slow grin spread across his face. "It seems to only be an issue when I become intimate as we were in the orangery."

"Then you have not..."

He wrapped his arms around her and pulled her close. His kiss was warm on the crown of her head. "I have no desire to be in such a state with anyone but you, Elinor."

Her entire body quivered from his touch. Taking a deep breath, she inhaled a mixture of spices and Michael. She longed to drown in the aroma. Her body and brain battled. She pulled away "I thought all men find their pleasure where they can."

"Not all men, Elinor." He caressed her cheek with the back of his fingers.

It was time to get to the heart of things between them. "I don't trust you."

"I know." He looked at the ground.

"You broke my heart."

"I'm sorry."

"That's not good enough." Her chest ached with wanting him and knowing she should walk away and never look back.

He touched her chin and met her gaze. "I know it isn't, and I shall endeavor to prove to you that I will never hurt you again."

A tear slipped from her eye, and she dashed it away. "I do not know if that's possible, Michael."

"I have to try." The pain on his face and in his voice hurt her.

He suffered as much as she did. She feared if she spoke she might cry. After a quick nod, she went to rejoin the ladies in the parlor for cake.

Dressing for a proposal that she had no intention of accepting turned out to be quite a difficult task. By the time Elinor finally left her room and crossed the lawn, she was hopeful that Middleton had given up.

His strong handsome figure, standing in the middle of the gazebo, quashed the happy thought. He looked out over the pond. Preston Knowles was a year older than Michael, but looked younger. The sun cast shadows against his skin and strong jaw. Preston had an ease about him. There was no pall hanging over his head. He was always smiling and chatting, a moment from hearing a good story.

Her heart clenched at all Michael had endured in the service, and the toll it had taken on him.

Elinor stopped several yards from the gazebo and considered running back and locking herself in her room for the rest of the house party. She could claim an illness, and only Dory and Sophia would know the truth. Mother would be a problem, but she could handle her.

Mulling over her options, Elinor looked up and found Middleton watching her. "I wonder if you will come the rest of the way since you have made it this far," he called out.

She had no choice but to meet his gaze and complete the journey to the gazebo. "I am sorry."

"Whatever for?" He offered his arm and led her to the side facing the pond.

"I hesitated."

His smile was warm and kind. "It is not a crime."

"Hmm." At the edge of the structure, she dropped his arm and put a few feet between them.

He moved behind her, only inches separating his mouth from her ear. "May I know what you are thinking?"

The grounds at Marlton were stunning, but her mind was occupied with more serious matters. "That my mother would disagree with you."

"About hesitation?"

"Yes. She would say that when one goes, one should go with determination."

Middleton touched the loose strands of hair around her neck.

She turned sharply, and he backed up a step, as she hoped he would.

"And does the Countess of Malmsbury always arrive in such a state?"

Elinor laughed. "Almost never."

He grinned and made way for her to precede him to the bench.

"You have a way of always putting me at ease, your grace." She sat.

"I would be honored if you would call me 'Preston.' Or 'Pres,' if you prefer."

"That is very kind."

Middleton paced, and it was the first time she had seen him looking troubled. He clasped his hands behind his back and faced her. "I realize that you have interests elsewhere, Elinor. I cannot say that I'm happy about that, but I understand, and there is nothing to be done. I would like to offer for your hand, but will not do so until I have your assurance that this is something you also wish. I do not want you to marry me because your parents forced the match. I am sure they would if I brought my contract directly to them. I am fond of you, and I believe you perhaps like me to some degree. While this is no indication of a grand passion, I think it is a good start and bodes well for a comfortable and happy life together.

"If you were my wife, I can assure you that you would always be treated with respect and you would, of course, be well cared for. You would want for nothing and would live by standards much higher than those you were raised with."

Elinor's heart pounded, and she had to catch her breath. *Had he just insulted her father?*

Her thoughts must have flashed across her face, for he addressed her concern. "I am certain your father has always provided for you amply, but this cannot compare to what my level of wealth can provide. I am exceedingly rich." Middleton took a deep breath and looked down. "My word, but I sound like an ass."

Elinor wished she didn't like him so much. It would make what she had to do so much easier. Preston Knowles was a fine catch and wanted to marry her. A large weight settled on her shoulders. "Is that it?"

His back straight and, wide-eyed, he looked about to laugh. "Except to say that I think it would be best if you did not answer me now. I realize that you have a great deal to think about. I wanted you to know my intentions at the start, and now you may have as much time as you need to make a decision."

"That is very kind of you." It sounded like a business dealing.

He sat next to her and took her hand from her lap. "You understand that I am proposing, don't you?"

The giggle that escaped was an accident, but the entire thing, her entire life, had become a tragic comedy and she couldn't help it. "You think we would be a good match because you are fond of me, and I seem to like you. You see, your grace, I heard you clearly."

He groaned and dropped his head in his hands. "I have really botched this, haven't I?"

She patted his arm. "Well, it was not the most romantic proposal a girl might gain during a given season."

"I apologize."

"It was well thought-out, though. And it could not come from a more worthy gentleman. I thank you very much, Preston. I am exceedingly flattered by your offer." It was the truth. If she had never met Michael Rollins, she would be jumping for joy at Preston's proposal no matter how unromantic.

He took her hand and met her gaze. "Then you will consider being my wife, Elinor?"

She wouldn't have thought her answer was important to him. He was a duke and could gain the hand of almost any young lady of the ton, but he really did wish to marry her. "I will think about all you have said, Preston, and I will give you an answer soon."

His expression relaxed, and the smile returned to his eyes. Lifting her hand to his lips, he kissed her gently.

"Thank you. Shall we join the picnic before we are too badly missed?"

Michael watched from the shadow of the line of trees. He couldn't hear what was said, but he imagined that he was in trouble. When Middleton sat and dropped his head in despair, elation shot through him. Not gentlemanly, but he hoped Elinor had refused Middleton. Then she touched her suitor's hand, and he kissed hers.

Michael neared his breaking point. He was tempted to rush out of hiding and challenge Middleton to a duel, but he held his position. If Preston was what Elinor wanted, then Michael would have to learn to live with her decision. Though, he had no idea how he would manage the task. He watched as they left the privacy of the gazebo and walked together toward the gathering on the lawn near the pond.

The pond was large and fed by a creek, which in turn led to a larger river that ran through the Marlton property. The river brought him back to his school days, when he would go home with Daniel rather than face his drunken father. As boys, they'd loved the spot where the creek met the pond.

He sought to be alone, but when he approached the place where he and his friends had gathered as boys, he heard voices. His brothers had found the best spot on the pond. "What on earth are the two of you up to? You are supposed to be picnicking."

Everett colored, but Sheldon spoke up. "We could take no more adult talk of nothing, Mike. Really, is that what we have to look forward to, sitting around eating and talking of the weather?"

The description was perfect. Michael laughed. "I am afraid

so, Shel. Once you reach the age of majority, you will have to learn to speak of things of little or no importance in order to be accepted into society."

"Dash that," Sheldon said. "I had better join the army. I do not think I could take a lifetime of such rubbish."

Michael frowned. "The army is a very hard life, and one from which I had hoped my fortune would save you."

Everett said, "But you were in the service, Mike. You are a hero. We heard of little else at school before your injury."

Sitting on the bank of the pond, Michael took off his boots and let his toes dangle in the cool water. "I had Father buy my commission so that I could stay away from his embarrassing behavior. I could not stand to watch him spend every penny that our grandfather had made over the years. He let the house go into disrepair, and when I commented or offered advice, it would send him into a rage.

"As your guardian, I would like to think that the two of you do not have that same anxiety. I hope that you know that I shall never be publicly drunk or take to the whorehouses."

"Of course, Mike," Everett said. "But do you regret your choice?"

The river flowed quietly, and he watched it for a few moments, listening to its soothing sound. "I have no regrets, save for my final mission. It was foolish, with so much to lose, to risk my life. And even though my wounds appear to be healing, I hurt the person who means the most to me, and I do not know if the damage can be repaired."

"She'll come around." Sheldon sounded like a wise old man rather than a boy.

Michael smiled. "What makes you think so?"

Sheldon shrugged. "I see the way she looks at you when she knows you do not see her. She loves you still."

"Shel, you really should mind your own business," Everett warned.

He wished he hadn't let so many years go by without seeing his brothers. He pointed up the creek. "I'll bet you that I can beat you both swimming up river to that old oak."

The two younger boys took one look at each other and began stripping off their clothes. Sheldon was the first in the water, followed closely by Michael. Everett took longer, as his concern for the condition of his clothes required him to take more care. Still, he gave Michael a good run and succeeded in a second-place finish.

The following hours were spent splashing around in a way that the three of them had never done together.

Chapter Fifteen

Something was wrong.

Elinor had gone to bed early, claiming a headache. Now the fire dwindled to ash, and she wasn't alone in the room. She felt eyes on her. She rolled over. A man sat in one of two large chairs by the hearth.

"Michael?"

"How could you be sure it was not Middleton?" He faced the dark fireplace.

She took her wrap from the end of the bed, put it on, and walked toward him. "He would never do something so inappropriate."

Laughing, he nodded. "That's true, I suppose."

"What are you doing here, Michael?"

He looked at her now. The wildness in his eyes reminded her of the man he'd been a year earlier when he'd courted her, but the joy hadn't returned to his gaze. "Have you accepted an offer from Middleton?"

"That is none of your business."

He stooped forward and added a log to the fire. With a few

pokes of the iron, the log caught and firelight filled the room. "He asked you to marry him, didn't he?"

"He did, but I do not know what business it is of yours. You should not be here, Michael." It would have been better if she managed some venom, rather than sounding as if she wanted him there.

"Did you agree?"

"Not yet."

"But you're considering it." His voice stung with anger.

Why did he always find the thing that would enrage her? "Why should I not consider a gentleman of good standing? A duke, for that matter. He is smart, kind, and seems to like me quite a lot."

The light in his eyes dimmed. "Of course, you are right. Preston is a good man with a lot of money and power. As his wife, you would be quite comfortable. So why have you not accepted his offer, Elinor?"

She turned her back on him. "You know perfectly well why not."

He came up behind her and pressed his body to hers. "Tell me, Elinor. Tell me why you haven't said yes to Middleton."

"Don't, Michael." She should slap him. She should run away, but he was an addiction she never wanted to break.

His hands rested on her shoulders, soothing the muscles she hadn't realized were tight.

She leaned back against his strong chest, reveling in his touch. Loving the feel of him.

"Don't ask you, or don't touch you?" He kissed her collarbone and up the side of her soft neck.

"Don't ask." Longing for his touch, she tilted her head to the side.

"I must know. Will you accept his offer?" Urgency rang in his words.

She turned the tables. "Why does it matter to you, Michael?"

"You know why."

"Tell me." Even as her mind screamed for her to break away, her body betrayed her. She couldn't keep her legs under her and leaned further into his strength.

His mouth was behind her ear, his warm breath on her neck, and just the slightest touch of his lips on the sensitive skin there.

"Because I love you, Elinor. I have always loved you, and I will always love you. You are my entire reason for living. I cannot imagine myself in a world where you are married to another man." Love and rage echoed in his words.

She should have been afraid, but she wasn't. He would never harm her physically, but emotionally this man could destroy her. Pulling away, she turned to face him. "How do I know you won't abandon me again? Twice you have left me to be the fool, both publicly and privately. Twice you have deserted me for the easy road."

Elinor still harbored the old anxiety relating to his disappearance. When caught in a scandal, he had fled London, leaving her to suffer the gossips alone. He had returned weeks later with an explanation, but by then her friends had come to her rescue. Still, he'd forced her to endure the sneering ton alone.

He squared his shoulders and narrowed his eyes, opening his mouth to speak. But no words came out. Slumping, he sat in the chair and shook his head. "I do not know how to convince you, Elinor. I love you with all my heart. The first time, I left you so I could settle my father's debts and earn enough money to be worthy of you. Perhaps I could have done that in some other way, but at the time, I could think of nothing.

"Then, after my injury, I was so angry and hopeless I did

not want to ruin your life by saddling you with a crippled husband. I thought I was being kind, but I see now I was only being selfish. I thought that your father's wishes reflected yours, and I was too embarrassed to confront you."

Michael appeared genuinely distraught, but Elinor had waited a long time to say certain things and get certain answers. She wouldn't waste the opportunity. "It occurs to me, in both cases, you did not consult me on your course of action. I did not even receive a note from you when our engagement ended, and the note I received when you left London last year was not adequate. Should I expect that if we are married, this same disregard for my feelings will continue? Am I to be discarded at the whim of your character?"

Looking at her with wide-blue eyes, he might have been lost. "I...I do not know what to say to this. I was a fool to think you would need no more information, and arrogant to have believed you would wait for me no matter the circumstances. It was cowardly and now all I can do is beg your forgiveness and swear that I will stand by you no matter what choices you make going forward."

This declaration piqued her curiosity. "Even if I decide to marry Preston?"

His expression filled with pain and anguish. "Even then, you may always count on my support. I shall stand down my efforts and respect your decision. If ever you should need me, you will only have to ask. Regardless of whom you marry, I am at your service."

She had to consciously make an effort to close her mouth. She dropped to her knees in front of him. Placing her hands on his cheeks, tears filled her eyes. "I have not accepted Middleton because I am in love with you and I always will be. Michael, how do we reconcile all that has happened? How do we go forward in society with all we have done? My parents will never allow me to accept you over Middleton, no matter your title."

She sat back on her heels. It was impossible.

"All these things can be overcome if you still love me." He brushed away her tears.

"It has just occurred to me that you have not said a word about marriage. It is customary to wait for the gentleman to ask before..."

Pushing back the chair, he fell to his knees and lifted her by the waist so that she was back on her feet. He looked up, his eyes brimming with tears. "It is I who should kneel before you, Elinor. You should always be above me. I know that I am not worthy of you but, by God, I want you so badly that I do not care about my worth. I am begging you to say no to Middleton and marry me. I will do whatever it takes to make you happy. If you want me to conquer countries, then I will do it. If you want jewels, then I shall sell everything to see you sparkle with diamonds and rubies. Tell me what you want, and it will be yours."

His eyes were liquid pools of blue.

She looked down at him and could think of nothing. She had never seen any man cry before, and Michael had always been so soldierly. He was strong and hard, and his emotions always hidden from everyone, including her.

She touched his short dark curls. Emotion shot through her, leaving pain and longing in its wake. The firelight danced on his skin and in his eyes. The warmth of the room was a cocoon around them. "I want babies."

His head fell forward. Tears finally escaped. "I am not sure I can give you babies, Elinor. My injuries..."

She cut him off. "I do not care where they come from, Michael. There are scores of children who need homes and love. If we cannot make them ourselves, then I want us to find them elsewhere. I want a lot of children. I love the way your brothers are together. You and I both missed that; I because my parents had only one child, and you because you were so much older than Everett and Sheldon. I want our children to have siblings, and a lot of them."

He smiled, dashing his tears away. "It is a relationship I am sorry to have missed, and I hope to gain with the time remaining. Having brothers is more important than I ever expected it to be."

"Then you would not mind having a few babies?"

"I would not mind." He took her hand and kissed the palm. "Does this mean that you will be my wife, Elinor?"

She knelt, wrapping her arms around him and pressing her face to the crook of his neck.

His arms enveloped her.

"I am yours, Michael."

His kiss was hard and bruising at first, but then more gentle. "Mine," he said against her lips. He pushed the light material of her wrap off her shoulders, and she adjusted her arms so that the garment fell to the floor.

He was still in his dinner clothes.

Desperate for more of him, she tugged at his neck cloth and pressed her lips to the base of his throat. His moan encouraged her, and she pulled at his blouse, kissing the sprinkle of hair on his chest.

"Elinor, do you know what you're doing to me?"

She looked, a wave of desire mingled with the excitement that they might be caught in her room so late at night. "I think so. Should I stop?"

His lips captured hers again, and he pressed his tongue deeply into her mouth.

Desire surged through her, settling between her legs. She touched her tongue to his and joined the dance.

His hands were on her hips, and he pressed her hard against his erection.

She gasped.

"Should I stop?" Though his words mimicked hers, there was no teasing from him. Breath frantic, sweat beaded on his brow. "I will stop this now if you wish, my love. I can wait until we are wed."

No one touched her heart the way he did. Nothing would ever be as perfect as the moment he'd shown her his true emotions. She never wanted anything more than she wanted Michael in that moment. "But I cannot."

He groaned and stood, lifting her into his arms. He took her to the bed and eased her against the plush mattress.

She expected him to put her on the bed. She'd expected him to immediately jump on top of her and she relished the notion. While some women complained about the act, she did not fear being with Michael.

He left her standing next to the bed.

She shifted, uncertain. Should she get herself onto the mattress? Should she wait for him? She leaned back onto the mattress.

He shook his head. "Do not move, Elinor."

In the flickering light, he removed his clothes one piece at a time. He wasted no time, but he did not tear at his clothes, either. Methodical and efficient like a soldier, his fingers moved deftly, and soon he stood before her naked.

Unable to take her eyes away from him, her cheeks burned. He was beautiful. Covered in muscles, but not bulky muscle like the strong man she had seen at the carnival, Michael was lean and powerful. His stomach rippled with strength, and his chest bulged and spread out to wide sinewy shoulders.

She touched the whitish puckered skin and traced the scar on his left shoulder.

"A bullet in Spain." He shrugged.

She looked in his eyes for a moment before touching a deep scar at the center of his chest. She pressed her lips to it.

A soft moan rumbled in his cheat. "A French spy a mile outside of London."

Her chest tightened. She had never asked him about his time working for the crown. It was as much her fault as his that she knew nothing of what he'd endured.

He took her hand from the chest wound. "A woman, but long before I met you."

"You could have been killed."

"More than once." He kissed her fingers before releasing her hand.

She trailed her hand along a rough patch of skin above his hip that stretched all the way to his ribs.

"Dragged by a horse after being shot in France. I am not certain who the shooter was."

She moved around to his back and touched a round puckered mark on his right shoulder blade.

"The bullet that knocked me from the horse. Might have finished me, but the shooter must have been too far away."

"Michael, why did you let them do this to you?" She touched another long, stretched-out scar across the middle of his back, imagining a whip or long knife that made the mark.

"It is what the enemy does, my love. I didn't let them, on those days they hurt me, but on most days it was the other way around."

"Not them." She swallowed down the tightness clogging her throat. "England. Why did you work for England for so long? Why did you put yourself through all of this pain?"

His laugh was ragged and humorless. He pulled her back around to face him again. "To be honest, I really don't know anymore." He touched her face as if she were a fragile flower. "When I was young, I joined the service to escape my father. Later, I stayed away and tried to distinguish myself so that people would look upon Rollins name with more than pity or loathing. As to why I took that last assignment—I wanted one last moment of glory. It was selfish, childish, and I have never regretted anything more in my life. Except for the day that your father came to see me while I was still recovering. I should have held my ground, Elinor. I should have made him honor our contract. Forgive me."

He cupped her cheek.

Part of her wanted to rail at him for allowing this to happen, and the rest wanted to coddle him until all his pain faded. She turned her head and kissed his palm. "He should have waited to see you. My father's arrogance since becoming an earl has escalated to the point that he is unbearable. He had no right to confront you before you were well. I forgive you, Michael, but I do not know if I can forgive him."

His mouth tipped up in a crooked smile. "He was only trying to protect you. Even if his motives were financial, they were still in your best interest. Let this pass, Elinor. Once we are married, none of it will matter."

She sighed, pushing back the anger she harbored against her father. There would be another time to deal with him. "You're right, though it won't be that easy. He has a lot to answer for."

"Do you really want to talk about your father?" He raised his eyebrows.

She looked down at his naked body. His shaft stuck out straight from his hips, only inches away from her center. Her stomach tightened and her core tingled. Still, worry invaded. "No, not really, but Michael, your headaches."

He looked away from her for a moment before refocusing.

"I feel fine. I think perhaps you are a better doctor than all those experts. I should have listened to you."

Boldly, she slipped the shoulders of her nightgown down. The white cotton shift puddled around her feet. She yearned for his touch. Her breasts ached with want.

He grazed the sensitive peak, following with his mouth. He pulled her nipple into his mouth, giving pleasure with just a touch of pain.

The attention pushed a moan from her lips that transformed into his name. Pleasure shot down her body and culminated between her thighs.

Pulling with his lips, he brought the little bud to a harder peak, and she gripped his head to pull him closer.

Everywhere he touched her sent new sensations through her body.

His hands were on her bottom, and he pulled her hard against him, bringing his cock to the place where she most needed him. His shaft slid between her nether-lips, and the delight made her lose her balance.

Elinor grabbed his shoulders for support as he slid forward and back, again and again, causing the air in her lungs to rush out. She gasped for more.

He walked her backward until she once again leaned against the bed. Then he knelt before her and pressed his tongue between her folds.

On fire, she arched her back. The entire world collapsed into this one moment with only the two of them. She parted for him longing for more.

He renewed his efforts, teasing at first, but then taking the hard bud in his mouth and sucking hard until she quivered.

Nothing had ever been more wonderful or more intimate. Every sense heightened. Nothing mattered, everything mattered. She was lost in him.

He lifted one of her legs so that it rested over his shoulder, then did the same with the other. He lifted her bottom until she was perched at the edge of the mattress. His tongue swirled and lapped, and his lips sucked gently, then harder.

Lightning shot through her and soared around her. Nothing was stable. The earth shook, and she bit her lip so as not to scream out and wake the household. Tension built at her center, tighter and higher.

His thumb slid inside her.

The world exploded before her eyes. Waves of pleasure flooded every inch of her body, which she no longer even recognized as her own. She clenched around his finger.

He muttered something she thought might have been "magnificent," but she was too caught up in her own pleasure to be sure.

She came to her senses in the middle of the bed. Michael was next to her with his head resting on his hand, and he smiled down at her with the most pleased smile on his face.

"Is something funny?"

"Two things are making me exceedingly happy." He trailed his fingers along her stomach to her breast.

She leaned up on her elbow and faced him. "What two things?"

Touching her from below her breast to her hip, he skimmed down her leg and up again. "The first is that you are the most magnificent woman in England. You respond like a siren. It is very gratifying to love you."

While her body called for more of his touch, her cheeks heated. "How can you say such a thing when you have not even taken your pleasure yet?"

"I say it because it is true, Elinor. And I shall never take my pleasure as you call it. We will give and receive pleasure together."

Her heart exploded with joy. She likely grinned stupidly. "Will you show me how to please you, Michael?"

"You already do please me."

She cocked her head and looked down his body. His shaft still stood erect between them, and she traced the bulging vein along the side.

He sucked in his breath.

"I think you know what I mean." She surprised herself with her boldness. In fact, she didn't recognize this wanton version either.

"What you are doing now is very pleasing." His breath grew short and fast.

Emboldened by his words and reaction, she wrapped her hand around him and squeezed softly.

He moaned and put his hand over hers, gently moving up and down in a steady rhythm.

His eyes closed and his head lolled back against the pillow.

"Beautiful" was the only way to describe him. Every inch of him, even the broken parts, were stunning, rugged, and made her long to kiss every inch.

He had given her pleasure with his mouth. She leaned down and ran her tongue along his shaft.

His breath was quickening, and he groaned.

Bolder, she traced the tip, sucking him. It was amazing, but he grew harder.

His eyes flew open, and he sat up. Grabbing her by the shoulders, he rolled her over and pinned her beneath him.

"Did I do something wrong, Michael?"

With a short laugh, he devoured her mouth. "Far too right, love. It has been a long time, and I cannot wait any longer for you."

He pressed against her opening, and she stiffened. Arms at her side, eyes closed, mouth clenched, she waited for his intrusion. She had seen farm animals copulate, and the female never seemed pleased with the process.

"Elinor."

"Yes."

"Open your eyes, please."

When she did, Michael's beautiful face strained above hers.

He held still. "I would like it if you would try to relax. I will not hurt you more than is necessary, and it will only be this first time. After that, it will never hurt again."

"Really?"

"I promise. Will you trust me?"

She wanted to trust him. It had been ages since she had. She nodded.

"Then relax and put your hands on me."

"Where?" she asked.

A joy filled smile spread across his face and lit his eyes. "Anywhere. My shoulders would be sufficient."

She did as he asked, looking into his striking blue eyes, and knew he wouldn't hurt her. She relaxed and parted her legs for him.

The tip of him stretched her, but the sensation wasn't unpleasant. In fact, once again her center tightened. She lifted her hips, pulling him in deeper. Pleasure surged through her.

"My love, I am sorry." He plunged the full length into her.

Burning pain flashed through her.

Michael froze in place.

The pain subsided, leaving in its place an ache of a different kind. Her body stretched to accommodate his size. She lifted her hips to him tentatively, and when he didn't move, she did it again.

This time he met her thrust. The base of his shaft rubbed her in such a way the pleasure built again.

Michael's breathing quickened, but he controlled his urgency and moved his body in and out of hers with languid strokes.

She lifted her hips to meet him, crying out with each thrust.

"My god, Elinor, you are magnificent. More wonderful than I could have even dreamed."

She tried to respond, but her words were stifled by the building pressure that was seconds from exploding. "I... I...Michael..."

Gripping his shoulders until her nails bit into his flesh, the orgasm engulfed her.

He crushed his lips to hers as her release came in a wash of feeling and emotion. Tears streamed down her face at the beauty of everything they did together.

Michael arched his back, groaning. His face a mask of pleasure, he collapsed on top of her.

Both in a mist of perspiration, he wrapped his arms around her.

Her body ached wonderfully. Sophia had told her that the marital act was nothing to be afraid of, but she hadn't expected such rapture.

He kept still.

Had his headache returned? "Michael? Are you all right?"

He rolled over onto his side taking her with him. His eyes had turned a deeper blue than she had ever seen. Smiling, he kissed her nose, her cheek, then her chin. "I am more than all right. It is more important to know how you are, sweetheart."

She blushed, wishing she could hide away, but there was nowhere else to look but into those piercing blue eyes. "I am fine."

"Fine." He leaned up on his elbow, wincing.

"I had not expected this to be so intimate."

"Are you embarrassed?" He kissed her cheek.

"I am too satisfied to be embarrassed."

"Good." Pressing his tongue to the seam of her lips, he encouraged her to open for him.

She did and sighed with pleasure as their tongues slipped together. Wrapping her arms around him, she wished the moment could never end.

With one last kiss, Michael got out of bed and crossed the room.

"Where are you going?" Panic pounded in her chest.

"I'm coming right back. Relax, sweetheart."

When he returned, he carried a cloth. Gently he pressed her knees apart and wiped the damp material along her thighs, stomach, and between her legs.

She gasped at the new intimacy. The coolness was both shocking and soothing.

"I can do that myself."

"Shhh. It is my honor."

He focused on her body as if he were washing a queen. The hands of a soldier, they were more gentle than she'd expected. It was a kind of worship, the way he attended her. Satisfied, he leaned over and pressed his lips to the center of her belly before crossing to the basin with the towel. He returned to the bed. "I am afraid the sheets will be telling. I hope your maid can be trusted."

Elinor's face was burning up. "I will speak to her. It will be fine."

He pulled the sheet over them and pressed against her side. Another wince shot across his face and was gone a second later. Gently, he combed the hair out of her eyes with his fingers. "You should sleep now. You must be tired."

"Actually, I feel rather wonderful. Will you stay with me?"

"Until the sun forces me back to my own room, sweetheart. If it were up to me, we would be married in the morning and I would never leave your side." A twitch flicked in his jaw.

She smiled. "That would be nice. Are you in pain, Michael?"

With a sigh, he pulled her tighter until her cheek pressed to his chest. "It is nothing like in the orangery, but I do have a slight headache. It will pass."

"Maybe this was a bad idea." Their lovemaking injured him. Sorrow suffocated her.

Pressing her back to the mattress, Michael gazed into her eyes with the intensity of a man going off to war. "This was the best night of my life. Please don't wish it away, Elinor. I love you. If I have to bear a slight headache to love you, it is no sacrifice."

Catching her breath, she ran her fingers through his tousled curls. "I just want our life together to be perfect, Michael."

"It will be, after we are married." He eased back onto the mattress, pulling her with him so that she lay against his side.

She traced a long scar along his hip. "It will not be easy to convince my mother to allow the marriage. She is keen on Middleton."

Every muscle tightened, and he pulled his lips into a straight line. "I will have you as my wife, Elinor, even if that means that we have to elope."

Another scandal would ruin her, even if she was married to a duke. They would receive no invitations and become notorious. She couldn't tolerate the idea. "Elope? No. I will convince her. If I need to, I will implore Middleton to retract his offer and back off from his courting. He is a good man, and he is already aware of my feeling for you. I think he would do as I ask."

"Perhaps, but I warn you, Elinor, if it comes to Middleton or me, I will snatch you up and haul you off to Scotland."

"That is romantic, but not very practical." Intending to be severe, she wished she could wipe the grin from her face. She was so happy, she couldn't stop smiling. Her cheeks ached with it.

As she did each evening, she recounted her day. Normally there would be a list, in the way some people kept a diary. She hadn't had time to make her list yet and considered getting up to do so. However, the feel of Michael next to her and his arms around her was too delicious to let end. "What did you do today, Michael? You didn't attend the picnic, so what did you do after you finished spying on Middleton and me?"

"Spying is a bit harsh. I was protecting you."

She stared at him until he laughed.

Kissing the top of her head, he shrugged. "I went down to the mouth of the creek and found the boys. We went swimming. It was the first time the three of us have ever had the chance to just be brothers. I was a man by the time they were old enough to play with. A shame, really, but today made up for quite a lot of missed opportunities. We had a wonderful time splashing about. They are both fine boys and will be good men, I think. No thanks to me."

Elinor turned to look at his face. "Are you mad?"

"Why would you say that?"

"You have set them an example for their entire lives. Do you think they used your father's example of what a man should be? They have been watching you since they were born and setting their caps at being men who will make you proud. You are entirely responsible for the type of men they will become, Michael."

His eyes were wide and teary. "I had not thought of that. I just felt I had missed their entire childhoods and had neglected them."

She nodded. "You may have missed them, Michael, but

they have not missed you. They followed every step of your career. They know every battle you fought and every honor you've been awarded. I sincerely hope you will get more chances to splash around with them. I agree that they are fine boys."

"Perhaps they can summer with us once we are married. We can go to the borderlands and enjoy the cooler weather of Scotland. I am the Duke of Kerburghe, after all."

Loving the idea of the future together, joy welled up inside her. "Yes, you are, and we will have to make certain that my mother hears that quite often over the next few days before you go to her with your offer."

"Sophia has enlisted her aunt for just that purpose," he said.

She rolled her eyes. "I know. Lady Collington brings it up at any opportunity."

"You do not think that's enough to sway your mother?"

"I am not sure anything will, to be honest." Mother's adoration of Middleton knew no boundaries.

"Perhaps we should enlist a few more of our friends to the task."

"Perhaps, but do not get overconfident. We need a plan."

"Why don't you make her a list?"

Her brows drew together. "First of all, there is nothing wrong with lists. They are helpful tools in both remembering and decision-making. Second, that is not really a bad idea. My mother is very responsive to lists. I shall give it some thought."

He kissed her brow. "You are quite adorable when you are angry with me. I am respectful of your list-making, Elinor."

It was likely a lie, but it did sound nice.

"I am. You always make the right decision. You are here with me now."

"I had no time for a list this evening."

He touched her nose playfully. "But I know that keen mind of yours was busy making all kinds of lists. You just didn't have time to write them down."

"How did you ever get to know me so well?" she asked.

"I love you with all my heart. I have made a study of everything about you, and I am delighted to know that I have not even grazed the surface. I will enjoy spending a lifetime learning every last detail of what is going on in that wonderful mind of yours."

"I do not know whether you are teasing me or if I should be flattered, Michael."

"Then choose the more pleasant option, my love." He kissed her so deeply, every last thought went out of her head. All she could concentrate on was the feel of him next to her.

He pulled back and stared at the fire.

"Michael, are you all right?"

He cocked his head. "My headache has subsided. I seem to have been cured. I shall put it down to your wonderful medicine."

They made love again, then slept for a few hours before Michael quietly slipped out of the room.

Chapter Sixteen

Break my fast
Tell Middleton no
Convince Mother to accept Michael
Lovely Michael

It would be quite a day.

Elinor woke up ravenous. She dressed and had an awkward and private chat with her maid, Josephine, who practically tore the sheets from the bed and carried them away like a thief.

Trotting down to break her fast, she was sore but deliciously alive. She took several sausages and coddled eggs. There was some lovely bread, and she popped several pieces on her plate.

Dory and Lady Collington were already in the room. Both stared at her as if she had three heads.

"Good morning Lady Collington, Dory." Elinor bobbed

and walked to the table.

Lady Collington frowned more severely than usual.

Dory's eyes were wide as saucers.

"Is something wrong?"

Dory leaned in. "I do not know, Elinor. You tell me."

"As far as I know, everything is fine. Are you feeling well?"

"I am quite well." Dory cocked her head.

"Perhaps you should sit down before the weight of your platter topples you over," Lady Collington said.

"Yes. Thank you, my lady." She sat next to Dory.

"You seem to have a hearty appetite today."

Elinor blushed. "Yes. I woke up with a frightful hunger today."

The older woman took one last sip of her tea. She gave Elinor another appraising look before getting up with only minor help of her cane. "I must go and find your mother. I have several very flattering things to tell her about Kerburghe, and I feel there is little time to waste."

Both women stared after the dowager before returning to their plates. Elinor could have sworn her dearest friend hid a snicker. Was it that obvious? Could everyone in the house tell that she had allowed Michael to spend the night in her bed?

Heaven forbid.

She had better avoid crowds for a while, just in case.

It was late morning, and they were the only two in the room. Elinor was grateful to learn the gentlemen had gone shooting and wouldn't return until luncheon. Then there were to be games outdoors to take advantage of the good weather.

She wouldn't have minded seeing Michael, but she did not think she could face Middleton that morning. She might blush, and he might get the wrong idea. Or the right one. Either way, it wouldn't be favorable.

A long silence filled the room. Dory was her oldest friend.

She could share anything with her. "Do I look so different?"

Dory patted her arm. "Not to worry, dear. I think your secret is safe. Though, I would recommend you stifle the constant humming and the daft smile."

"What?"

Dory lowered her voice. "You came into the breakfast room humming, ignored that we were sitting here, and turned from the buffet with the most ridiculous smile on your face. I shall not even mention the quantity of food you procured. Suffice to say, at this rate Sophia will have to send the servants to market on a more constant basis."

"Oh." Elinor wanted to crawl under the table.

"Should we take a long walk after you've finished that troth? Perhaps you could stand a talk between friends?" Dory smiled.

It was exactly what she needed. "I would like that very much."

It took a significant amount of time, but Elinor finished every bite of food on her plate.

The two ladies walked to the far end of the gardens, where there was a lovely fountain and some bushes that were not so high as to conceal prying eyes. A series of benches lined the square, and there were several varieties of flowers in bloom.

They sat, and Dory looked from one end of the garden to the other before turning back to Elinor. "So you have slept with Michael Rollins."

"Yes." Elinor liked her directness and loved that she could answer honestly without the worry of recrimination or judgment.

Dory watched her for several moments. "You do not seem devastated by the event, at least not in the negative sense. Does his grace intend to marry you?"

"Yes."

"And you wish this as well?"

"Of course. I love Michael. You know I do. I am still working out my anger over him abandoning me, but last night went a long way toward that goal. The problem is Middleton."

Dory waved it off. "I see no issue. Kerburghe has offered. Middleton has not. You have only one option. Your mother can't argue with that."

Elinor stared at the pebbled path at her feet.

Dory's legs swung back and forth. She stopped them. "Oh, I see. Middleton has also offered. Has he gone to your mother?"

"No. He said he would wait for my answer before he did."

"Then perhaps this will all work out. You will have to tell Middleton that you will not marry him." Dory lowered her voice. "It is imperative that your mother never knows he has offered."

"Yes. I know."

"And, forgive me for saying so, but your mother is easily influenced by the ideas of others. We must start to talk up Kerburghe until she thinks him a saint."

"Yes. I agree. I confess I planned to ask for your and Sophia's help with that."

"Consider it done."

"Thank you."

She and Dory had been friends since infancy. Their families' country estates were next to each other. They had been through everything together. Elinor cleared her throat. "Shall I tell you everything, or would you prefer to be left in the dark?"

Dory grinned and clapped her hands. "I thought you'd never ask. I want to know every detail. From the look of you, I can see that it was not what my mother describes as a horrible experience."

Elinor placed her palm against her cheek. Something would have to be done about all that blushing. She willed any embarrassment away. "It was the farthest thing from that, Dory. It was spectacular."

For more than an hour, Elinor related every detail of the previous night. When she wasn't asking questions, Dory sat wide-eyed and listened intently.

The hour grew late. The gentlemen would have returned from shooting. Elinor bubbled with the memories of the previous night.

Dory pulled on her hair and wrung her hands. Her eyes grew wide and her cheeks pale.

"Should I not have told you, Dory?"

Dory blinked several times and shook her head. "Of course you should. It's about time someone did. All this speculation cannot be good. I am happy to hear it is pleasant, but astonished that what you have described could be."

"I think lovemaking is something better experienced than described. I do not know how to explain it, but I promise it was extremely rewarding and much more intimate than I'd expected."

With a long sigh, Dory stood. "I suppose I shall have to wait for my own husband to fully understand, but I appreciate your sharing your experience. I must say, it puts my mind at ease. I know you would never lie to me, and perhaps my mother's experiences are colored by her distaste for my father."

"I imagine so." Elinor took Dory's arm, and they walked the garden path back to the house.

Elinor jumped at the opportunity to go down to the river and fish with Michael's brothers rather than play lawn games.

The three of them trooped down to the river and cast their

lines.

Shelton caught a small trout within a few minutes, but after that, it was slow going.

Finally, there was a tug on her pole. She shouted out her excitement.

Sheldon and Everett came running, both of them laughing.

"Pull it in, Lady Elinor," Everett said.

"Give me the pole. I'll get it." Sheldon reached for her pole.

"Don't you dare touch my fishing pole, Shel. I can do this myself."

Her arms strained against the fighting trout. She pulled the determined fish ashore.

Sheldon leapt on the slippery, flapping creature.

Exhausted from the fight, Elinor collapsed on the grass.

Sheldon managed to wrangle the fish and held it up for viewing. "Are you going to marry my brother?"

"Sheldon," Everett scolded. "That is none of your business."

Sheldon attached Elinor's fish to the stringer. He wiped his hands on the grass before turning toward his brother. "Don't you want to know?"

"Yes. But it's not appropriate to ask questions that are not your business."

"Michael is our business."

Before the argument got too out of hand, Elinor broke in. "It's all right. Yes. I am going to marry your brother. But this information is only for the four of us. We must keep a secret until Michael has an opportunity to speak with my mother. You do understand that, don't you, Sheldon?"

The boy's grin was contagious. Covered in water, mud, and fish scales, he was a sight. "I can keep a confidence, Lady Elinor. You need not worry about that."

He looked just like Michael, dark hair and blue eyes

sparkling. Did Michael smile that brightly before he went into the army? Had Michael ever been so carefree? She didn't think so. He was serious and haunted, the price of being his father's eldest. He always had a lot to overcome.

The bushes behind them shook and something crashed through.

Certain they were about to be attacked by a wild boar, Elinor screamed.

Everett shielded Elinor and Sheldon.

Three men with guns burst through the row of overgrowth.

"That is very touching, Lady Elinor," a short, round man said. His skin was freckled, and what was left of his red hair stood straight up on top of his bulbous head. Blue eyes bugged out from above his fleshy cheeks. If it hadn't been for the two enormous men with guns flanking him, he might have been a circus entertainer.

Elinor moved beside Everett. "Who are you, and what do you mean, bursting in on private land?"

He came closer and Everett stepped out again.

"You are in no position to ask questions, my lady. I have the guns; therefore, I have the upper hand." He might have been reading instructions from some kind of "attacking innocents" handbook.

It would do no good to panic. The man must want something, and it was better to discover what it was from the start. "May I inquire as to the nature of your visit, sir?"

He smiled and bowed as if she were a queen and they'd met at a ball. "I have come to take you away from all of this." He gestured to the surroundings.

"The hell you say." Sheldon pushed forward, trying to get past Elinor and Everett.

She put out her arm and stopped Sheldon, who now had guns pointed at him. "May I have your name, sir? You cannot expect me to run off with a man to whom I have not even been introduced."

"Indeed." The bow that followed was so low, that his face turned cherry red, and his hair flapped in the breeze. "I am Carter Roxton," he declared.

She almost laughed.

"Lemmy's brother? Pretender!" Sheldon renewed his effort to push through.

It was all Elinor and Everett could do to hold back Sheldon.

"Sheldon, be calm. Those guns are not toys. Stay back now," she whispered.

"Better listen to her, boy. I do not want to kill you, but I certainly will if need be."

"And if I do not wish to go?" she asked Roxton.

He sighed. "I am afraid that is not an option, my lady. You must come with me in order for justice to be served."

"What justice?" Everett demanded.

Roxton had been gazing at Elinor as if she were the moon, but now he turned to Everett. His eyes narrowed, and his voice clipped. "Justice your brother has denied me until this point."

It made no sense. Elinor looked at Everett, who shrugged. Clearly, this man was deranged.

"Hold these whelps while I load the woman," Roxton ordered the armed men.

The two brutes rushed forward, grabbing Everett and Sheldon in their meaty hands. Both boys fought, but they were no match for the ruffians.

Elinor beat on the arms of the one holding Sheldon. "Let them go."

Sweaty arms wrapped around her waist and pulled her away.

She clutched Everett's arm.

Roxton tugged harder, robbing her of her breath and her

grip. "Time to go."

"You're mad if you think I am going anywhere with you." Turning, she scratched his face only a hair away from his eye.

His hand lashed out and struck her across the face with such force, that her own eye might become dislodged. Pain seared her cheek and she tasted blood. Shocked, she clutched her cheek and stared wide-eyed at her assailant.

"Terribly sorry you made me do that, my dear. Please refrain from such behavior in the future. I should hate to have to harm you." He spoke in a calm voice that sent chills up Elinor's spine.

He grabbed her by the hair and dragged her toward the trees.

The boys hollered and called out.

Praying they would not be harmed, she struggled to free herself.

Once the trees were behind them, Roxton threw her up into a waiting carriage. A third gun appeared, held by the driver. He was slightly smaller than the others, but still as big as the carnival man who lifted the elephant. A moment later, she heard a loud whistle and the rustle of trees. Roxton climbed into the carriage and sat across from her.

"I hope you are comfortable, my dear, it is a long drive."

"Where are you taking me?"

"To my lands. I have a lovely castle in the lowlands. You and I will be happy there."

The weight of the carriage shifted as the other two kidnappers leaped on its back.

Already moving, the carriage tottered back and forth as if being shook. Someone screamed. As Roxton stuck his head out the window, Elinor tried to open the other side door. It was locked or stuck. Everett lay on the ground, wrestling with one of the kidnappers.

A gun fired.

Elinor screamed.

The man got up, looked down at Everett's body, shook his head, and ran toward the still-moving carriage.

"No!" Elinor watched Everett getting smaller and smaller as her kidnappers took her away. He didn't move. Sheldon ran out of the woods as they turned a bend in the road.

She sat back down. Tears were streaming down her face.

"That is a shame." There was too much joy in Roxton's voice for him to sound sincere.

"You'll hang for this," she said.

"I do not think so. I am a duke. Dukes don't hang."

There was no possibility this idiot was a duke. "The duke of what?"

Unbelievably, he tried to make a bow from the seat. "Duke of Kerburghe, at your service."

He was mad. That was the only explanation. She would have to think of what to do, but first, she had to get more information. And getting that from a madman wasn't going to be easy.

"Mike, is that your young brother running like the devil?" Thomas leaned on his crocket mallet.

Sheldon ran toward them, legs and arms pumping like mad. His face was red, and neither Elinor nor Everett was behind him.

Something was wrong. The hair on the back of his neck stood as it often did when he was on a mission. Michael's heart sped up. *Elinor. Had something happened to Elinor? Where was Everett?* He ran toward Sheldon.

Thomas's footfall was just behind him. By the sound of

shouts and running, a few others followed as well. Daniel, he was sure, and perhaps a few more.

When he reached Sheldon, the boy collapsed to his knees, gasping for air.

"What's happened, Shel?" Michael grabbed Sheldon's shoulders.

"She's been taken, Mike. We tried to stop them, but they took her, and now Everett is shot. There was so much blood." Tears ran down Sheldon's filthy face.

"Taken, shot, blood," echoed in his mind.

Daniel arrived on horseback with another in tow. His friends from Eton always knew what was needed.

Sheldon cried into his hands.

Michael pulled him into his arms, and, in spite of his own panic, kept composed. "Sheldon, can you show me where Everett is?"

Sheldon nodded.

Michael swung onto the horse, then lifted Sheldon behind him.

"I'll send for a doctor," Daniel called out and relinquished his horse to Thomas, who followed Michael.

They found Everett exactly where Sheldon had left him in the clearing. His skin was sickly white, and his left leg bled through a tightly bound field dressing made from a torn piece of Sheldon's jacket.

Michael jumped from the horse and cradled Everett's head. His heart pounded, and what had started as the best day of his life plummeted into horror. "Everett, talk to me."

His eyes fluttered open. "I tried to stop them, Michael. I am sorry. I really did try."

"I know you did, and I am very proud of you. Now stay with me until we get you back to the house, you hear me. Don't you dare die. I forbid it."

"Yes, sir," he whispered.

Thomas knelt at Everett's leg. "Who tied this dressing?"

"I did," Sheldon said.

"It's a good job, boy," Thomas looked for something to splint the leg with.

"How did you learn to do that?" Michael asked.

Sheldon colored. "I've read all your war reports."

The fact that his youngest brother had invaded his privacy and read his papers would have to wait. The fact that he had gotten anything useful out of them was astonishing. Michael exchanged a look with Thomas, who tore his blouse, then used the fabric to tie a long stick to Everett's leg.

Middleton arrived with a large carriage carrying Lady Rollins, who was near tears but kept her composure as she helped get her middle son into the transport.

Daniel followed on horseback.

The carriage started back to the house, where a doctor would be waiting to tend to Everett.

Michael, Daniel, and Thomas stood and scanned the tracks of the carriage that had taken Elinor away.

Thomas said, "I will follow the tracks so they don't go cold. You go back to the house and see to Everett, Mike. Send for Markus and James Hardwig. We will need some law, I suspect."

Daniel added, "I know Sheldon is distraught, but someone will need to question him and find out who is responsible. It will help to have a motive here."

Torn between going to see about his brother and finding Elinor, Michael nodded. "I won't be more than a few hours behind you."

They all nodded, and twenty years of friendship linked them.

Chapter Seventeen

It had been over an hour since Elinor's kidnapping, and Michael was dying inside. Thomas hadn't returned with the kidnapper's direction, and no report had come from the doctor on Everett's condition.

Tears streaming down his face, Sheldon clung to the edge of his chair.

"Tell me everything that happened, Sheldon." Michael held his fists tight at his side to keep from shaking him.

Sheldon cried. "I told you already."

"You have to remember more," Michael screamed. What he really wanted was to scream at Everett to stand up and tell him he was fine.

"I cannot."

Markus stood in the library doorway.

Daniel sat behind the desk, rubbing his eyes.

"Sorry to interrupt." Markus stepped inside the room. "How is Everett?"

Slumping, Sheldon wiped his face.

Daniel said, "The doctor is still with him. He's lost a lot of blood, in spite of the excellent field dressing that Sheldon managed before running over three miles to get help."

"I see," Markus said. "Then he is in God's hands now."

Michael glared, but Markus slapped his gloves against his hand and strode closer. "Perhaps it would be best if Sheldon and I had a chat, and you sat and took a rest, Mike."

This was his family and his responsibility. Michael was about to tell Markus to shove off.

Middleton entered the room. "It's been raining an hour now, Markus. Thomas has probably lost the trail."

Markus nodded. "Yes. Therefore, we will need good intelligence before we begin. Hello, Preston, didn't know you were in attendance."

"Markus," Middleton said with a nod.

Markus sat next to Sheldon on the couch. "Sheldon, why don't you tell me what happened today."

"I already told everything," Sheldon whined.

"I am certain that you have, but humor me and tell it to me. It is possible that in your brother's desire to get Lady Elinor back, he has flustered you, and some critical information has been left out."

Markus's gentle brand of interrogation was exactly what the situation called for. Beginning from the time Elinor caught the big fish, Sheldon told everything in great detail.

Sheldon described the carriage and the two men with Roxton. He told them about how he and Everett had been smacked hard enough to send them both sprawling before the two guards left the clearing by the river. He hadn't had a good view of the driver since he was already moving away by the time Sheldon had emerged from the trees. Earlier accounts left out the part where Elinor admitted to the boys that she intended to marry Michael.

Middleton nodded and listened.

When Sheldon had finished, Markus patted his back. "Very good, Shel. Why don't you go up and have a bath? Then you can go see about Everett and bring us a report."

Sheldon jumped up and ran from the room.

Middleton rose and closed the door behind Sheldon.

"So Roxton knows that Elinor is yours," Markus said.

Middleton flinched.

"Yes, but why would he take her and where?" It was unbearable to think of what Elinor was suffering in the hands of that worm.

"North," Thomas opened the door and dripped in the threshold. A puddle formed beneath him as the butler arrived with towels. He thanked him and entered the study. "I lost them on the north road. I think he's headed for Scotland, but I cannot really be sure."

"Why on earth would he go to Scotland?" Middleton asked.

"Perhaps he intends to marry Lady Elinor," Markus said.

This was all his fault. He'd put her in danger, put them all in danger. Why hadn't he taken that ridiculous Roxton more seriously? He had failed, and the people he loved paid for it.

"Sorry, Mike, but it would be the best way to destroy you, and I am assuming that is Roxton's goal."

The apology didn't help.

Middleton shook his head. "Then what? He cannot come back to town with his new wife in tow. The marriage would be annulled immediately. I don't know this Roxton, but he cannot be so stupid as to think that he can force a woman to marry him and get away with it. I think we can assume that Lady Elinor is not willing."

Michael walked to the window. The rain continued to run down the glass, blurring the view. It didn't make sense to take her to Gretna Green. Middleton was right. He would take her somewhere he thought he could stay long-term. "Daniel, have you sent for James?"

"Yes. I wrote him a detailed account after we returned. I am sure he will arrive in the night. What are you thinking, Mike?"

"Write him another note and send a runner to intercept him."

Daniel took a piece of foolscap out of his desk and wrote.

Middleton pounded his fist on the desk. "I realize that the four of you have been friends a long time and I am not in this particular club, but it would be helpful if someone would inform me of what the hell is going on."

"Sorry, Preston. Old habit," Markus said. "Roxton has gone to Kerburghe. At least that is what we think. Our guess is, he is trying to set a trap for Michael."

"But aren't you the Duke of Kerburghe?" Middleton demanded.

Michael wished he had never been given the title. If he were still Sir Michael, Elinor would be safe. "I have not had the opportunity to travel to Scotland and make my face known."

Middleton's eyes widened. "You think that Roxton is posing as the duke?" Silence fell over the room, then Middleton blew a low whistle.

"I understand the grounds are quite a fortress." Michael recounted what he had read in the paperwork describing the castle.

"Then we will need a sound plan of attack." Thomas ran the towel over his hair.

"I've been the bait in worse situations," Michael said. It was more than he could bear. Everett and Elinor. He couldn't lose them both. Hell, he couldn't lose either of them.

"Am I to understand that a duke of the realm is planning to

use himself as bait to draw out this Roxton?" Middleton's eyes narrowed, and his spine was stiff as the chimney.

Markus smiled. "You are starting to get the hang of this, Preston. I am quite impressed."

"The four of you are mad, you know."

"Mad to want to recover her?" Michael faced Middleton.

Preston stood his ground, his fists on his hips. "Mad to go about it without the authorities."

"We did call James," Markus defended. "He is the authorities."

Michael and Preston stood nose to nose. "By the time James arrives, it may be too late. How long do you suggest we leave her in the hands of a man who is insane?"

"I want her back as badly as you do, Kerburghe."

As much as he needed Middleton's help, he hated that another man wanted his Elinor. "Even if she has agreed to marry me?"

Pulling his shoulders back, Middleton shook his head. "I am fond of Lady Elinor. Regardless of her choice, I shall assist in recovering her. I always knew that there was a good possibility she would choose you. Love cannot account for taste."

Michael couldn't argue with that. "Indeed. I should have chosen you over me out of hand, but for some reason that only God can explain, she has picked me."

"It's ridiculous, really," Markus agreed.

"Absolutely." Daniel shook his head.

"I cannot understand why such an intelligent woman would have made such an error in judgment," Thomas said with a straight face.

"That will do." Michael raised his hand to stall further insult.

The door burst open and a panting, still-dirty Sheldon rushed in. "Mike!"

Michael's heart stopped.

Sweating, Sheldon gasped for air and held his knees.

"Sheldon?"

"He will live. The doctor thinks he will live. He's awake now, but they said he has to rest." Sheldon's color was high and his eyes bright.

Michael hugged him and when Mother appeared at the door, he opened his arm and included her in the embrace.

When they separated, all three were teary-eyed.

Tabitha dabbed at the corners of her eyes with a lace handkerchief. "He's asking for you, Michael. He won't rest until he sees you."

Kissing Mother's cheek before he left the room, he took the steps two at a time. He reached the landing and sprinted down the hall to the room Everett and Sheldon shared.

Everett looked tiny in the bed.

He ached seeing his brother sickly, but it wouldn't do to show weakness. He took a deep breath. "You gave me quite a fright, boy."

Everett opened dark eyes ringed an even darker purple. "Me too."

Michael's chest tightened painfully. He might have lost his brother. He moved into the room and sat on the edge of the bed. "I am terribly glad that you're going to be all right, Everett. I do not know what I would have done..."

Everett gripped his arm with surprising strength. "I know, Mike."

Their eyes met, and Michael saw a man before him. He loved his brother, and he'd come close to losing him to an idiot. It could have been one more tragedy caused by his desire to have a title. One more item on the list of why he shouldn't have taken that last assignment.

"Lady Elinor? No one will tell me anything."

"Roxton took her, and we have not yet found them."

Everett's eyes closed in what looked like pain. "I am sorry, Mike. I tried to stop them."

"I know you did. None of this is your fault. We are going after them now. I just wanted to see you before I left."

"You'd better go, then," Everett said.

Michael squeezed his brother's arm, then on impulse dropped a kiss on the boy's forehead.

Everett looked stunned, then he smiled.

"I'll see you when I return." Michael rushed from the room.

The sun slipped lower on the horizon to Elinor's left, so she knew they traveled north. Her bottom ached from the poorly sprung carriage and worn cushion. It had taken hours to become accustomed to the stench of sweat and cloying perfume.

As if it wasn't enough to be kidnapped, Roxton never stopped talking and never said anything of any interest.

"Pardon me, Mr. Roxton, but where are you taking me?" She interrupted his monologue about how long it had taken to make his coat and how many stitches were in each sleeve.

His lips twisted unhappily, but then he smiled, showing his horribly crooked and yellowed teeth. "Home, of course. Technically you should address me as your grace, but since we are to be married, I shall forgive this cut and permit you to call me by my Christian name."

He did not supply her with the name, and since she had no intention of using it, she continued on as if he hadn't mentioned it. "You have a house in the north of England?"

"In Scotland," he said.

"Not Kerburghe. Surely you can't be mad enough to take me to property not your own."

His hand jutted out before she could defend herself. His meaty fist wrapped around her throat, and his feted breath assaulted her senses. She scratched at him, but he held tight, cutting off her air. She continued to fight him, but he was far stronger than he looked.

"It will be mine soon enough, and so will you." He released his hold.

She gasped for air, clutching her throat. It was foolish to underestimate him. He had kidnapped her, shot poor Everett, and stolen Kerburghe. The man was insane.

Elinor made a list in her head of things she might do to free herself: Jump out the door. Scratch Roxton's eyes out. Feign illness. None of them were good ideas, but they kept her mind occupied.

Elinor sat in silence until they arrived at an inn. She was ordered to remain in the carriage while the horses were changed. A terrified-looking young girl placed a hot brick at her feet. Elinor stared at her, hoping to convey that she wasn't traveling of her own free will.

The girl only bobbed her head and ran off.

Where was Michael? Why hadn't he come for her?

It rained for hours. The carriage slipped around in the mud, but they still pressed northward. Elinor prayed for a broken wheel or for the carriage to overturn. She hoped a bridge might wash out, but to no avail. They continued to plod along until the next day, at noon, they arrived at a fortress.

The rain came down in buckets, but Elinor was too exhausted to care. A bridge spanned to the front gate, and the empty moat stank of filth and muck. The walls sprawled upward hundreds of feet. Men walked the tops of the thick walls.

Elinor had stepped into an insane medieval storybook and had to find some way of escaping.

First, she needed rest. It had been a full day since she had set foot outside the carriage, which needed new springs. Her body ached from the bouncing of the road. She was sure she had a bruise on her face from where Roxton had hit her. Her throat still ached from the near- strangulation. All of that, and she hadn't slept in two days.

Escape was her only hope, but nothing came to mind. She had to think of something, since there was no sign of Michael.

Sleep first.

Roxton walked through the keep and inside without a word.

A young woman showed her to a chamber and helped her into a nightgown. She was too tired to ask where the garment came from. The soft bed lulled her, and her aching muscles wouldn't be denied rest.

Warm yeasty bread filled her senses and pulled her from her restless sleep.

Heavy-headed, Elinor pulled herself from the soft down mattress. The room was sparse. The bed, which was exquisitely comfortable, a chair, and a small table filled the tiny chamber. Nothing hung on the walls, and no rug warmed the floor.

A petite red-haired girl in tattered clothes fed the blazing fire, humming.

"Have I slept through to morning?" Elinor asked.

Gasping and clutching her chest, the girl spun.

Elinor held up her palms in what she hoped was a peaceful gesture. "I am sorry to frighten you."

The girl relaxed. "Oh, 'tis nothing." She had a lovely smattering of freckles along the bridge of her nose. "You did indeed sleep clear through to morning. I've never seen anyone as tired as you were. I scant got your—" She rushed forward and touched Elinor's cheek. "What on earth happened to your face? Did you fall?"

Pain shot across her face and she pulled back. "Roxton was angry with me."

Eyes wide, she took her hand away. "His grace did this to you?"

"He is not the duke and, yes, he struck me." *He had nerve to call himself by Michael's title.*

The girl's eyes welled up, and her face colored bright red.

Elinor changed the subject. "Is that delightful-smelling bread for me?" Smiling brightly, she threw her shoulders back.

Elinor's mother always said to stay on good terms with the cook so you would never go hungry should the rest go to Hades. Elinor wished she could see her mother at that moment.

"Of course, miss, you must be half-starved. Here, sit." She pulled out the chair by the table.

Elinor's stomach rumbled in anticipation of her first food in days. Had it been that long? The light buttery bread melted in her mouth. The mulberry jam's tart sweetness tasted like heaven. A steaming cup of tea warmed her. If she hadn't been kidnapped by a madman, it would have been a pleasant morning.

She was so famished that plotting her escape would have to wait. When every scrap of food was gone from the tray, Elinor took the last sip of tea.

Watching, the maid sat on a window seat. If she hadn't been gaping, she might have been quite pretty.

Elinor blushed. "I was starved."

"I can see that you were," the girl said.

"What is your name?"

"Brianne, miss."

"That is a lovely name. Brianne, my name is Elinor Burkenstock. My father is an earl in England. I assume that I am in Scotland now?"

Brianna picked up an old tattered gown from a bin and brushed it out. "Yes, you are in the lowlands at Kerburghe Castle."

"The man who brought me here?"

"The duke?"

"He is no duke. He is only pretending to be the Duke of Kerburghe. The real duke will show up at any moment and rescue me from him." She wasn't even sure Michael would be able to find her. Poor Everett had surely been shot and would need attention. She prayed for Everett and for herself.

Brianne pulled a needle and thread from the box on the window seat and threaded the eye. "His grace explained that you might say such a thing. He is generous to have taken you for a wife in spite of your infirmity.

"My infirmity! What infirmity would that be?"

Brianne's skin pinked and she wouldn't meet Elinor's gaze. "He told us that you were touched in the head."

Elinor held her temper. Obviously, Roxton had told lies to keep her a prisoner. She changed tactics. "What do you think of his grace?"

Tasting lemons would have produced a sweeter expression. She pulled the fabric together and sewed a hole in the dress. "His grace is a fine lord."

"Chases the maids about the castle, does he?" Elinor asked.

Brianne looked away and smoothed the gown.

"I hope you are a fast runner, Brianne." Elinor walked to the window.

"I am quite fast, miss. I also know my way about the castle a far cry better than his grace. I've had to lose him more than once." Her smile faded. "I am sorry, miss. I am always shooting my mouth off that way. Mother often tells me to keep my thoughts to myself. I am sure your betrothed is a fine man."

Though she tried not to, Elinor laughed. "Brianne, I am going to tell you the truth, but you'd best keep it to yourself. No one is going to believe me, anyway."

"I'll believe you, miss."

"I am not crazy. I am engaged to the Duke of Kerburghe, but that man, Roxton, is not him. Michael Rollins is tall with dark brown hair and blue eyes, and he was elevated to the rank of duke not two months ago. This man is an imposter, and I really could not tell you why he is doing all of this. I was taken here against my will and would be grateful if you would help me avoid Roxton until Michael arrives to save me."

Brianne smiled, but her eyes remained sad. Returning her attention to the now-mended gown, she gave it a shake. "It's just wedding jitters. The Father will come and marry you soon. You will see that everything will be fine."

"I have no intention of marrying that pig of a man."

Brianne gathered more bolts of ancient clothes out of a trunk and shook each one out.

"What is that?" Elinor waved the dust from her face. Motes swirled in the light from the window.

"Why, 'tis your wedding clothes, miss. They belonged to the last duchess, but that was years ago. She died in childbirth with the babe. That's why the title went to the current duke, who's only a distant relation."

Hoping to make sense of the situation, Elinor absorbed Brianne's report. "Is there a shortage of women in Scotland?"

"No." Her freckled nose scrunched up. "Why do you ask?"

"I just wondered why Roxton would steal an unwilling woman from England when there are ample women here at Kerburghe."

"He must be in love with you." Brianne cocked her head and gazed dreamily out the window.

It would be a miracle if the food stayed down, the way Elinor's stomach churned at the idea of Roxton. "I had never met him before yesterday when he snatched me away from a house party, so that seems unlikely."

Shrugging, she brushed dust and dirt from the wedding gown.

"How far is England from here?"

"About twenty miles, I suppose. But you shouldn'a think of running for the border, miss. It's a rough road for a woman alone." Brianne's eyes widened, and she paled.

"I cannot very well marry this pretender. He's abhorrent, has injured me, and may have killed Everett."

Clutching the fabric to her chest, Brianne gasped. "Who's Everett?"

"Michael's brother."

"Why would his grace kill this Everett?"

"The boy was trying to rescue me from the kidnapping."

"Boy? Is Everett a child?" Practically tearing the gown, she leaned in for more of the story.

"No. I suppose not any longer. He is seventeen. Since he is Michael's younger brother, I suppose I have thought of him as my brother as well. I pray he is well."

Brianne frowned, looked at the gown, and back at Elinor.

Chapter Eighteen

Michael road as if an inferno was at his heels. He could already be in Scotland if not for his friends' extraordinary amount of preparation. First, the letter to James had taken forever to write and send. Then, Thomas had insisted upon gathering more firearms than they would ever require. Mother had delayed him by an hour with words of warning about being careful and not taking unnecessary risk.

Once she finished, Virginia cornered him. She had been hysterical since her daughter's kidnapping. "You must find her and bring her back. I know that my husband and I have not been as kind to you as we might have been, but that is no reason for you to make my darling girl suffer. I could not stand to lose her."

Michael couldn't blame her. There were moments when he wished he had the luxury of hysterics himself. "Lady Malmsbury, be assured, I shall find her and bring her back."

"I do not want you to think my family heartless. We liked you very much, but then you were injured and his lordship thought it best if Elinor found another husband. You must understand."

Michael did understand, but his temper still edged near the surface. He had believed himself as unsuitable for the lady as her parents had. Only Elinor remained loyal throughout the past few months. She had come to him in the night and begged for a reason for his betrayal. All he had done was insult her and send her away.

He shook himself. That was the past. She loved him still, and she was his. He would go and get her, then deal with the problem of her parents. None of that mattered. The only important thing was that Elinor was brought home safely.

Michael took Virginia Burkenstock's hands and looked her in the eye. To his amazement, she stopped weeping. "My lady, I will do whatever it takes to bring her back to you. I would give my life for Lady Elinor. If it is in my power to retrieve her, then I shall no matter the cost. You must believe that."

"I have faith in you, your grace." She turned and walked up the curved steps to her chambers.

Interesting that she'd spoken to him alone. She hadn't gone to Daniel, whose property they were on, nor had she spoken to Middleton, whom she intended for her daughter. She had come to him, knowing his feelings. Perhaps, like her daughter, Virginia Burkenstock played at being simple-minded. What else might she be aware of? But thoughts of his sweet Elinor lying in his arms made him lose focus, so he brushed them away.

In the courtyard, Michael and his friends mounted their horses.

Daniel rode beside him. "We'd best get moving. With any luck, James is close to Kerburghe by now."

Michael kicked his horse into a trot. It would do no good to kill the beast, and they had a long ride before they could change horses.

~

Before luncheon was served, Brianne stuffed Elinor into miles of wedding gown fabric and pulled her through the castle. "Come on, miss."

The gown stank of mold and some other odor that she couldn't identify. If the style was any indication, it had been in a trunk for forty years.

The halls were a blur of gray stone and cobwebs. Dust tickled Elinor's nose as they ran through, and she sneezed. "What is the hurry?"

"His grace has a bit of a temper. If we're late, there will be the devil to pay." With a shaking voice, she tugged harder on Elinor's hand.

They must have traversed the entire span of the castle before arriving at the chapel. Elinor's feet ached with the pounding from the stone floors.

She had to admit that it was a lovely chapel with tall ceilings and stained glass. Under any other circumstance, she would have enjoyed visiting such a place. If the marriage had been to Michael, this would have been lovely.

Jowls jiggling in an unnatural and disgusting way, Roxton bounced around the altar like a misbehaving child. Between that sight and the stench of her gown, Elinor's stomach churned. Bile rose in her throat as one of the men who had helped to capture her prodded her up the aisle.

The other guard stood near the altar.

The dower-faced priest stood behind them. Holding his Bible in one hand, he tapped the cover with the other. He was red from too much sun.

Where were the guests? Why were no neighbors present? Elinor's heart pounded in her ears. Panic rose up from her gut. This couldn't be happening. Her feet hurt from traversing the castle and courtyard wearing ancient, ill-fitting slippers that matched the wedding gown. If the guard's vice-like grip hadn't held her up, her legs might have given out. She would have bruises on her arm to match the one on her face.

Elinor said. "You cannot actually believe that I shall go through with marrying you."

Roxton frowned. "You do not seem to understand. I have not asked you, because the choice is not yours. I am in command here at Kerburghe. You will do as I say. Everyone here does as I say."

"You have no business here. This is not your holding. Michael Rollins is the Duke of Kerburghe, and you are most certainly not him. He is a hero for the crown, and you are nothing."

Before she could flinch, Roxton slapped her across the face. She immediately tasted the blood.

"This is a house of God!" The priest stomped his foot and raised his bible.

Roxton turned on him eyes bulging and spittle on his chin.

They were about the same height. Roxton carried more fat around his middle, and the priest wore spectacles.

The priest stood his ground. "Am I to understand that the young lady does not consent to this marriage?"

"I do not. I have been brought here against my will. I—"

An enormous meaty hand clamped over her mouth and blocked her breathing.

She struggled, but it was useless, and the bruises on her face stung from the added pressure.

"Of course, she wished the marriage. I am a duke." Roxton's

voice took on a sing-song quality. "All women want to marry a duke."

The priest sighed and removed his spectacles. He closed the Bible and rubbed his eyes. "I cannot marry you if the lady is not willing. You shall have to release her and allow her to go."

"Go! Where can she go? She is mine. I will never let her go." He advanced on the priest and pointed his finger in the man's face. "You will marry us, or I will put you out of Kerburghe. You will be left without a living."

To his credit, the priest merely frowned. "I shall pack my things, for I shall not go against the church and marry an unwilling party."

For a man who had obviously overindulged in food and drink for most of his life, Carter Roxton was surprisingly quick. He pulled out a long thin knife from his boot and pointed it at the priest.

The cleric only narrowed his eyes. "I cannot be threatened, my son. I do not fear death as it only brings me closer to my Lord. I would only fear for your soul should you kill me."

Roxton's freckled face spread into a grin. He turned the knife away from the man and toward Elinor.

Elinor also preferred the idea of death to marrying the fiend. However, the hand blocking her mouth kept her from voicing this.

"I wonder if those brave words hold up now."

The guard continued to hold Elinor. He let go of her mouth and held both arms behind her back. Her shoulders ached from the strain.

"Father, I would rather die than marry him."

Now Roxton pressed the edge of his blade against her neck. Cold steel sent a shiver up her spine.

"You are not going anywhere until this marriage is complete. I shall have her, or I shall kill her. You see, Father, I am in love with this woman, and I cannot stand for another man to have her. I am quite desperate."

He didn't sound at all desperate. In fact, his voice was almost melodious as he described her two possible fates. It was a game to him. His ruddy face colored a deeper red and puffed out. He would kill her, and he thought he could get away with the murder.

The priest looked at Roxton, then at Elinor. She could see that he too believed that she was in peril. "I am sorry, my child."

"Father, you cannot." It was unbearable. *Where was Michael?* She would have screamed if a blade hadn't been threatening her life.

The priest spread his hands and looked hopelessly down the steps at Elinor. "I cannot be the cause of a mortal sin."

"So you would be party to a forced marriage—a sacred oath that I cannot keep. How is it that this pig's immortal soul is of more value than mine? I would rather die than allow that piece of dung to touch me."

He pressed the blade.

Blood trickled down her neck, staining the low collar of the yellowed dress.

"Don't test my patience." Roxton blew stale putrid breath in her face.

"My child, please," the clergy begged.

Any fear Elinor might have experienced had been overshadowed by rage. She would plunge that dagger into Roxton's heart if she had the chance. "Is there nothing I can say, Father? Nothing that will save me from this person?"

The priest sighed and shook his head.

"Good." Smiling, Roxton removed the blade and slipped it into his boot with practiced ease. He nodded to the guard, who released her arms.

A cry escaped before she could stop it, and Elinor slumped forward, rubbing her aching shoulders.

Roxton pulled her upright. "I am sorry for all of this unpleasantness, my dear."

She wouldn't be able to count the bruises by the end of this insanity. She was about to be married to a complete madman, and there was no way out of it. Running wasn't an option with his hired guards looming over her.

Not even the priest would help her.

The ceremony began, and bile rose in her throat. She did not have any idea whose ancient gown she had been swallowed up in, but she begged their forgiveness.

"Do you, Lady Elinor Arabella Burkenstock, take Carter Smythe Roxton, Duke of Kerburghe, to be your lawfully wedded husband..."

Her ears rang. The walls closed in like a nightmare.

Perhaps she had become pale, because the priest stopped and asked, "Are you all right, my child?"

She vomited the lovely bread from her morning meal all over the gown and the priest.

After that, everything blurred. Hands gripped her, and there was shouting. She tried to focus on what was going on, but nothing made sense. *Why was Michael not charging in to save her?*

More shouting.

The priest was again refusing to continue.

The room righted itself and stopped spinning.

"I now pronounce you man and wife."

She never said, "I do," but it didn't seem to matter.

"Take the priest and lock him in the dungeon until after Rollins is dispensed with."

Maybe she was in the midst of a nightmare and would soon wake up and realize she was still at Marlton and Michael was just down the hall. Then her biggest problem would be convincing Mother she should marry Michael rather than Preston.

Roxton wore a cat-like smile, and she almost vomited again. The urge to sprint from the church and run until this nightmare was over almost overwhelmed her.

"Take her to the lady's chambers and have her cleaned up. I plan to make this marriage official before the sun sets."

The beefy guard dragged her from the church.

Elinor sat on the edge of the bed as footmen carried a large ancient tub into the room. After it was in place, they filled it, which took an hour. As bewildered as she was, her mind still raced, thinking what to do next. The servants all thought she was daft. How could they not? In the last twenty-four hours, her life had gone from pure joy to complete horror. That would be enough to drive most women mad.

She looked at the window and knew immediately that she was far too high to jump. The hallway was crowded with guards and servants. The wardrobe connected to the master's chambers, and she assumed that Roxton would be through there. The servants' passage through the back of the house was the only way out, but she would need help.

When the tub was full, the room cleared except for Brianne, who was adding some kind of oils to the water.

"Brianne, what are the servants saying?"

The girl turned with wide eyes.

"Come now, I know that there must be some gossip in the back stairs. It's not possible for what is going on here to be completely secret."

"I am not supposed to tell tales, your grace."

Elinor cringed at the title. She had to get out. Letting Roxton touch her wasn't an option. "That is commendable, but please tell me what you've heard."

"The rumors have run wild. They are saying you are a runaway princess and your father will send his knights to rescue you. I heard that the duke put a knife to your throat. I even heard that there is a priest locked in the dungeons. It's like a fairytale, the way they are all going on." Her red curls bobbed as she giggled.

Elinor smiled. "I am no princess, Brianne. But the other two rumors are quite true. The priest who was forced to marry me to that pig of an impostor is locked in the dungeon." She pointed to the small cut on her neck. "You can see for yourself that I was cut by the knife at my throat."

Brianne rushed forward and touched the cut. She frowned, tugging at the collar where blood stained the dress. "Goodness. I thought you made up everything."

"I need your help, Brianne. I have to get out of here before Roxton comes for me. I will kill myself rather than have the man touch me. Do you understand?"

The maid nodded, but tears filled her eyes. "But where will you go? It's only a matter of time before you're found out. Then he will take you, and I will be put out in the street or worse."

She took the girl's hands in hers. "Listen to me. I do not need to be hidden for long. I told you the truth when I said that the real Kerburghe will come for me. I only hope he has figured out where I am."

Brianne's eyes grew even larger. "Then the story of the boy who was shot was also true?"

Sorrow washed over Elinor, and she dashed away her tears. "I am afraid so. I only pray Everett survived. I shall never forgive myself if I am somehow the cause of Everett losing his life. There is no time to think of that now. We must get me out of here."

"Can you get yourself out of that dress?" Brianne asked.

"I think so." Elinor tugged at the ties running up the back.

"I shall go and fetch you some of the servants' clothes."

Relief flooded Elinor. "Please, be quick."

Chapter Nineteen

Michael crawled over a rocky hump toward Kerburghe Castle. "Hardwig," he whispered.

Crouched behind a row of hedges and rocks, James and his men startled.

"Good Lord, Kerburghe, You've nearly caused me an apoplexy." He looked around. "Where are the rest?"

"Looking for other ways into that pile of rocks."

The castle's towering walls and single gate complicated entry. Luckily, the overgrown grounds surrounding the fortress offered places for a man to hide and watch. Look-outs walked the battlements. If properly executed, an attack could succeed, but Michael had to work out the details.

James shook his head. "Built in the old style, it won't be easy to get in without causing a commotion."

Michael smiled. "That's exactly what we need, Hardwig."

"Pardon?"

"Did you happen to bring any explosives?"

James smiled. "No, but I'll wager my eyes that Thomas

Wheel has a bit tucked away somewhere. The man's a fanatic when it comes to firepower."

Michael shared a knowing smile with the inspector. Thomas loved his weapons and munitions. "I'll go find him. When you hear the signal, rush the front gate. It should be clear for you. Roxton doesn't have enough men to keep the front covered while the rear is being attacked."

"Can I assume the signal will be obvious?"

"You won't miss it, James." Michael took one step, then turned back. "Be careful of the servants, James. They probably think Roxton is the duke. They have no idea what's going on. These people are under my protection, even if they don't know it yet."

Hardwig edged closer to Michael. "I hate to bring this up, but the church bells rang a while ago. We may be too late. They may have married already."

If Roxton had harmed his Elinor in any way, he would pay the price. "If that is the case, then the lady is about to become a widow. If that is a problem for you, Inspector, then you had better leave now."

James narrowed his eyes and nodded. "We'll move on your signal."

~

Brianne pinned the hem of the plain gray dress so Elinor could move without tripping.

"Where did you get this dress?" Elinor asked.

Shrugging, she said, "I borrowed it from Nel, the scullery maid. She won't notice for some time, and my other dress would have been far too big for you. This one is just slightly long."

"I shall make it up to Nel when this is over." Elinor made a mental note. Lord, how she missed her list book.

Brianne leaned in and whispered, "You must take the back stairs down two flights. Then turn to your left and go all the way to the end of that hall. It's dark, so be careful. You should not run into anyone down there at this time of day, but keep your face hidden just the same. No need to take a chance. When you reach the end, you will see stairs to your right. Go up one flight down that hall to the end, then you can take the stairs on the left all the way down to the kitchen garden."

"I've got it." Excitement and terror rocked Elinor. Making it out of the castle before Roxton found her was unlikely. If he did catch her, the consequence would be dire.

Pointing to the door, Brianne said, "When you step into the hallway, keep your head down. Those dolts he has guarding won't notice it's you and not me. Here, take this with you." She handed Elinor a bundle of laundry, including the wedding gown she had bled and vomited on.

"This is the worst thing I've ever smelled."

Brianne laughed and clapped her hands. "Good. It will keep them from investigating too closely."

They went to the door. "I do not know how to thank you, Brianne."

Blushing, Brianne smiled. "You're not out of it yet, mi'lady."

Someone pounded on the master chamber's adjacent door. "Your grace," Roxton called. "Your dear husband is about to make all your dreams come true."

"Go." Brianne pushed her toward the other door.

"What about you?"

"I will manage the pig." Brianne lifted the candlestick off the hearth.

Elinor hugged her.

"Go, before it's too late." She kissed her cheek.

Elinor ran into the hall. She kept her face tucked down so far that the sour smell in her arms made her gag.

The two guards paid her no mind.

Once in the dark, stale, servants' corridor, she took a deep breath. At the first door, she knocked. Once assured no one was inside, she opened it and placed her laundry inside, silently apologizing to whomever the small room belonged to.

As she scurried down the two flights, she saw no one. In the long corridor, a young man carrying an armful of wood strode toward her.

She ducked her head down and pulled on her cap.

He hallooed, and she nodded and mumbled while hurrying past him. She resisted the urge to look back and see if he recognized her.

Elinor climbed up and down stairs and halls until the final stretch of her escape. The walls shook with a loud boom. She covered her ears. Bits of the castle crashed in on her. Covering her head with her arms, she tried to run, but tripped over the hem of her borrowed dress.

She lurched toward the ground. The stupid castle had waited hundreds of years in order to collapse on her head. Pain seared her arm and shoulder an instant before everything went black and silent.

The explosion opened up a large hole in the back side of the castle. Michael and Middleton raced through and up the stairs toward the central keep. The others rushed to the outer walls to deal with the guards patrolling up there.

Even in the chaos, Michael noted the castle was outdated and damp.

To the right of the first landing, a man roared. A guard as tall as the doorframe raced toward them.

Michael threw the giant over the railing.

"Not exactly subtle," Middleton said.

Michael shrugged. "I am a soldier. To let a man of that size get the better of you, for even an instant, could be fatal."

Middleton looked over the railing. "I suppose that is true. What now?"

Feminine screams echoed down against the stone walls.

They bolted down an adjoining hallway.

The screaming woman was behind the first door. Middleton tried the knob, but it was locked.

"Keep trying." Michael rushed down the hall.

"Where are you going?" Middleton rammed his shoulder against the door, but it did not give.

Silently, Michael slipped through a door down the hall.

"Open the door this instant! I demand you open this door!" Middleton shouted, pounding on the door.

It was a good distraction.

Michael slipped into a dressing room, then ran and burst through the door on the opposite side.

Roxton seemed to be wrestling with a writhing curtain.

"Get your filthy hands off of her!" Michael shouted.

A writing desk and chair had been overturned near the window. On the other side of the room, another chair lay in ruins. Near the bed, the side table was shattered. Glass shards and liquid littered the floor. The bedding was tossed in every direction, and the curtains had been ripped from around the bed.

Against the far wall, the screaming woman was using the drapes to shield herself from Roxton, who was bare-assed and groping at his prey like a swine going after a full troth. A leg kicked out from the cloth and caught the pig in the chin. His bulbous head snapped back, and he cried out.

Michael grabbed a handful of red hair and propelled Roxton across the room.

Middleton appeared in dressing room door just in time to see Roxton crash to the floor in a heap.

Roxton shook his head and blinked. Then he smiled. "Rollins, you are interrupting our wedding night. You will have to call another time. My wife and I are not receiving guests at this delicate point in our marriage."

Michael lifted Roxton with one hand and punched him in the stomach with the other. Then he tossed the pretend duke across the room.

Roxton landed in front of the windows, curled into a ball holding his bloody face and crying. "Guards? Where are my guards?"

Michael turned toward the bed. "Elinor?"

The fabric mound whimpered.

"Elinor, it's all right now. I am here."

Still no response.

"It's Michael, my love."

A freckle-faced red-haired girl peeked out and her eyes widened. "You're real. My lady told the truth. Are you the real Kerburghe?"

Baffled, he pulled her from the drapes. "Where is Lady Elinor?"

From the corner, Roxton screamed for his guards.

The girl wept loudly.

Battle chaos bubbled up from the floors below.

"Kerburghe, she is just a girl. Please put her down. You will get nothing from scaring the child." Middleton put his hand on Michael's shoulder.

He set the girl down. "Who are you?"

She erupted into a fresh bout of hysterics.

Michael threw his hands up and turned away. He considered beating Roxton some more. It wouldn't help the situation, but it would most definitely make him feel better. Rolling his eyes, he turned to Middleton. "Perhaps it would be best if you spoke to the girl."

Middleton gave a half smile, picked up the unbroken chair from the floor, and placed it in the middle of the room. "Please sit down and tell me your name, miss."

The girl sat, but she had her hands over her eyes. "I am Brianne. I'm the maid."

He knelt in front of her. "Where is the Lady Elinor, Brianne?"

"She made a run for it. I was to distract his grace while she tried to escape."

"I'll kill you, you little bitch." Roxton hauled himself up and rushed toward the girl.

Brianne's piercing scream filled the room.

Michael picked up a piece of the broken chair and whacked Roxton on the back of the head.

He landed with a thump and did not move.

"Is he dead?" The girl hugged herself and rocked back and forth.

Michael examined Roxton. "No. Unfortunately, he lives still."

Turning back to the girl, Middleton asked, "How was the lady to escape, Brianne?"

Now that Roxton was silent and Michael leaned against the wall, Brianne spewed forth the entire plan of escape. She told the two men the entire route that she had explained to her lady, ending with the small servant's door at the back of the house.

Michael asked, "How long ago was that?"

The girl wrinkled her nose. "Not long, your grace. She left here just before that one came in and attacked me."

"The explosion." Michael's heart stopped. What had he done?

"Go," Middleton commanded. "I will take Roxton down with the rest, then I will follow."

Michael was out the door before Preston had finished his sentence.

Chapter Twenty

Dust filled Elinor's lungs, and she coughed herself back into consciousness. Sprawled in a pile of dust and rubble, she eased up, pushing away pieces of rock and mortar. Considering she'd thought the entire castle had fallen on her head, it was nice to wake up at all.

Her arms, legs, and head all seemed to be in the proper place. Tentatively, she touched the side of her head where a substantial bump had formed. She winced, then brushed her hair out of her face. She had little pain and only bruises and scrapes.

Not twenty feet beyond where Elinor had lain unconscious, the passage had collapsed, leaving the hallway exposed to the outside. It was a miracle that she was alive and uninjured. Crawling to her right, she used the wall to steady herself as she tried to stand.

Far in the distance, voices raised.

Footsteps clattered down the stairs behind her.

Her heart banged loudly in her chest, and her head throbbed. How she yearned to lay down on her soft bed at home and cry until the tears would no longer come. One of those tears escape down her cheek, and she dashed it away. "No time for that now." The possibility of winding up back in Roxton's bed pushed Elinor beyond her normal limits.

When she steadied herself on all fours, rough stone cut into the soft skin of her hands. Thankful for Brianne's sturdy boots, she climbed over jagged pieces of rock. She made it outside with a few more bruises.

Clean air was a relief, but the open courtyard and garden left her nowhere to hide. A wall stood thirty yards away, but she knew she couldn't make that run unseen.

She picked up a good-sized rock and rushed behind the edge of the exposed wall.

Shuffling and footfall sounded on the other side of the rocks.

With all her might, she raised the stone above her head, her arms shaking with effort.

A dark head came into view. Without a thought, she hurled herself forward with the rock, intent on cracking the man's skull.

He dropped to the ground and rolled forward, knocking her to the ground. The stone tumbled harmlessly away.

Elinor screamed as her shoulder hit the ground.

He leaped on top of her.

She screamed louder and thrashed her head, kicking her legs.

"Elinor!"

One of her hands slipped from his grip, and she lashed out with her nails, cutting deep scratches in his neck.

He took a firmer hold of her arms. "Elinor, it's me, Michael. You're safe."

She stopped thrashing and looked up. It took several seconds to recognize that it was indeed Michael who held her. It was Michael she'd nearly killed with a rock. "Michael?"

"I am here." He released her hands.

She slapped him soundly across his face.

He stared down at her with all the sweetness and love they shared shining in his eyes.

"You are too late. I am married to a monster." The hysteria she'd been holding back tumbled out in large tears and wracking sobs.

Michael rolled to one side, pulled her into his lap, and held her tight. "Don't worry. We will take care of whatever Roxton has done."

"I am truly ruined now." An entire year of planning and disappointment swallowed her up.

Cradling her in his arms like a child, he rocked her and kissed her forehead. "I love you, Elinor. Everything will be fine, I promise."

She stiffened and pulled away far enough she could look at his face. "You make promises too easily, Michael."

He released his grip on her and stared with wide eyes.

She leaped from his lap.

His face was a mixture of confusion and sadness but most of all, he looked tired. His normally tanned skin was pale and sickly. His bright eyes were ringed red with dark circles underneath. Sitting on the ground amongst the rubble, he almost looked fragile.

"Are you ill?" She was torn between worry and exhaustion. She needed him to be the strong one.

Finally, he got up off the ground. He took a step closer, but she backed away an equal distance. He did not pursue. "I am just tired."

"Everett." She'd forgotten. She must have hit her head harder than she thought. She grabbed Michael's arms.

He crushed her to him. Her ribs ached, but not enough to break the contact. Desperate to be near him, she clung tightly.

"He was alive when I left Marlton. I spoke to him, but he was very weak."

Utter sorrow engulfed her. "He's just a boy. He tried to save me, but he's just a boy. You have been through so much. I'll bet you have not slept, and here I am being churlish."

He eased her away and lifted her chin. "I think, my love, you have been put through quite an ordeal yourself, and it is all because of me. I shall not censure you for being put out." His voice filled with humor. "After all, you were kidnapped and forced to marry against your will."

Where was her brain? "The priest."

"What priest?" Michael's face filled with confusion.

"The one who married me, of course. He's locked in the dungeon. My God, I hope the dungeon did not collapse as well. He can attest to the wrongness of the entire marriage. He knows that I did not wish to marry that...that...mongrel. He was there when I vomited. He will testify, or whatever it is one must do to dissolve a marriage."

"A priest. I suppose we'll have to go to the pope." Michael shook his head. "Come, love, we'll find the others and the priest, then we can head for England."

When they stopped at an inn, it was midnight. Elinor fought to keep her eyes open. The tavern was a blur. She vaguely remembered Michael paying a large man with a bald head and an apron for several rooms, including one for the priest. She did not see Roxton again and worried about where he had gotten to.

She remembered the weightless feeling of being lifted into

Michael's arms and carried upstairs. He gently kissed her forehead and left her sitting on the edge of the bed.

She must have dosed off, because some time later, a bath appeared in the middle of the room, and two maids helped her out of Brianne's dirty but serviceable dress and into the tub. They scrubbed her for an eternity before putting a soft shift over her head and tucking her into bed.

When her eyes opened again, the candle flickered. She scanned the small, clean room. The sky outside was still black and the tub was gone, as were the two women. She had no idea how long she had slept, or even if it was the same night. Her dress was nowhere to be seen, which was concerning, but she slipped back to sleep.

His scent warmed her before she opened her eyes and confirmed that Michael had slipped into the bed beside her. Snuggling in deeper, she sighed and smiled at the little moan of contentment that rumbled in his throat.

"Was there something wrong with your room, your grace?" she asked, her lips touching his bare chest.

"Yes. You were not in there. I didn't want to wake you, but it was torture to not touch you. Forgive me."

"Is it nearly morning?"

He nodded against the top of her head. "Another hour until the sun is up."

She kissed the hollow of his neck, then stuck her tongue out, licking his warm skin and kissing his corded neck.

He moaned. "Elinor, do you know what you're doing?"

She giggled. "I think so. What are you going to do about it, your grace?"

His hand moved down her shoulder and caressed the side of her breast before he took her nipple between his thumb and forefinger and pinched.

She gasped with the pleasure that shot from her breast to where her thighs met.

Then, he dipped his head down and took the same nipple between his lips, sucking gently.

Elinor moaned as his tongue swirled around and around at a maddeningly steady pace. His head came up, and she moaned again, this time with disappointment.

His cool breath skittered across her wet skin, and she gasped at the new pleasure.

"I am going to assume that you like that." His voiced filled with laughter.

"Mmm," she said, pulling gently on his face to bring it back up to hers. Boldly, she put her lips on his, imitating the kisses he had shared with her. It was the first time she had ever taken control of their intimacy. She found it both wicked and wonderful to wield such control.

"Have I created a wanton?"

She looked into his eyes, then a wave of shyness overtook her, and she looked away. "Would you mind?"

He did not answer with words only took her hand and placed it on his shaft. In truth, he had only meant to hold her. He yearned to be near her and feel her heart beating, but she was so warm and responsive that his gentlemanly thoughts were long forgotten.

She was tentative at first. Her soft fingertips ran gently down his length and up again. She lingered around the ridge, swirling around the tip before descending again.

Michael didn't move. He found it difficult to breathe. Her innocent ministrations were driving him mad. He wanted to give her time to explore him, but if this continued for much longer, he would surely explode in her hand. Under different circumstances that might have been enough, but he yearned to be inside her and didn't want to wait for another time.

Suddenly, she gripped him harder.

He cried out; not sure if he should let her continue or take her immediately.

She let him go. "Did I hurt you?" Her voice shot to a higher pitch.

He took her hand and returned it to his shaft. "No. You are wonderful."

He put his own hand over hers and showed her how to pleasure him as he closed his eyes and leaned back.

She traced her fingers along the corded vein that protruded down his length.

"Oh, Elinor, you're killing me." He took her hand away and rolled over on top of her, his shaft perched at her center.

Unable to bear her strained expression, he relaxed down next to her. He leaned his head on one elbow and touched her cheek. "I will not hurt you, Elinor. I told you it only hurts the first time. Don't you believe me?"

"Yes." Her voice sounded small and strained.

He laughed. "That was not very convincing, my love."

She shrugged.

"I shall have to prove it to you." He slid down the bed.

"Michael, where are you going?"

Desire and joy filled him to overflowing. "I am setting out to prove a point. Now, don't interrupt me."

When he reached the bottom of the bed, he crawled forward, pushing her legs apart as he came up between them. He reached the juncture between her thighs and puffed out a small breath.

She gasped. "Michael, I thought you were going to..."

"Patience."

He slid his finger between her folds, moving up and down. She was so wet and touching her so erotic, he closed his eyes to savor the moment.

She gripped the bedding and arched up for more attention.

Michael replaced his finger with his lips and tongue, then slid his hands up her torso to plucked at her hard nipples.

She thrashed and bit her lip.

The priest was just down the hall, so silence was important.

Michael licked her folds from the bottom to the top, then down again. He focused on the bud at the top of her sex, first kissing then suckling it. He pinched and tweaked her nipple.

Opening her legs wide, she arched her back, giving him better access.

Every reaction from her left him achingly ready to take her. He rubbed her entry, and she gasped.

She threaded her fingers through his hair, pressing his mouth harder against her core.

Sucking harder until she was close to rapture, he stopped, making her groan.

When she opened her eyes, he covered her body with his, and entered her in one smooth gliding stroke. He pulled out and slid in again and again.

She raised her hips to meet him. The pace was slow and steady as the tension built.

She cried out again, and Michael covered her lips with his own, plunging his tongue into her mouth with the same ferocity he plundered her sex.

His climax was close. He reached between their bodies and stroked her sensitive bud between his thumb and forefinger.

She cried out, arching into him. She pulsed around him, sending him over the edge as he thrusted deep inside her one last time.

Waves of pleasure hung between them until Michael

relaxed his arms and rolled over, taking Elinor with him and landing her on top of his chest. "Did you feel pain, my love?"

She sighed, satisfied. "Pain. No."

"Then you will not be afraid in the future?"

"Never." She kissed his chest.

Nestled against him, she snuggled deeper. "You never answered my question."

Eyes closed his head lolled. "What question?"

"If you would mind..." She couldn't bring herself to complete the thought.

He laughed. "Mind if my wife was a wanton in the bedroom? Oh, my love, you are every man's dream. To have a wife who is a harlot in the bedroom and a lady in the parlor is what every man wishes for and few actually achieve."

She turned away from him. "But I am not your wife. I am the wife of a crazy man."

He tugged her shoulders until she faced him. "Elinor, listen to me. First of all, you are my wife in the eyes of God. You will be in the eyes of the law as well. This entire situation is my fault. I should have taken Roxton more seriously. I thought he was only a fool. I never imagined he was dangerous. If I had, I never would have left you or the boys alone. I should have protected you better, and Everett. I do not know what I'll do if he dies. I have failed entirely as protector of my family. I promise you that I shall make this all right again. I will pay whomever it takes, whatever it takes, to have you for my wife. I will never let anyone hurt you again. Forgive me."

She cupped his cheek. "This is not your fault, Michael. You are not responsible for the actions of another man."

He pressed his lips to her palm.

Daylight created shadows at the window.

Sighing, she said, "We had better get up, and you had

better get back to your own room before the maids come back with my dress."

He kissed her forehead. Sitting on the chair, he tugged on his boots, pulled his blouse over his head, and tucked a long knife into his right boot.

"Do you always have that?" Wide-eyed, she pointed toward his boot.

He shrugged. "It's an old habit. Perhaps one day I will not feel the need, but for now, it's still prudent to be prepared."

She frowned but agreed.

"I will see you in the carriage, my lady." Then he made a courtly bow, picked up his trousers, and walked half-naked into the hallway.

Chapter Twenty-One

Hooves thundered into the yard outside the inn as Michael handed Elinor into the carriage. The horses brought with them a cloud of dust, obscuring the view of the riders.

He secured Elinor inside the carriage and stepped forward. The hair on his neck stood in anticipation of news he wouldn't like.

Markus had taken the priest in a separate carriage and headed to London at first light. Thomas, Daniel, and Middleton waited for the dust to settle from the hasty arrival of James and his two men.

Breathless and grim-faced, Hardwig dismounted. "Your grace, I came as soon as I could to tell you Roxton escaped."

"Escaped. You had ten men watching a fat pig of a man, and you couldn't manage to keep hold of him for the trip to London?"

James's face colored brightly. "I am sorry, your grace. He stabbed one of my men with his own sword, then ran into the woods with the weapon before anyone knew what had happened."

"Your man, was he killed?" Preston asked.

Inspector Hardwig shook his head. "No but it will be some time before he's fit for duty. That ridiculous man cut him and left him for dead."

Thomas said, "I assume you are searching the area."

"We've been searching all night. I brought in twice as many men. We have checked every farm house and stable, but have not found a trace of him beyond one hundred feet from where we lost him. I came to tell you to be alert."

"I should think the man would get as far away from here as he can, while he can," Preston said. "He's probably headed for the coast."

Michael knew that wasn't the case. Roxton had a grudge, and losing Elinor only added to it. "No. James is right. He'll come for me. He's mad, and he thinks that I am the cause of his ruination. He won't stop until he destroys me, and he will hurt anyone close to me to do it."

From the carriage window, Elinor watched and listened. Her face had turned sheet-white and filled with fear.

Hell, he too was afraid for her safety.

Hardwig remounted easily. In spite of his protruding belly, he was an accomplished rider. "I have to get back to the search, but you may want to hold up here until Roxton is found. The open road might offer him more opportunity."

"I wish we could, James, but my brother's injuries force me back to Marlton with haste. I cannot wait. Perhaps we can lead this horse to water on the road."

James nodded. "I thought you might say that. I will leave these two men with you for extra protection. Have them scout ahead on the road."

"Thank you. Any additional men can be useful. Hopefully,

we won't have need of them. I wouldn't mind if Middleton were correct, and Roxton did the prudent thing and made for the coast."

"I think we both know that is unlikely, given his state of mind," James said.

Surveying the horses and carriage, Michael sent the two guards ahead to scout. He looked from Thomas to Daniel, and they nodded. Preston took his place behind the carriage with them, while Michael climbed into the vehicle and took the seat across from Elinor.

Sighing, she looked out the window and watched as the inn disappeared and the woods obscured any view.

The road was dangerous at the best of times. Highwaymen were lurking in the shadows. A party of their size was normally quite safe, but not today.

Elinor sighed again as she pushed her stubborn hair from her face. "I feel as though I'm a child again, with monsters lurking in the wardrobe."

Michael took her hand. He forced a smile, but it was a struggle to hold it, and he let it fade.

Wariness clouded her eyes.

The forest rolled by as they took the road to London.

At midday, the rain began. The light drizzle tapping on the carriage roof lulled her to sleep. They galloped down the road, but the rain slowed them.

Her sleep was fitful, and her dreams of crumbling castle walls and red-haired madmen disturbing.

The carriage shifted, and Michael pulled her close. He warmed her and chased away the visions. Her sleep deepened, and she snuggled in closer, breathing in his warm male scent.

The carriage jerked to a stop, waking her. The rain was rapping on the roof harder. "Is something wrong, Michael?"

He kissed the top of her head. "Just changing horses. You can go back to sleep."

As Michael left the carriage to help with the horses, the warmth left with him. The cool dampness was raw against her skin, making her clothes clammy and uncomfortable.

She made a mental list of all the warm comfortable things she would enjoy once they reached Marlton, and Everett was safe and well. A roaring fire, a fur pelisse, maybe some hot soup, and Michael wrapped around her.

Michael returned to the carriage, face strained and clothes soaked.

"Something is wrong."

His jaw tightened, and his lips pulled back in a straight line. He shook off the water and climbed in. "I cannot help thinking that this weather is perfect for an ambush."

"Do you really think that Roxton would attack us by himself? His men are still in custody. How can he hurt us? He needed those muscle men just to kidnap me, with only two boys for protection. Now he is helpless against seven men."

Frowning, he watched warily out the window as the carriage started forward. "I am sure you're right."

She knew he was only trying to ease her concerns. Her anxiety heightened, and she joined him in watching the pouring rain out the window. Between the heavy trees, dark clouds, and rain, it was impossible to see anything beyond a few feet. Elinor strained her eyes looking for shadows, but there was only rain and the rising fog. Soon she could see nothing at all and closed her eyes against the strain.

An hour after they'd changed horses, the fog closed in on them. "Why is it so quiet?" Elinor asked.

Michael stuck his head out the window. He did the same on the other side. "I do not see the others."

"What do you mean? Where could they have gone?"

"I don't know. It's foggy. That can sometimes dull sound and cause a party to separate."

He knocked on the roof. "Wallace, do you see the others?"

No answer.

The carriage sped up.

Wet roads and speed created a rocking that tossed Elinor from side to side.

Michael lifted her and placed her on the carriage floor. "Hold on," he commanded as he slipped through the door.

Elinor screamed his name but did not move from the floor. With the horses at a full run, the carriage tossed her back and forth. She braced her legs between the benches. They shook with the effort.

The rain dwindled to a drizzle but the fog grew thicker, making it impossible to see the driver clearly. Michael climbed up to the top of the carriage, heading for the driver. After he told the man to stop, he would worry about finding the others. He was only inches from him when the carriage rumbled over something in the road. Michael clung to the roof, air whooshing from his lungs.

The driver turned. The face that looked back was Roxton's. His initial shock transformed to a wicked smile as he tossed the reins aside. Roxton pulled out his sword, stood, and hacked madly at Michael.

As the sword came crashing down an inch from his neck, Michael rolled to one side, barely escaping the loss of his head

The carriage rocked wildly. Elinor screamed.

With no one directing them, the horses ran blindly into the fog.

Michael had little hope that he could survive a crash, but Elinor might make it safely home if he could toss Roxton from the roof.

Roxton took another wild swing with the sword.

Michael grabbed his legs. Off balance, Roxton fell forward on top of Michael, and together they crashed through the carriage roof.

Elinor screamed, rolling out of the way just in time. She curled up in a corner of the back seat.

Roxton kept chopping at Michael.

Michael blocked, putting himself between Roxton and Elinor.

Roxton screamed, "I'll kill you. I'll kill you."

The carriage rocked so violently, it could topple any second, killing all three of them.

Michael pressed his forearm against Roxton's throat, but he couldn't get hold of his sword arm and stop the idiot from hacking.

The men landed on the floor of the carriage with Roxton on the top. Elinor wished she could see Michael's face, but only his boots were visible, pressed firmly against the carriage floor.

The carriage lurched, and she toppled across the bench.

Steel glinted from Michael's boot.

Elinor pulled the thin knife free, lifted it high, and plunged it into Roxton's back.

The world froze.

Elinor pulled the knife from his back.

Red spread across his jacket.

The sword stopped moving.

His face a mask of surprise, Michael looked around Roxton.

Elinor dropped the knife.

Michael pushed Roxton's body to the side and squeezed out from under him. He stared at Elinor, then jumped up through the hole he and Roxton had made in the roof.

Hollering to the racing beasts, Michael slowed the carriage. The horses neighed before the carriage stopped.

Elinor stared down at Roxton.

His back was dark with blood, and he hadn't moved from the floor.

No.

The door opened, and Michael pulled her from the carriage and into his arms.

"Did I kill him?"

"You did what was necessary. I am very proud of you, Elinor." He caressed her back.

She closed her eyes. "Should we go and look for the others?"

"They will find us." He took her hand and walked her to a fallen tree beside the road.

The rain had stopped, but the silence was just as thick as the fog.

Elinor voiced her only coherent thought. "I suppose I am a widow now."

"You were never really married to that pig, Elinor. It would have all been resolved, and we would have been married regardless. This just makes things easier. You did the right thing. He might have killed me, then you would have been in real danger."

She nodded, but her mind was a jumble of images she wanted to push away.

"Really, it's a miracle that the carriage stayed upright through all of that."

She nodded again and looked at the blood on her hands.

Michael removed his neck cloth and wiped the blood away. The white cloth turned reddish- brown. He was serious about his job, and a deep crease formed between his eyes.

Could he love a woman who was a murderess? "What are you thinking?"

"I was just thinking that I have never had my life saved by a woman before." He tucked the cloth inside his jacket and pulled her closer.

"I didn't know what to do. I saw the knife in your boot, and I acted without thinking." The same sense of panic that gripped her in the carriage returned.

He kissed her forehead. "You did exactly the right thing, love."

Voices and pounding hooves penetrated the fog. A moment later, Thomas and Daniel rode up.

Thomas dismounted and looked inside the carriage.

"Are you two all right?" Daniel asked.

"A little bruised, but otherwise we're safe."

Thomas shook his head. "I guess that solves that problem. You took care of him."

The three men exchanged a look.

Michael said, "Yes. I took care of him."

Thomas and Daniel both looked at her.

Grateful that Michael kept her part in the incident a secret, she kept quiet, though she suspected their friends knew the truth. She had done the only thing she could, but still her stomach lurched and her hands shook.

Thomas went to find Inspector Hardwig to manage Roxton's body and report what had happened.

Middleton arrived last on the scene, but said he would send

notes to people in high places, assuring that Roxton's death was unavoidable. He shook his head. "The man was clearly mad."

Due to the carriage's severe damage, Elinor rode the rest of the way on horseback with Michael. While she could have ridden on her own, she was glad for the safety of his arms. Sitting in front of him, she leaned into his chest and tried not to think of the events of the past few days. The heavy haze afforded them some small bit of privacy.

Wet and tired, Michael, Elinor, and the rest of the party returned to Marlton Hall just before dark. The moment they entered the yard in front of the tall wide doors of Marlton's estate, Elinor's sense of quiet was shattered.

The butler had the door open before they'd finished dismounting.

Grooms rushed forward to take control of the exhausted animals.

Sobbing, Virginia Burkenstock ran from the door, down the steps, and crushed Elinor in her arms.

"It's all right, Mother. I'm all right." She patted her mother's back.

"I was so worried. I was sure you were dead." Virginia wept.

"All is well, Mother. I have been rescued."

At that, her mother broke away and turned toward Michael. She opened her mouth to speak, but closed it again and threw herself against him, sobbing once again. "Thank you, your grace. Thank you. I do not know how to thank you."

Michael stood with his arms wide and an expression of utter confusion. It was comical, but Elinor's energy was too sapped even for a laugh.

He looked to Elinor for help, but she just smiled and shrugged.

He patted Virginia's back. "It is my pleasure to deliver Lady Elinor back to you safely."

The butler cleared his throat. "Your grace, your brother's health has taken a turn. Your mother asked for you to come above stairs as soon as you are able."

Virginia disengaged herself and rushed back to Elinor.

Michael looked at her.

"Go to Everett, Michael. I'm fine. I shall bathe and change before I come to see him."

He nodded and bolted up the stairs two at a time.

Elinor put her arm around her mother's shoulder and moved into the house.

Sophia and Dory waited to see her, but after giving them each a heartfelt hug, she asked to be allowed to go upstairs alone and wash.

The rain had chilled her to the bone, and she needed to scrub away the filth of everything she had done and seen. She indulged in a lengthy bath, but the memories haunted her.

Once dressed, she went to see Everett.

Tabitha sat in a chair near the bed. She looked small and worn next to the large bed Everett was tucked into.

Closing the door behind her, Elinor entered the room unnoticed.

She walked to the bed and touched Tabitha's shoulder. "You should get some sleep, my lady. You will make yourself ill, then who will care for him?"

Tabitha rose, and a smile touched her brown eyes. She took Elinor's hand. "I am so relieved you are safe, my dear. Everett will be relieved as well. He frets over you in his sleep."

Elinor's heart broke looking down at Everett's pale face. "Where is the doctor?"

"Gone to get more laudanum. He will return shortly. An infection of the blood, he says. All we can do is wait and pray."

Tabitha looked like she hadn't slept in days. The dark rings framing her eyes and her pallor were a testament to her vigilance over her son.

Elinor hadn't had much rest either, but she squeezed her hand. "I will sit with him until the doctor returns. Go and rest."

Tabitha hesitated, but then took a breath, nodded, and left. Michael's mother had always been kind to her, but some invisible barrier had broken between them. She trusted her with one of her most precious things.

Everett lay still in the bed. Seventeen, he was a man, but his illness made him look small and helpless.

She sat by his side and took his hand. "Oh, Everett, I am so sorry. Please live. You really must get better. I will make you a list of reasons to get better. First, your mother would not recover from your loss. Sheldon would be lost without you. You have your school work that you love and must complete. There is an entire world for you to explore when you are older, but you must get older to see it. Think of all the exotic places you will see. One day you will fall in love. You do not want to miss that. I do not know what Michael will do if he loses you. He was just telling me how he wishes to spend more time getting to know you and Sheldon. He plans for you to stay with us during your school breaks after we're married. Oh, and you will miss the wedding if you do not get better." She stopped her list to catch her breath.

"You could be a duke one day, you know. Michael and I shall adopt children, and you or your son will one day be the Duke of Kerburghe. Won't that be something? I shall have to call you, 'your grace.' Of course by then I will be an old woman with grown children and a dozen grandchildren running about. Perhaps you will be kind to me and allow me to call you by your Christian name. What do you think? Shall I be allowed to be familiar with the great duke?"

"You may call me, 'Kerburghe,'" Everett grumbled.

She looked up, and his eyes were open.

The hint of a smile touched his lips.

"Everett, you're awake. How long have you been listening to me babble?" It eased her worry that he still had his sense of humor.

He tried to shrug, but it was more of a twitching of his thin shoulders. "I do not know, but it was a good list. I will do my best to see it through."

"Good." She wiped the tears from her face. "How do you feel?"

"Hungry." He grimaced.

Joy spread through her. "I'll ring for something." She pulled the cord near the bed. A few moments later, the door opened, and the maid rushed in followed by half the household.

Michael was first in. He'd washed and changed. He stared from Elinor to Everett and back again.

She couldn't contain her tears. She squared her shoulders. "Everett would like something to eat."

The doctor, a bald burly man with an overgrown beard, pushed through the lords, ladies, and servants crowding the doorway. He put his hand on the boy's head, then took his wrist between his fingers. He smiled, and the strain on his face eased. "The infection seems to have abated. He is out of danger."

The crowd cheered.

Tabitha pushed through and hugged Everett.

The doctor turned to the maid. "Get him some broth and nothing too strong for a few days. See he's fed a small amount every couple of hours." Narrowing his eyes, he turned to Everett. "No jumping about, boy. Go slowly for a while until you get your strength back. The wound will need time to heal."

"Yes, sir."

"Now, everyone out of the room, the boy needs food and rest," the doctor commanded.

The group dispersed and chattered happily as they left the room. Michael and Tabitha stayed behind. Elinor made to leave as well, but Michael took her arm and pulled her close as he addressed the doctor. "Is there anything else we should do?"

"Just keep him quiet for a few days, your grace. He's young and should make a full recovery. It would be best if you didn't travel for a least a week. The last thing he needs right now is to be jostled around in a carriage for hours."

Tabitha whispered to Everett and brushed the hair from his forehead.

He smiled up at her.

"Thank you, doctor," Michael said.

He nodded. "I'll check on him daily for as long as you stay here at Marlton Hall. I assume you have a family physician in London you can call upon when you leave."

Michael confirmed that they did, and the doctor left the room.

He looked at Elinor and his bright blue eyes swam with unshed tears of joy. He touched her cheek, and smiling, she nuzzled deeper into his hand.

Weariness swamped her. Her legs wobbled, and she longed for somewhere soft to lay her head. "It's late. I am going to bed, and you should get your mother to sleep as well. She's exhausted."

Michael went to the bed. "Mother, go and rest now. You heard the doctor. Everett is out of danger. I will stay with him a while."

Tabitha Rollins nodded and kissed both her sons. "Sheldon is in bed, but he will be happy to see you in the morning."

Everett smiled for his mother.

Tabitha touched Elinor's cheek as she left the room.

Holding onto the doorframe to keep her feet, Elinor marveled at how similar the brothers looked.

Michael shifted from foot to foot before he finally sat. "I am glad you are all right."

"I am happy to see you recovered, Lady Elinor," Everett said.

Michael nodded mutely.

"Was it an adventure?" Everett asked.

Michael looked over his shoulder at Elinor, and his expression warmed. "It was. If you will try to rest, I will tell you all about it."

Everett closed his eyes.

Michael began the tale from the point where Sheldon ran toward them.

Unable to listen, Elinor stumbled down the hall to her bed.

Chapter Twenty-Two

It wasn't like Elinor to take a meal in her room, but she was too tired to face an entire house of people wanting to know what had happened. What would she tell them? She had already decided not to tell anyone other than Sophia and Dory about having killed Roxton.

Michael seemed willing to let it be his hand that had done the deed, and the scandal of her having killed a man would be terrible. However, she couldn't lie to her two best friends. Besides, they could be trusted to keep the information private. Elinor suspected that Marlton and Thomas Wheel already knew the truth. The four men often communicated in some silent way.

Unable to eat, she sipped her tea. Michael hadn't come to her last night. She worried that he might have changed his mind about the marriage after seeing her kill Roxton.

Her stomach knotted. What man would want to marry a woman who had murdered? She had potentially saved his life in the process. Would he take that into account? When he spoke to the doctor about Everett, she'd stayed by his side. It was like she was part of the family and should be present for any important conversations. That was a good sign. Perhaps he was just tired last night and that was why he hadn't come.

She was startled out of her reverie by knocking at the door. "Come in."

Dory poked in her perfect gold-blonde head. "We did not have a chance to talk yesterday." She opened the door further, admitting herself and Sophia to the room. "May we come in?"

"Of course." Elinor was glad for the distraction from her troubling thoughts. She accepted hugs from her two friends.

The three of them sat at the small table.

Sophia picked at Elinor's untouched breakfast.

Dory took charge. "Are you all right?"

"Yes." It was what she had told her mother and anyone else who asked. "And no," she said honestly.

"Tell us," Dory said.

"I do not know where to start. It was only a few days ago, but I feel as if I have lived years in that time. I fear everything has changed."

Sophia stopped eating. "Perhaps you should start at the beginning. Then Dory and I will have more of an idea how we can help you to sort this all out."

Elinor nodded and began the tale from the lovely time she had fishing with Michael's brothers by the river. She ended with plunging the knife into Roxton's back and arriving back at Marlton.

Dory gasped and reached forward, taking Elinor's hand.

Sophia nodded. Perhaps she'd already heard the information from her husband.

"I fear that everything has changed." The thought plagued her.

Dory squeezed her hand. "What do you mean? You are safe now. No one outside our circle need ever know."

"I do not think that Michael will want to marry a woman who is a killer. I cannot say that I blame him. He might think that I could do the same to him whilst he slept." She wiped her tears.

Dory's eyes widened. "He is a fool if that is what he thinks, and he does not deserve you. You saved his life and—"

"I do not think you need worry about that." Sophia scowled at Dory, and then smiled at Elinor. "In fact, I am certain that he still wishes to marry you."

"How do you know?" Elinor sniffed into her napkin.

Sophia had a way of making her feel good just by being present. She had come to her rescue when she and Michael had been caught in a compromising position, and now she had the key to free her from this tragedy as well. "Michael asked Daniel for the use of his study in order to speak with your mother this morning."

Elinor jumped from her seat. "When?"

"They are together right now."

"Oh no! Why didn't you tell me sooner? Here I have been sitting and telling stories and my future is hanging in the balance. What if Mother says no? I must go." She looked in the mirror, tucked an errant hair behind her ear, and ran through the house.

When she got to the study, Elinor pressed her ear to the door, but heard nothing. Catching her breath, she lifted her hand to knock, but instead squared her shoulders, put up her chin, and walked in.

Mother frowned across the desk at Michael, and Michael frowned back. They both looked up.

Elinor was tired of being bullied. "I understand my future is being decided. I would prefer to be the one making those decisions from now on."

"Elinor, really. You have no business being here." Mother's scolding did not have the effect it usually did.

Michael smiled, bolstering her courage.

"I have every right. I am not a child, Mother. I will make my own decisions." She was an adult and would act as such. The last few days had changed her as much as the events of the last few months. *No more waiting for someone else to change her world.*

Mother glared. "I have already told his grace that a marriage agreement between the two of you is out of the question. Your father was very specific in his instructions before he left." She took on the monotone she used whenever quoting Father verbatim. "You are not to marry Michael Rollins. I do not think he has changed his mind, and I have no way to contact him at this time. He has an essential job and cannot be bothered with trivialities."

"My future is not a triviality. Nevertheless, I do not wish for you to contact Father. His business is what he really cares about, anyway. If he cared about me then he would have asked my opinion before he created this mess in the first place. Michael and I would already be happily married, and Father would not have dishonored our family by breaking his word to a duke of the realm."

Mother gasped. "Elinor, how dare you speak of your father that way?"

Michael beamed at her. It was nice to see pride rather than pity or shame in his eyes.

Virginia gaped at Elinor, then cried.

With a sigh, Elinor sat next to her. "I am sorry, Mother. I know that you think Father is always right."

"That's not true. He is rarely right, but he is still your father," Mother said.

Elinor laughed. "Well, I am telling you right now that I will marry no one if I am not allowed to marry the Duke of Kerburghe. I would rather grow old and be pitied as an old maid than to marry a man whom I do not love. It is not fair to me and certainly unfair to the poor man I am forced on. I will marry Michael or no one at all."

Mother sputtered. "Elinor, you do not know what you're saying. It is obvious to me that the events of the past few days have caused you some sort of trauma. I shall call the doctor back for another look at you."

"I am not ill, Mother. I mean what I say, and no amount of doctoring will change my mind."

"Middleton is a good man, and he may well make an offer."

"You are correct. Middleton is a good man. However, whether he makes an offer or not is irrelevant. I will not have him. I love Michael, and marrying anyone else is out of the question. Besides, do you really think that Middleton wants a wife who is in love with someone else?"

Mother got up and walked to the other side of the room, shoulders slumped and shaking.

Michael's eyes smoldered with desire.

Reading his mind, she blushed, thinking of all the wondrous things he had done to her and how she wanted to do them all again.

At the window, Mother gazed into the gardens. "I do not know where you got the idea that marriage and love had anything to do with each other, Elinor. Marriage is a contract. It's business."

Elinor wished for some kind of divine intervention. Being disobedient wasn't what she wanted, but she would have her way. "I do not know where you got the idea that marriage was about anything else but love, Mother."

Virginia spun, wide-eyed. "I do not know who you are anymore. You look like my daughter but everything else about you is a mystery to me. When did you become so forward? Where is the sweet girl I raised to be a lady?"

"You and Father gave me little choice. When Father became an earl, I stopped recognizing the two of you." She had to proceed without hurting Mother too deeply. She rose and walked over to Virginia. "I don't know Father. He was always gone on some mission to Spain. So when he became overly enamored with the idea of being an earl, I was not really surprised. He always had an opinion of himself that outstretched his reach."

"Elinor." Mother gasped.

She put up her hand to stop Mother from saying more.

Behind her, Michael chuckled.

"However, Mother, you have taught me everything about life and love. You have been with me every day for my entire life. If I believe that marriage is about love, it is because you taught me that, in spite of the state of your own marriage. I know that you love Father. His feelings are a mystery to me, but yours are obvious."

Mother slouched, dabbing her nose with her lace handkerchief.

"I was not surprised by Father's attitude, but I was surprised by yours. All my life, you have been my constant ally, until the moment I needed you most. When I needed you to stand up to Father and tell him what he was doing was wrong and dishonorable, you abandoned me. I can only assume you too had become full of yourself over being a countess."

Head down with shame, Mother sighed and nodded.

"You left me no choice but to take control of my own life. I will admit, it has not gone as I had planned, and Michael's first response was unfavorable." She turned to Michael, whose apology was written all over his face.

It was unfortunate that she was hurting the people she

loved most, but at the moment, it seemed inevitable. "I had wanted to spare you this information, but I will have the man I love for my husband. I am no longer a virgin."

Mother's face fell and she stumbled to a nearby chair.

She wanted to go to her and comfort her but couldn't show weakness. "At this moment, I could be carrying the heir to the Kerburghe dukedom. So you see, Mother, you really have no choice but to let us marry as soon as possible."

Mother stared at Elinor as if she had two heads.

Michael moved across the room, put an arm around Elinor's waist, and kissed the top of her head. He whispered, "I could not be more proud of you."

She might lose her mother's love, but at least she hadn't done it all in vain if it meant something to Michael. Living her life as Mrs. Micheal Collins was all she'd ever wanted.

Mother closed her eyes and took a deep breath. When she opened them, she dabbed her cheeks. "I suppose you are right. You leave me no choice but to allow the marriage. I expect you will wait at least long enough to have the banns announced and a proper wedding arranged. I expect it would be best if the matter of your marriage to Roxton was kept quiet, but even if it gets out, you will be married to a duke, so no one will shun you for marrying so soon after being widowed."

"I am hardly a widow, Mother. I do not consider the marriage to Roxton as valid."

"Nor do I," Michael said.

Virginia got up and faced them. "Be that as it may, others will talk, and you will be on the negative end of that talk." She kissed her daughter on the cheek and did the same to Michael. "You have my blessing."

Elinor let out the breath she'd been holding. "Thank you, Mother."

Virginia crossed to the door.

"What will you tell Father?" Elinor wouldn't mind telling her himself, but she doubted she would get the chance.

Turing back, Virginia waved a hand. "I see no need to bother him with trivialities. After the wedding, I will inform him of the event. I am sure he will wish to give his felicitations at that time. Now I am going to rest. It has been a trying few days."

"Of course, Mother. Shall I come and call you for luncheon, or shall we announce at dinner?"

She sighed. "Dinner will be soon enough. Have a tray sent to me at midday."

Once the door had closed, Michael whirled her around the room, laughing. "My god, you are incredible."

Elinor laughed as well. "Michael, put me down."

He did as she asked, then kissed her hard on the lips.

She expected it to be a quick kiss, but his arms wrapped around her and his warmth filled her as the kiss deepened. She caressed his neck and shoulders. Tipping her head to one side, she accepted and joined the deepening kiss. She loved the rumble in his chest and the way his hands skimmed up and down her back.

He eased her away, his breath coming in short gasps. "If this continues, I will take you on the settee."

"I do not think I would complain if you did." Breathless herself, she longed for more of him.

His smile was the happiest she'd ever seen him. His eyes lit with it and reflected her own joy.

She was his in body and soon she would be his by law as well. The idea made her giddy.

"I have not truly appreciated you, Elinor. I am the luckiest man in all of England to have you love me. I will never make that mistake again. Losing you was terrible, but might have been the best thing that could have happened to an arrogant ass like me. How could I have been so stupid? I nearly ruined both of our lives by taking that last mission. Somehow, I thought I needed to prove one last time that I was the best in the field. My arrogance could have cost me everything. I am as bad as your father."

"Not quite. Father has still not figured out his flaws. You have recovered brilliantly." She was bursting with happiness.

Once again, he took her in his arms and crushed her until her ribs ached. His desperate hold continued and showed no signs of letting up.

"Michael, are you all right?"

"I am the luckiest fool alive."

"Not such a fool. You came for me, and you came to your senses."

Releasing her, his smile filled his face and her heart. "True. I cannot believe you said all of those things to your mother. She had unequivocally refused me before you entered. I even gave her the 'but I am a duke' argument. She was unimpressed and told me that while she appreciated all I had done in rescuing you, Middleton would make a much better match for you."

Elinor's heart ached. She had hurt her mother with an unwinnable argument and more truth than Virginia liked to hear. It would take her weeks to recover and dozens of lists.

"Is something wrong, my love?"

"I just wish it had not been necessary to say such harsh things to my mother in order to facilitate our marriage."

"Elinor, do you believe your mother could have been swayed any other way?"

"No." She was awash with regret.

"Look at me," he commanded, tipping her chin up with one finger. "Was anything you said untrue?"

"No." She let out her breath.

"Then how can you be wrong? Your parents have lived

their lives in a sort of fantasy, where your father pretends to go off and be an important counsel to kings and your mother pretends to miss him. In reality, I think they are both content with the kind of detached marriage they have. I think your mother was so keen on Middleton because he would offer you the same life that she has."

"And our marriage will be different?" she challenged.

He took her hand, pulled her over to the settee, and sat her in his lap. "I will never take a mistress, Elinor. I will only leave your side when absolutely necessary, and only if there is no way for you to come with me. I will make all my efforts to make you happy."

Her sight blurred with tears. "I love you, Michael. I will never wish you away from me. I would not like it if you took a mistress, though I am not so naïve as to think it is not common amongst the men of the ton."

He took her chin again, forcing her gaze to him. "I will not take a mistress, Elinor. I have neither the need nor the desire to bed anyone other than you."

"When you did not come to my room last night, I thought it was a sign that you were disgusted by my killing Roxton."

A burst of laughter exploded from Michael's lips.

"It's not funny!"

He dropped to his knees in front of her. "Oh, Elinor, I think you are the bravest woman I have ever known. And I have known women who kill for a living. I had no idea six months ago that you had the courage of a lion, and I love you more after seeing your measure. In the last two days you escaped a madman, were crushed by a castle wall, killed to protect the man you love whilst being nearly killed yourself by a runaway carriage, and still found the audacity to come in here and stand up to your mother and secure our happiness. I repeat, I am the luckiest man in England. What other man can boast of such a woman?"

She rather liked the sound of that. "When you put it that way, I sound like Catherine the Great."

They laughed, then he kissed her cheek, then her lips. He kissed her chin and her nose, and continued to scatter light kisses across her face and neck. "I love you. I love you."

"Michael?"

"Hmmm?" Another kiss on her eyelid.

"I have to go and speak to Preston."

Murmuring something to himself, he stood. "I can speak to him later."

She shook her head. "I think it would be kinder for me to tell him my decision. He has been wonderful through all of this and has not said a word, though I am sure he knows most of what has transpired. I would like to speak to him."

He frowned, clenching his hands into fists before relaxing and meeting her gaze. "As you wish."

Chapter Twenty-Three

Elinor found Preston Knowles, The Duke of Middleton, in the stables rubbing down a horse.

"I would think there are many grooms here who could manage that task, your grace." Elinor stepped around a pile of straw.

He smiled. "There is something about the care of a horse that always calms me. I often go out to the stables on my property in Kent and act a groom for an afternoon. The world always appears more reasonable after a day with these animals." He brushed the mare's black coat.

"Do you require calming, your grace?" she asked.

"I thought we had agreed that you would call me 'Preston,' or has our friendship dwindled to the point that we must revert to titles, Lady Elinor?"

She walked over until only the horse's lead separated them. "No, Preston, forgive me. I...we are still friends."

"I am glad to hear it." He smiled, but his eyes were sad and distant. The usual open regard closed away, as he continued grooming.

She found herself without any words to convey why she had come.

He crossed under the lead. "I assume you have come to tell me that my suit is being rejected."

She looked at her feet. "I am sorry, Preston."

He put down the brush and patted the mare's neck. "Kerburghe has made you an offer?"

"Yes."

"Your mother has accepted him, as have you?"

"Yes." She focused on his hessians, unwilling to gaze into his eyes.

"Elinor?"

She looked into his strong face.

Only disappointment shone in his eyes. "Michael Rollins is a good man. We have already discussed your love for him. I have only one question."

"What question?"

He brushed a stray hair from her forehead.

It was an intimate gesture, but there was nothing forward in it. His familiarity was more brotherly than of a lover. Whenever Michael touched her, she longed for more. Even the slightest caress made her skin tingle and warm. There was no such sensation at Preston's touch.

"Is he what you really want?"

"I beg your pardon?" She had told Preston from the beginning of their acquaintance that she loved Michael and was devastated by their separation.

The horse whinnied.

Preston cooed and rubbed her nose. "I just want to make sure you are happy with this outcome, Elinor. I really do care for you. I would not have traipsed all the way to Scotland after a madman for just anyone. I would still marry you, even after all the drama of the past few days."

A groom entered the stable and cleared his throat. "Are you finished with Moonbeam, your grace?"

Preston inclined his head. "Yes. Thank you, John. The lady and I were just leaving." He offered Elinor his arm and they walked out into the haze of the late morning toward the house.

She waited until they were away from the stables and wouldn't be overheard. "You are too good to me, Preston. I have not even thanked you for helping in my rescue."

Before she finished her sentence, he shook his head. "No thanks are necessary. You are safe. That is all the matters."

"Still, I could not be more grateful," she said.

They walked into the house gardens from the back and strolled along a cobbled path.

"Michael is all I've ever wanted. I love him, and I am happy. Is that what you needed to hear?"

He stopped and took her hand. He bowed down and kissed her fingers gently. "That is exactly what I needed to hear. Sadly, I stand down my offer for your hand. I think we would have suited very well, but I understand your choice. Kerburghe is a lucky man. I am honored to be the first to wish you joy."

"Thank you, Preston. I am sorry, though I do not think we would have been truly happy together."

"Oh, why not?"

"I like you, but I think we are better suited as friends. You are more brotherly to me."

"Ouch." He gripped his chest feigning a wound.

She smiled. "I think you will survive."

"Perhaps but it will be a struggle." He smiled, but again there was no spark there.

~

The next few weeks passed with long, tiring days. The difficulty in getting the banns announced, and arranging a wedding in as short a time as was respectable, created more tension between Elinor and her mother.

Virginia was constantly worried that the events at Marlton Hall and in Scotland would become known amongst the peerage, and all would be lost. She reminded Elinor of this several times a day in dramatic fashion.

The parlor was silent. Mother had gone shopping and thankfully left her at home alone. Elinor picked a book off the shelf and curled her feet under her. The fire burning in the hearth was delightful.

She was just becoming absorbed in the book when the butler announced, "Lady Dorothea Flammel to see you, miss."

Clapping the book shut, she put it aside.

Dory's perfect hair and perfect figure were clad in the perfect dress as usual, but her face was pale and her expression near panic.

Elinor's chest clenched, and she rushed forward. "What is it, Dory? You look as if someone has died."

"Then you have not heard?" Dory took her hands.

"Heard what?"

"Somehow the incidents of Scotland have become known. It's all over town. The afternoon paper is said to be printing a story that will tell the entire tale."

"No," Elinor said. "How could anyone know? It's not possible."

The door flew open, and Virginia ran in. Her hair was half out of its coif. The lace at the bottom of her dress was torn and dragging on the carpet. "We are ruined!" She flung herself onto the settee and threw her arm over her eyes.

"Mother has obviously heard," Elinor said.

"Oh, Dory, thank God you're here. We must make a plan of what to do," Lady Burkenstock urged, but she did not move from her dramatic position.

"Mother, it would be best to wait and see what people actually know. Let's just see what is written in the paper before we do anything rash."

Putting down her arm, Virginia looked at Elinor. "How can you be so calm? Don't you understand? We are ruined! We will have to call off the wedding. We might have to leave the country. We shall never be allowed to show our faces in good society again!"

Elinor raised an eyebrow. Why had the news of her repeated ruin not sent her into fits as it would have done a year ago? "We will not call off the wedding. I am marrying Michael next Saturday. If the chapel is empty for the service, then so be it, but the wedding will go on."

Mother sat up. "Do you really think that Kerburghe will want to marry you now that your reputation is destroyed? He has his own family to consider. After the scandals that his father created, he will run for the hills the moment he hears of this. After all, that is what he did at the last sign of trouble."

Elinor narrowed her eyes at her mother. "He will not run, and that is not what he did last time. We will be married next week regardless of what the papers know or do not know, Mother. Is that clear?"

Mother gaped. "I do not think I really like this new side of you, daughter."

She shrugged and sat on the settee to wait for the paper to arrive.

Dory sat next to her, smiled and patted her hand. "Good for you."

When the afternoon edition arrived, Mother snatched it off the silver tray that the footman had delivered it on. She fanned it and swallowed. Opening the paper, she closed it again before giving in.

She read aloud.

More secrets are lurking behind the walls of the Earl of Malmsbury's home. It would seem that the young miss of that household was recently married in Scotland, in spite of the fact that she is about to marry a prominent member of the peerage next week. I have further learned that the sudden marriage was followed by an even more sudden death, making the poor girl a wife and a widow in a matter of hours. The only mystery here is why the laws of our country allow such a person to walk the streets with honest people of importance.

This reporter is appalled.

Virginia threw the paper aside and burst into tears.

Elinor rubbed her forehead. She could take little more of the ton and their gossip.

Dory picked up the paper and read it again. "None of this is true."

"None of it is a lie, either," Elinor said.

"Who could have told?"

Elinor shrugged. "A servant, the priest, or one of the officers who helped in my rescue could have been paid to tell. The story is vague, so it's likely whoever it was did not really know all that had happened."

"How can you be so calm? We're ruined. No one will have you now!" Mother's wailing was annoying.

"Well, there is no point in getting hysterical. It won't help anything if we cannot keep our wits about us."

"What should we do?" Dory asked.

"I will wait for Michael. He will come. You should go home so as not to be associated with me. We don't want this to taint your reputation." Elinor patted Dory's shoulder.

Dory looked horrified. "I will not go. You are my oldest and dearest friend, Elinor. I will not abandon you when you need me most. If my friendship with you is not suited to some man who wishes to receive my dowry, then he can go to Hades."

"Dorothea, language," Mother scolded.

Elinor and Dory exchanged a private smile. "Thank you."

Dory nodded.

They didn't have to wait long. Michael's arrival was announced only thirty minutes after the newspaper's arrival.

Virginia didn't even bother to hide her surprise. "I thought you would have left the continent by now, Kerburghe."

He smiled crookedly. "I would be happy to leave England for a while, but my bride-to-be has insisted on Scotland for our honeymoon. It seems she worries over the state we left the property in the north. Though I have assured her I have sent a steward to see to the repairs."

Elinor stood at his side and gazed at him.

He kissed her nose.

Pacing frantically, Mother said, "We shall cancel the wedding and you can elope. The scandal will be much lessened by your absence. I will go now and start writing letters."

Holding up a hand, Michael stopped Mother's exit. "No. We will go on with the wedding as planned. To run now would be an admission of guilt. We have done nothing wrong. Certainly Elinor is not culpable for the actions of a madman."

"I do not know if society will see it that way, Michael," Elinor said. "Perhaps Mother is right. We could disappear for a while, and the talk would eventually stop. The ton becomes bored with these things so easily. Once it has passed, we can come back to London."

"Elinor, it's not fair for you to have your wedding spoiled by ignorance. You should not run. I don't like it one bit." Stiff with rage, Dory walked across the room to the window.

"It really doesn't matter, Dory." As long as she ended up married to Michael, she didn't care about the rest. *Well, not much.*

Michael took Elinor's hand, and they sat as far away from the other two women as possible. "I don't want you to be disappointed, my love. I still think it's better to stay and face the scandal. I'm a duke, and that should be worth something to these people."

"I just want to be with you. I do not care how we get married. The fact that you are here is the most important thing to me. The rest is trivial."

He smiled. "I could be nowhere else."

Voices raised and doors slammed in the foyer. It sounded like an invasion. A moment later, Sophia and Daniel burst in.

Kendall trailed behind and announced them. The stout little man rolled his eyes as he left.

Giving the butler's back a stern look, Sophia slapped her gloves across her palm.

A deep frown marred Daniel's handsome face.

Before the new arrivals could be informed of the couple's decision, a footman appeared with a note.

Virginia made to take the note, but the footman turned and delivered the missive to Elinor.

She read the note, and the rest of the room stood in silence, watching. "It's from Middleton."

Michael frowned and grumbled something that she couldn't understand.

"Well, what does it say?" Sophia put her fists on her hips.

"He says he thinks he can be of some help. He advises that Michael and I attend Lord and Lady Brasher's ball tomorrow night. He advises us not to run or take any steps that might confirm the statements in the paper." She looked up from the note and shrugged.

Daniel stepped forward. "May I see the note?"

She handed Daniel the message.

He read it. "He says that if you have not been invited he can arrange an invitation."

"We have one." Virginia reclined on the chaise and maintained a dramatic pose. "I had planned to decline since we were so busy with the wedding plans."

Daniel said, "Michael, I think you and Elinor should do as Middleton advises. I am sure he has a plan."

"And if his plan is to make a fool of me and take her away from me?"

Elinor touched his arm. "He would not. Even if he could, I do not believe he would do anything to hurt us, Michael. He is my friend. I think he only wishes to help."

Daniel nodded and took the note from Michael. He looked it over. "He is influential amongst the ton. His friendship could be enough to silence the masses."

"We should all go," Dory said.

"I agree," Daniel said. "I will contact Thomas and Markus as well and see if they are available. I cannot stand for the malice of such a report. We must push back, or the reporters begin to run our lives."

"They have been running mine for years." Elinor should have kept her thoughts to herself, but she was tired of being a good girl. It had never gotten her anything.

Michael squeezed her hand. "I know it seems that way, Elinor. We shall find a way to put all of this behind us. I am quite tired of every nuance of my life being put to print for the entire world to read and interpret. It is time to put an end to it. Then, once we are married, we will no longer be of such interest to the gossip of London.

"I will go and see Middleton today and find out what he has in mind."

"You will be nice, won't you, Michael?"

He smiled. "I will be nice."

~

The Brasher ball was one of the biggest events of the season. Elinor had attended the event before, but she took special pains to look her best. She had no idea what Preston had in mind, but the fact that a duke of his influence was supporting them would go far amongst the meddling ton.

She had chosen a sapphire blue gown trimmed in silver. The soft fabric hugged her body snugly, and the bodice's design pushed her breasts up, showing just enough cleavage to inspire the men to great things. At least, that is what the dressmaker had professed when Elinor picked out the confection. It had been twenty minutes since her maid had informed her that Michael was waiting downstairs, but she wasn't ready.

Her hair was coifed and curled with strands of silver that caught the light. The gown was exquisite and needed no alterations. She had even dowsed her eyelashes with a special black soot that was all the rage. It made her blue eyes even brighter. As she looked at herself in the mirror, she had no idea who the woman was looking back. She took a deep breath, and the movement made her breasts push higher.

She liked this new person more than the old Elinor, much more.

Pushing her shoulders back, she turned from the mirror and

left her room. At the top of the stairs, she spied Michael in the foyer. He was stunningly handsome, all in black with a crisp white cravat. He spoke to Mother, but they were too far away for Elinor to hear the conversation. Whatever they were discussing, he didn't like it. He frowned at Virginia, but his stance stayed relaxed, with his elbow leaning on the finial at the bottom of the handrail.

She moved forward, and he turned and looked up at her.

His mouth hung open, then a slow smile spread across his face.

She floated down the stairs, with only Michael in her sight. He was her sun, and she reveled in his heat.

She closed the gap between them. Her heart in her throat, she wanted to run away with Michael and leave all of the ton and their silliness behind.

He looked at her as if she were the most beautiful woman he'd ever seen. Yet he was magnificent, like a star shining through on the darkest night.

"Really, Elinor, that dress borders on obscene." Mother shook her head and pursed her lips.

Michael's grin was wicked and delicious.

"Well then, Mother, it shall give them something else to talk about. I will not slink through and try to go unnoticed. If we are to make a statement this evening, it shall be a bold one."

Mother sighed and accepted her wrap from the butler. "Shall we go?"

Michael smiled and wrapped Elinor's hand into the crook of his elbow. He leaned down and whispered, "You are stunning."

"Not obscene?" She joked, but her heart pounded with trepidation.

"I have never seen a more beautiful woman in my life. If I

could, I would whisk you back up those steps and take you this minute."

Her cheeks burned, but she loved the way he wanted her, and kept her gaze on his.

Virginia was already out the front door and walking down the steps.

Elinor stopped their progress at the door. "Everything is going to be okay, isn't it, Michael?"

"Of course, my love. The ton does not run our lives. They are merely an inconvenience that we have to deal with."

She nodded, and they moved toward the waiting carriage.

Virginia used the entire carriage ride to vent her opinions of Elinor's behavior over the past few months. She droned on and on.

Elinor stared out at London as it passed and reminded herself she had only one more week to deal with her mother's disapproval, then she would be Mrs. Michael Rollins, The Duchess of Kerburghe. Though she suspected Mother would still find fault with her.

Michael sat like a statue. He dug his nails into the wood on the carriage's sill. "Lady Malmsbury, if you do not stop berating my future wife, I shall have to resort to severe measures. Kindly refrain from further blather. If you cannot think of a kind word, it would be best if you did not speak at all."

Heart leaping in her chest, Elinor had to hold back her glee. He had defended her when she couldn't defend herself.

Virginia huffed, crossed her arms over her chest, and pouted for the remainder of the ride. However, she was silent, and that in itself was bliss.

As was the case in many homes in London, the Brasher townhouse was overdone. The ceilings were gold and red. Thick plaster columns meant to imitate the great temples of Greece adorned the walls. It was horrible, but Elinor tried to focus only on what was in front of her. She didn't want to see the contemptuous looks of the people around her as she, Mother, and Michael walked through the crowded foyer and into the even more crowded ballroom.

Once inside, they were immediately approached by the Dowager Countess of Grafton. Lady Daphne Collington could be quite harsh, and many called her the Cruel Countess, but she was Sophia's great aunt and a good friend of Mother's. The crowd held their breath, expecting some scalding set down. Silence descended, which in itself was amazing considering the awful cacophony usually present at one of these crushes.

Even Elinor found herself on the verge of bolting from the room. The Countess had been at Marlton Hall and knew most of what had transpired. It was possible that she disapproved and would set in motion a series of events that would ruin both her and Michael.

Michael put his hand over hers. "You can't run now, love."

Lady Collington had taken to using a cane in the last year, and she used it now to whack a young man in the calf as she plowed through the crowd. The man stumbled, grabbing his leg, and the countess said, "Out of my way, foolish boy."

Even Virginia looked worried that her friendship with the dowager might not hold up to this level of scandal.

With a flair for the dramatic, the Lady Collington stood a full ten seconds in front of the three of them and scowled before she took the last step. "Virginia, my dear, so good to see you." She kissed her friend's cheek.

As she stomped past Elinor, she whispered, "You had better take that horrified look off of your face, dear. You look like you've swallowed a bird."

Elinor actually laughed and hugged Lady Collington.

"It was very wise attending tonight. Sophia informed me, and I immediately accepted the invitation."

"Thank you, my lady." Elinor kept her voice down and her affection brief.

"Bah! I know what happened up north, and you are certainly not to blame. But it is not me you should be thanking." She walked away without elaborating.

Middleton pushed through the crowd, took her hand, and kissed it longer than was strictly proper. "My dear, Elinor, how wonderful to see you."

Elinor's eyes widened, and she looked from Preston to Michael. Calling her by her given name in such a public setting was outrageous, and kissing her hand as he had cause for a scandal in itself. However, it was the forlorn look on his face that shocked her most.

Michael's face filled with rage.

Preston had lost his mind and Michael was about to kill him.

She began at a stutter. "I...I am pleased to see you as well, your grace. How have you been?"

"My wellbeing is of no consequence as long as you are well. May I have this dance?"

She looked around the room. Every eye was trained on the three of them. She couldn't refuse but her fiancé was grimacing like a feral dog. She could claim a twisted ankle. No one would believe it. They had all seen her walk in. She looked up at Michael's furious face and for an instant caught something in his eyes that wasn't anger. Amusement?

Elinor put on her best demure smile for Preston and nodded once to her fiancé. She took Preston's arm, and he led her onto the dance floor. The music started as they reached the crowded floor, and Preston's hand settled on her back.

It was a waltz. Elinor rolled her eyes, imagining the crowd's gossip as she took Preston's hand and allowed him to begin the dance. "What are the two of you up to?"

Preston smiled down at her. He was still too handsome to doubt, but she fumed at him and at Michael for keeping her in the dark on whatever they'd plotted.

"We are restoring your reputation, my sweet."

"Don't call me that, Preston. I nearly fell over when you approached me as if I were your fiancé and not Michael's. This will only add to the scandal. Society will call me a loose woman."

"I think not."

When he didn't elaborate, she stomped on his foot, making him lose a step.

He frowned at her, then laughed. "Smile, Elinor."

She glanced around the room. Everyone was still watching. She smiled and laughed at him as if he had made an amusing comment. He was right. They had to put on a show.

"That's better. It is better to have the ton think you are being pursued by two dukes than to think that you had to run off and get married due to some horrible mishap in the north."

"There will still be scandal. I will still be shunned, and so will Michael after the wedding," she said.

He shook his head. "I don't think so. No one will believe the rumors about what happened in Scotland or on the way back. They would never believe that I would still be after your hand if I thought those rumors were true." He whispered, "Better to be thought of as loose than as a murderess."

She gasped.

His hand pressed at the small of her back, lower than was proper.

"And are you still after my hand, Preston."

"Is it available?" He raised an eyebrow.

"I love Michael. I will marry him next week if he will still have me." She continued smiling for the crowd.

A sad smile marred Preston's lovely full lips. "I thought as much. Then I shall be thwarted, you and Kerburghe shall marry, and your reputation will suffer little more than a hiccup. I suspect even that will have passed by the time you return from your honeymoon."

She couldn't hold the fake smile any longer. "Why are you doing this?"

He gripped her tighter. "I think you know the answer to that question." The intensity in his gaze was replaced by a light smile. "We are friends. I want to help you."

Tears of gratitude welled in her eyes. "Thank you, Preston."

"I am at your service." As the music ended, he bowed, then took her hand and kissed her fingers lightly. "I always will be available for you if you need me, Elinor."

Torn between gratitude and shame, Elinor could think of no response.

Middleton delivered her back to her mother's side. "I will make sure that by the end of the evening, the entire party thinks the story in the paper was rubbish spread by an unhappy servant. I am sure this will pass quickly." He bowed and turned to walk away.

"Your grace," she called.

He faced her.

She whispered, "Will you attend my wedding?"

He smiled and bowed again. "It would be my honor."

Middleton strode away and disappeared into the crowd.

She had seen something sad in his eyes. The possibility that two men were really in love with her was too much to think about.

Michael stood near the doors to the gardens, watching her.

She took a step toward him, then turned back to Mother. "Mother, I am going to get some air."

"Yes, dear. It's terribly hot. Don't stay away too long. It's best to be visible tonight."

She was already heading for the door. People stared at her as she passed. She smiled and nodded to each of them. Some were acquaintances and others gossips, but she treated them all the same. *Let them think what they wanted.* She wouldn't be made to hide at home and cower. She picked her head up even higher.

Once she was at the back of the room, she quietly slipped out the open door. Even fall's cool air couldn't cut through the stuffiness of the ballroom.

The fine weather had coaxed a few people outside. Elinor moved into the shadows. No one turned to see her, and she continued quietly along the outside of the dim patio, descended several steps, and rounded a shrubbery into the darkness of the gardens.

A full moon provided the only light. The white pebble path shone, but the manicured bushes did not allow her to see much beyond it. She walked for a few minutes. Every bush looked the same, and the path gave no clues to how far she'd come. She wouldn't find Michael and would never find her way back to the house.

An arm snaked around her waist and pulled her hard against a male body. The warm scent of soap and vanilla mixed with Michael's distinctly male aroma sent a shiver down her back.

"Michael," she whispered and leaned back against him.

His mouth was just at the curve of her ear. "How was your dance?"

"Are you jealous?" She pushed her bottom into him.

He moaned. "You're damned right, I am jealous."

Turning, she put her arms around his neck. She leaned

forward and kissed his lips softly, allowing their breath to mingle. "There is no reason for you to be."

"No?" He pushed her an arm's length away. "Middleton is in love with you. You must know that."

"He has not made any declarations of the kind." She pressed against him from knees to neck. "I am in love with you. Preston is our good friend who is helping us out of a difficult situation."

He mumbled something.

"I thought you went and saw him yesterday. Didn't the two of you discuss what would happen this evening?"

"It is one thing to sit in a library and discuss the idea of another man showing desire for one's fiancé. It is quite another to see her in that other man's arms."

"I am in your arms now, as you knew I would be. And next week, I will be your wife and in your bed every night for the rest of our lives."

"Mmm. That is worth even the price of watching you dance with Middleton." He kissed the skin between her shoulder and her neck.

She tilted her head to give him better access and sighed as her desire blossomed.

"We should return to the ball." He kissed a line from her throat to her shoulder.

She yearned to rip off her clothes and press against him like the wanton she'd become. "You are probably right. We are supposed to be disrupting a scandal, not creating a new one."

His laugh rumbled deep in his chest. Feeling the vibration, she pushed herself tighter to him. He warmed her through their clothes.

"Elinor, you are driving me mad." He groaned.

"I am driving myself mad as well." She took a breath to steady herself.

"It's only one more week."

"It will seem like an eternity." She pressed her hips hard against his obvious desire. It sent glorious sensations shooting through her.

Michael ran his hand up along her waist to the side of her breast, then gently caressed the swell of her breast above the gown. His fingers slipped beneath the fabric, pinching the rigid nipple.

She pushed her chest forward, unable to resist the delight he provided.

Gently, he tugged her bodice until her bosom popped free. Immediately, he lowered his head and took her into his mouth.

She had to bite the inside of her cheek to keep from crying out. Wantonly, she arched against his suckling mouth, wanting more.

Far too soon, he raised his head and returned her gown to its proper position.

She was about to complain, but his hand had moved to her hip, then lower to her thigh, where he eased up her dress. Once he had reached the bottom, his hand caressed the sensitive skin of her thigh through her light chemise. He ran his fingers over the delicate fabric, lifting it as well.

When his skin met hers, her legs quivered.

His hand ran down the back of her thigh and up again, squeezing her bottom and pulling her against his erection.

A familiar tightening flooded her. She would let him take her in the garden with half of London within earshot. She wanted him, wanted this.

He traced down to the back of her knee and up again until two fingers settled between her thighs.

Gasping, she clung to his shoulders, burying her face in his chest.

"Oh, Elinor, so soft and wet, so beautiful." His voice strained.

Her own passion was so intense, everything else faded away. She thrust against his probing fingers.

Moments might have passed, or it could have been an hour. She erupted against his hand.

His mouth covered hers muffling her cries. He crushed her to him until the wave of ecstasy flowed gently away, leaving her like a willow in his arms.

She shook and clutched his shoulders until the orgasm calmed.

"We will have to go inside soon, love. People have probably already noticed our absence."

"Yes, I know." She remained clinging to him in the garden's darkness.

"Elinor?"

She sighed and took a deep breath before stepping out of his arms. "I have to find an alternate entrance, one that is not so public. I am sure I look as if I've been ravaged."

"Let's see if there's a servant entrance." Laughter rang in his voice, but he took her hand and led her down the path.

She stumbled along beside him. "How can you see anything? It's dark as pitch out here. I can barely see the path."

"Practice, I suppose."

Elinor quaked with the notion of all back alleys and woods he must have slunk through as a spy. She shuddered at the danger he had put himself in for so many years.

"Are you cold?" he asked.

"No."

"Well, here is a door. Stay here a moment and I'll check where it leads."

She nodded in the darkness, but he must have seen her, because a second later she stood alone in the dark. She should have been frightened, but the delight of what transpired in the garden kept her happy.

The door opened, startling her out of deep thoughts of rapture. Michael took her hand and pulled her inside.

"This seems to be a private family entrance. The Brashers must have felt a need for a discreet entrance." He looked down at her with a wicked grin.

Elinor giggled.

"There is a small lady's parlor through that door." He pointed to the door on the left. "It is empty. I believe that if you follow this hall to its end, you will arrive back at the foyer."

"I see." She would need a few minutes to gather her wits.

"Will you be all right?"

Loving him so intensely would make for many such entrances over their lifetime. Unable to contain her joy, she smiled up at him in the shadowy hall and touched his cheek. "I will be fine. You had better go."

He kissed her lips, then went back out the private doorway.

Chapter Twenty-Four

By the time the Kerburghe carriage had delivered Elinor and her mother home in the early morning hours of the next day, any rumors of what might have happened in Scotland were pushed aside as impossible. Elinor was the talk of the town. No woman ever had two dukes bidding for her affections at the same time. It was unheard of. At least, that's what the paper printed. The only explanation was that the lady was extraordinary. All eyes should be focused on the wedding of the season, to take place on the next Saturday.

Virginia was ecstatic with joy as she read the paper the following morning.

Elinor couldn't have cared less about the gossip. All she cared about was making it to the following Saturday without anything going wrong.

The crowd outside the St. George's the following Saturday was the largest in memory. The streets were so thick with people that the carriages couldn't pass. Elinor chewed on her fingernails looking out the window. How would they ever get to her own wedding?

Making matters worse, Virginia screamed at the driver to push through. "Move forward, man!"

"Mother, stop yelling. If Jones could move, he would. I do not want anyone killed by our carriage on the way to church."

"We will never get through. How long do you think the congregation will wait?"

Elinor thought about that and smiled. She had a vision of the entire sanctuary being empty, save Michael and the pastor whom Michael had forced to wait. She laughed aloud.

"I see nothing funny," Virginia scolded.

"Michael will wait. That's all I care about."

"I wish your father were here."

That wiped the smile off Elinor's face. "If Father were here, the two of you would be yelling at poor Jones, and we still would not be moving."

"I sent him a letter this morning." Virginia pursed her lips and crossed her arms.

"I am sure Father will be thrilled to hear of my happy nuptials."

"Don't be so harsh, Elinor. Your father loves you very much."

"He loves money and power more." It was bitterness, but Elinor couldn't help it. She had not yet forgiven her father. Perhaps she never would.

A commotion in the street turned her attention toward the window.

Eyes wide, Elinor watched as the unwilling crowd made way for three riders to advance toward the carriage.

Markus Flammel, Thomas Wheel, and Daniel Fallon were all mounted and heading to the waylaid carriage.

Inch by inch through the complaining onlookers, the three made progress until Thomas Wheel, smartly dressed for the wedding, arrived at the carriage door.

She couldn't help the joy welling up inside her. These friends of hers and Michael's were extraordinary.

He made a half bow in the saddle. "My lady, I am afraid when you marry one of us, you must accept all four as family."

She laughed. "You say that as if it is a bad thing, Mr. Wheel."

He smiled brightly. "Today you will be happy to have us, but I expect that there will be a day in the future that our presence will become a nuisance."

"Mr. Wheel, if you can get me to my wedding, I will forgive you any transgressions in the future."

Tugging on the horse's reins, Thomas nodded, his eyes full of amusement. "You may come to regret those words, but we will get you there."

The three riders moved into position in front of the carriage and nudged the throngs of people aside enough to allow for the carriage to roll forward. It still took over an hour to make the short trip to the church, but they did arrive, and everyone was still there waiting for the bride.

The people in the street oohed and aahed as she descended the carriage. Great cheers rose up as she walked into the church. Then the doors closed behind her, and there was silence.

Hundreds of faces stared, but the only one she cared about had bright blue eyes that twinkled in the candlelight of the altar as they looked down the center aisle at her.

Markus Flammel, Dory's brother and longtime family friend, walked Elinor down the aisle.

When he handed her over to Michael, she gasped for the breath to thank him.

He smiled and joined his wife, Emma, in the second pew.

Elinor took her place next to Michael.

"Are you all right?" he whispered.

"I am here now. That is all that matters."

The pastor cleared his throat to get the bride and groom's attention. He was obviously annoyed by the long wait.

He spoke of duty and obedience, and the perils of desire and depravity.

Elinor listened but heard only a word here and there. She and Michael faced each other, and she was lost in his eyes. When it was her turn to answer, she turned to the pastor momentarily before turning back to those stunning eyes and saying, "I do."

Michael never took his gaze from hers as he too answered in the affirmative. The ornate church filled with murmurs as he said the words that would make Elinor his for a lifetime.

The moment after they were pronounced man and wife, they rushed from the church.

The people still waited in the street.

Michael turned toward his bride, pulled her to him, and kissed her soundly on the lips.

A roar went up in the crowd.

Elinor blushed the prettiest shade of pink.

It took two hours to make the twenty-minute ride to the

Burkenstock townhouse, where the wedding breakfast was served later than expected.

After two hours of laughing and speech-making, Michael had all he could take of the celebration. His only desire was to have his wife to himself.

His wife. He couldn't believe she was his.

He looked around the room at each of his three best friends.

Each looked back and nodded. Their silent communication had always come in handy. Now they let him know that they understood he was leaving the party.

At the far end of the table, Preston Knowles sat talking to Daniel's younger sister. He broke from his conversation with the lovely Cecilia Fallon and looked over.

To Michael's surprise, he also nodded his understanding.

In all the years since Michael, Daniel, Markus, and Thomas had met, no one else had shared their special communication. It would seem now there were five of them. Elinor had described Preston as their friend. Perhaps she was correct.

Michael nodded back.

He leaned down toward his new bride. "I think it's time to go, love."

She looked up smiling. Without a word, she took his hand, and the two of them quietly left the reception.

Much to her maid's distress, Elinor did not even change into traveling clothes. The luggage was already loaded, so the couple put coats over their wedding clothes and climbed into the carriage waiting outside.

~

When Elinor and Michael arrived at Kerburghe, repairs on the castle were already underway. It would take a while, and the colder weather was already slowing the progress, but soon enough the ancient structure would be whole again.

It was late and they had been on the road for days.

Michael woke for the first time in the master's chamber. It was stark, with no rug and stone walls, but it was his. He breathed deeply the scent of fresh linens. The night before permeated his mind and his arousal returned as well. He rolled over to pull his sumptuous wife to him and found only more linen.

His heart beat tripled in an instant, and he leaped naked from the bed. The room was empty.

"Elinor." She might have gone to use the privy. He held back the panic building in his gut.

No reply.

Throwing on his trousers and blouse in an instant, he was still pulling on his boots as he rushed through the door and crashed headlong into his valet, Peters.

"Your grace?" Peters called from the hallway floor.

"Sorry. Have you seen her grace?" Michael helped him from the floor. He was thin and tall and dressed as a valet should be, with every piece of clothing starched and clean. Even after the collision and fall, he remained impeccable.

"No, sir, should I look for her?"

He heard laughter from the window at the end of the hall.

"What is that?"

"The church children are playing in the courtyard. Do you want me to send them away?" The valet looked almost eager to shoo the children from the premises.

The bubble of bliss filled him, and he slapped Peters on the shoulder. "No. I think I can guess where my wife is."

Michael followed the sound of the children's laughter until he arrived in the front courtyard. Half a dozen children, ranging from two to about eight, played with a small dog and a stick.

Wrapped in an ermine fur-lined cape, Elinor sat on the steps watching them. The sweetest smile tugged at her lips. She shivered on the cold stone steps. Winter fast approached, even in the lowlands.

Kneeling behind her, he pulled her from the stone and slid his body beneath hers, so she was in his lap protected from the chill.

"Michael." She relaxed into his lap.

"I woke to an empty bed and thought you had been whisked away from me yet again."

"Never." She kissed his chin.

The children tossed a stick to a small dog that yapped and dragged the thing around the courtyard. Laughter filled the air as they chased the dog to get the stick back.

"Who are they?" Michael asked.

"Orphans that the priest looks after while he tries to find them homes." She pulled the ermine tighter.

"So many from such a small village." Michael had a lot of work to do to learn about the people under his protection. He would start after they broke their fast.

She nodded. "There was a fire a few months ago, and several people were killed. Their parents were among the dead. I am told four of them will go to some family that has been located in the far north. They are coming down to get them, but cold weather in the highlands has delayed their arrival."

"And the other two?" Michael hated to think of any child growing up without parents, but these children were now his responsibility. Guilt for not trekking to Scotland immediately after he'd been elevated settled in his chest.

She shrugged. "Jimmie, the older boy, and Sarah, the baby, are brother and sister. No family could be located for them. They will stay with the priest until he can find a family willing to take one or the other in."

"They'll be separated?"

She nodded, and a tear dripped on his hand. He looked up and saw tears quietly rolling down Elinor's cheeks.

Michael's heart wretched at the idea of siblings being separated. Having almost lost Everett, he couldn't bear the idea. Had the gunshot wound killed his brother, he wouldn't have been at his wedding, nor would he have lived to stand at his own. One day, in the not-so-distant future, he would watch Everett take a bride. It would give him great joy knowing his brother's child would inherit a dukedom. He had to stay a bout of his own emotion.

"I think it might be nice to spend some time with those two, Elinor. What do you think?" His throat remained tight, making the words rough and stunted.

She turned in his arms and looked at him. "What do you mean, Michael?"

"I was considering the idea of adding a nursery and seeing if they would care to live with us here."

Her eyes were so wide, he almost laughed. "You want to take in Jimmie and Sarah?"

"Only if you think it's a good idea."

"For how long?"

He frowned. "Jimmie looks to be about seven or eight. He'll have to go off to school in a couple of years. I went to Eton when I was ten. Of course, he will still come back during breaks. Sarah will marry in, say, sixteen years, then she will surely move away."

Tears ran freely down Elinor's face. "Are you sure?"

He wiped away her tears. "If the boy is willing to give it a try, then I think we should take them in and give them a family, my love. I cannot stand the idea of them homeless or separated from each other. I did promise you a family. I see no reason why we can't start that family now."

"Oh, Michael!" She clung to him.

Nothing would ever be as perfect as the strength of her embrace or the joy one small gesture brought her. "Does that mean you agree?"

She looked up. "I can think of nothing that could make me happier."

"I will speak to the priest and Jimmie later today."

"I am so happy."

"I am glad you are. Do you think I can convince my lovely wife to rejoin me in our bed?"

She blushed and said coyly, "I might be persuaded."

He kissed her neck, and she giggled.

"I can be more persuasive, but the yard is full of children and the priest sits in the shadows of the chapel."

She spun and looked at the shadowed figure standing at the side of the chapel across the yard. "Perhaps we should retire to our rooms, your grace."

"I am so pleased to have married such a smart woman."

"And to think, just months ago you thought me a dunderhead."

"No. That is too harsh. I thought your mind was occupied with simpler things, but I am delighted to have discovered that you are as brilliant as you are beautiful."

"Simpler things? Delicately put, your grace." She laughed.

He heaved her between his thighs. "If you do not stop calling me that, I will have you right here on the steps with an audience."

"Michael, you wouldn't." Her eyes were wide and her mouth agape. Standing, she straightened her dress even though it was the same one she had been wearing the night before and was wrinkled beyond a simple smoothing. She brushed out the skirts as if she were standing in a ball room. "Husband, it is time to go inside."

"A marvelous idea, wife." It was too much of wonderful to hold back his laugh. He rose and offered his arm.

They looked back toward the courtyard, where Jimmie held the puppy still so that his baby sister could pet the rambunctious animal.

The pup licked the little girl's face, and she screamed with laughter.

"There is a lot to do to ready the house for children."

He would bet his heart she was making one of her lists. How he loved those lists and everything else about her. He kissed her head and gently pulled her toward their bedroom. "Later."

She sighed deeply. "Yes, later." Elinor took off at a run toward the master bedroom.

Letting her win this race was no hardship. He caught her at the edge of the bed and they tumbled in together.

Epilogue

From the next room, Elinor screamed a word that Michael didn't think she even knew.

"Papa, is Mama all right?"

He looked down at Jimmie's cherubic face and wide eyes, and ruffled his hair. "She is fine. These things take some time, and we will have to be patient."

Jimmie nodded and propped his chin on his knees, wrapping his arms around his legs.

A cry of another kind came from down the hall, and the harried nurse rushed in with Sarah's chubby body clutched in her arms. The young woman's hair stuck out from under her cap, and her dress was wrinkled and stained.

"Mammaaa," Sarah cried.

"I am sorry, your grace. I tried to keep her quiet in the nursery, but we can hear her grace, and the child will not be still."

Michael reached for Sarah. "It's all right, Miss Jones. I will take her. You may go and rest."

Miss Jones cocked her head and put her hands on her hips.

"I'll be all right with her," Michael said. "She is my

daughter after all. We will just sit here and wait for Sarah and Jimmie's new baby brother to arrive."

Another piercing cry erupted from the bedroom across the hall.

Sarah's eyes widened, and she looked up at her father.

"It's fine, sweeting." He kissed her head, but something in his tone must not have been convincing, because the baby broke into a cry.

Michael couldn't help but think about Markus, and how Emma had been so healthy when she had become pregnant. Now Emma was gone, and Markus couldn't stand to even look at his infant daughter. He had become a madman, and his friends had taken turns keeping an eye on their wayward comrade.

The nurse continued to stare in doubt.

Michael stood and paced until another heart-stopping scream tore through the hallway. He handed the baby to the nurse and rushed into the birthing room.

"Elinor?"

"You should not be in here," the midwife scolded.

"Michael?" Elinor gasped from the bed.

"You must push." Sweat dripped down the midwife's ruddy face, but she would brook no argument.

Michael went to the side of the bed and leaned down next to Elinor. He never dreamed he would be able to father a child after his injury. They would have been content with Jimmie and Sarah. Everett would have inherited the properties and titles, and his children thereafter.

When Elinor had announced that she was pregnant a few months after they were married, he had been shocked but ecstatic. He would have a son to inherit, and he would also have Jimmie and Sarah to love and raise as his own. No man could be so lucky.

Now, looking down at Elinor, enormously rounded with the baby and covered in sweat, he wished she had never become pregnant. He thought of losing her, and his throat closed up until he couldn't breathe.

He took her hand. "You have to push now, love."

She looked up at him, gripped his hand like a vise, and pushed until the effort lifted her from the bed. Another piercing scream tore through her.

"There, there, there," the midwife said.

The next sound was the unhappy wail of the baby coming into the world.

"It's a boy." The midwife cut the cord, swaddled babe, then rested him on Elinor's chest.

Michael's heart contracted, then expanded.

Elinor cooed to the infant, who immediately stopped crying and looked up at her expectantly.

Too soon, the midwife took the baby to a basin on the dresser.

He had to clear his throat to speak. "What will we call our little man?"

Her face was covered in sweat. He plucked a cloth from the side table and wiped her brow. There were dark circles under her eyes, but she was the most beautiful he had ever seen her.

"We could name him after your father," she suggested.

Heavens, no. "Never after him. What about 'Rolf?'"

She wrinkled her nose. "My father deserves no such honor. If it had been up to him, we would not be married, and that would mean that this little nugget would never have existed. Not to mention that Jimmie and Sarah would be up in Scotland with no one to care for them. No, not 'Rolf.'"

The midwife returned the baby to them. He was clean and fussy.

"All right then, what?" he asked, touching his son's face with the tip of his finger. His skin was so soft.

The baby looked toward him, and his eyes widened just as Elinor's always did when surprised.

Pure sustained joy welled up, making Michael laugh.

"We could name him after you, Michael."

His son should have his own name and his own path to follow. He hoped it wouldn't be the path of a soldier. "How about 'John?' 'John' is a good, sturdy name for a sturdy boy."

"John," Elinor repeated. The baby turned his little head and looked at her again.

"See, he likes it." Michael's heart was near to bursting.

A small scratching at the door broke them from the trance that John had them under. "Come in."

The nurse opened the door, and two little heads poked through.

Michael marveled at his wonderful life. "Come in and meet your new brother, John."

Jimmie and Sarah rushed through the door and up to the bed. Jimmie reached out his hand to touch the baby, but Sarah had eyes only for her mother.

"It's all right, Sarah." Michael lifted the little girl and put her on the bed next to Elinor, then he lifted Jimmie onto his lap.

The midwife said, "You make a fine family."

Elinor looked up and smiled. "Thank you, Mrs. Jennings, for everything."

Mrs. Jennings nodded, bundled up the soiled bedding, and left the room.

A few minutes later, the nurse returned and took Jimmie and Sarah.

In the early hours, Michael held his new son and looked out the window at the coming dawn. His wife lay sleeping in their bed. When the baby had stirred, he got up with him so he wouldn't wake his exhausted mother from her long-needed sleep.

The child had stopped crying immediately, and now stared up at Michael with great concern as a small crease formed between his brows.

"You have your mother's eyes, you know. I'll tell you a little secret, John. I cannot say no to that woman when she looks at me the way you are looking at me now. I suspect that you will have that same power over your poor father. Try not to abuse the old man though, will you."

John gurgled, and a smile tipped his tiny lips.

"Okay, you win. What do you want, a new pony? Your older brother just had his first riding lesson. You cannot be jealous already."

"Michael? What are you telling him?"

The baby's head fit comfortably into Michael's palm, and rest of him neatly in the crook of his arm.

He brought the infant to the bed, easing in next to Elinor. "I am just giving him some fatherly advice."

"It sounded as if he was manipulating you. Whatever will you do when John learns to speak?"

He brushed the back of his knuckle across John's soft skin. "I imagine I will spoil him just as I do his brother and sister."

Elinor smiled. She kissed his cheek, then John's. "Have I told you how happy I am to be your wife?"

Those were the most satisfying words his wife ever said. She had said them before, but he never tired of hearing it. "Not today, but it is early."

"I shall have to remember to tell you later then." She nestled her head against his shoulder.

He kissed the top of her head. "I shall be glad to hear the news, my love."

They reveled in a few minutes of peace. It wouldn't be long before the thunder of little feet started down the hallway, and the wet nurse came to take little John away to be fed.

"Michael?"

"Hmmm?"

"I am deliriously happy."

"I know. I am also happy beyond what is fair for one man to accept."

"Do you think it will last?" Her concern was evident in her voice.

"I think that we are lucky and should just enjoy our happiness without looking for an end to it. Life has been good to us, in spite of our shortcomings."

"Indeed it has. And to think of what a rocky start we had. I never dreamed of this much happiness." She kissed John's head as he dozed.

The door flew open, and Jimmie leapt onto the bed.

Sarah toddled in, and her brother hauled her up as well.

Crawling up, they peered at John.

Elinor's laughter filled the room. She pulled Jimmie and Sarah onto her lap, and they all leaned on Michael side.

John opened his eyes.

"Can we stop time right now, Elinor?"

"Yes. I never want to let this moment go."

Ready to read more Forever Brides? Next up is Dory and Thomas's story in Desperate Bride.

Desperate Bride

An unexpected promise... an everlasting passion.

An accomplished musician, Dorothea Flammel has refused more proposals than any London debutante; her only true love is her music. Dory's shimmering talent and beauty have long been adored from afar by Thomas Wheel, an untitled gentleman who can only dream of asking for the hand of a nobleman's daughter. But when her father, the insolvent Lord Flammel, arranges for Dory to marry a lecherous Earl in order to pay off a debt, she runs to Thomas—and proposes marriage to him.

Eloping to Scotland saves Dory from a disastrous fate, but what is for her a mere marriage of convenience proves more passionate—and more complex—than either imagined as rumors, scandal, and buried emotions come to light. And when a vengeful challenge from a drunken and embittered Lord

Flammel puts Thomas's life on the line, will the fragile trust between husband and wife be enough to save them both?

Chapter 1

More than an hour reading the Westgrove Estate titles and entailments left Thomas Wheel with an aching neck. If he acquired the property, those two fields neighboring his two family estates would be perfect for the Dutch four-crop rotation method. Increased productivity could mean putting the local children in a schoolroom rather than laboring for pennies to help feed their families. The little barn on the property could be converted into a schoolhouse.

Crowly cleared his throat. The butler was tall and wide and occupied the entire doorway. "Yes, what is it, Crowly?"

"Sir, I know you said you didn't wish to be disturbed, but you have a visitor." Many visitors found the unseemly size of the man intimidating. Crowly was quiet and efficient and that was good enough for a bachelor of Thomas's standing.

Thomas pulled the watch from his pocket. Nearly midnight, no decent person called so late. "At this late hour? Send whoever it is away. It is too late for callers."

The butler shuffled his feet but did not leave.

"Is there a problem, Crowly?"

"Well, sir, you see, the visitor is a young woman of apparent good breeding. She arrived in a hack, and I am reluctant to put her back out on the street."

Thomas stood. "She is alone?"

"It would seem so, sir."

"Who is it?"

"The lady refused to provide a card and wishes to speak to you rather urgently."

After pulling his jacket from the back of his chair, he dressed himself. "I suppose you had better let the mystery lady in."

"Yes. Thank you, sir." Crowly's shoulders relaxed.

Within seconds, a woman draped in a black cape with a hood hiding her face entered the study.

Thomas stood behind his desk and waited for her to speak, but she fussed with the edge of her cape and shifted her feet. He suspected that she was contemplating running away. "How may I help you?"

Her head snapped up and her hood fell away. There, standing in his study, was Lady Dorothea Flammel. The amber in her blond hair came to life in the firelight and Thomas had to

grip the back of his chair for balance. He did not know what he had been expecting, but in his wildest dreams he never thought to see Dory in his home. Well, maybe in his dreams, but never in reality.

Compared to the burly Crowly she looked lost in the doorway. She was petite and her green eyes ringed red as if she'd been crying.

His initial excitement overshadowed by her distress, his concern mounted. He crossed the room, stopping only when he realized that she backed away from him. "Lady Flammel, what is wrong? Is it Markus?"

Markus Flammel, Dory's older brother and one of Thomas's closest friends, lost his wife during childbirth a year before. The child had lived, but losing Emma had sent Markus into a desperate depression.

"No. It's not Markus. He is in the country as far as I know." She stared at her feet.

Thomas waited for her to say more, but she pressed her lips together while avoiding his gaze.

"Perhaps you would like to sit," he suggested.

When she looked up, he thought again, that she might run, but then her expression softened and she nodded.

When he offered her the chair in front of his desk, she skirted away from him to reach the seat. Never had he seen her so out of sorts. He rounded the desk and sat in his office chair.

The silence in the room was palpable. Thomas cleared his throat and the sudden noise made her jump in her seat. Dory had always appeared so calm and in control, his interest piqued. "Lady Flammel?"

"Yes?" Snapping her head up, she revealed her wide eyes and pale skin.

He smiled. Most women found his smile engaging, but she looked at him with wide eyes and trembling lips, like he'd bared his teeth for the kill.

He leaned forward, resting his arms on the desk. "I can only assume that you have come to me for some reason. You risk quite a lot coming to a bachelor's home, in the middle of the night, in a hack, and all alone. You must permit me my curiosity at such an unorthodox act. I have known you most of your life and this is the first time you have arrived on my doorstep. What can I do for you?"

She sighed. "Perhaps it was a mistake."

"Was it?" he asked.

She stared at him. He had watched her play the pianoforte dozens of times over the past few years. She was an artist of the highest order. Her emotion when she played was enthralling, but away from her instrument she always appeared so calm and controlled. Here in his study that seemed to have escaped her. She was near tears. He wanted to stand up and go to her but he did not wish to scare her.

The last thing he wanted was to allow his height to intimidate her.

"I am in trouble," she said.

Anger seared through Thomas. "Who was it? I will cut out his innards." He pounded his fist on the desk.

She flinched then waved her hand in a dismissive motion. "Not that kind of trouble, Mr. Wheel."

His fury seeped away. Watching her from the shadows for years, her music had drawn him in but those full eyelashes and deep green eyes kept him mesmerized. For a long time, he had yearned to touch the soft skin of her cheek and kiss those delicate ears. It was impossible.

She was the daughter of an earl. She would marry a man of her own station, not Mr. Wheel of Middlesex.

"Perhaps you should just tell me why you are here since you have made the trip. I will help you in any way I am able. I assure you that your presence here will remain our secret. My staff is very discreet."

She frowned. "I suppose as you are a bachelor, they would have to be." There was a bitter twist in her voice.

He did not comment, though her distaste rang through her statement and the twist of her lips.

She took a deep breath, making her full bosom rise.

Distracted for a moment, he then steeled himself and watched her eyes, which he found almost as intriguing.

She cleared her throat. "I am in need of a husband, and I have decided that, if you would not mind, you and I would suit nicely."

It took a full count for her meaning to penetrate his mind. "Perhaps earlier you didn't understand my anger." Anger rose again in his gut. He didn't want to frighten her. "It would seem that I must be blunt. Are you with child?"

She picked up her chin. "I understood you, Mr. Wheel. I

am not with child nor have I been ruined. It is only that I need to marry immediately."

He sat back in his chair and scratched his chin where the late hour had left him with a shadow of a beard. No one intrigued him as Dorothea Flammel did, but she was the unattainable. Now, here she was in his home offering herself to him. Saying yes and rushing off to Gretna Green rumbled through his mind, but doubt reared its head and he asked, "Why?"

Those beautiful eyes drew together. "I suppose you have a right to know." Staring at her shoes, her hair fell in loose curls around her neck and shoulders. She shook her head. Some inner turmoil etched on her face. "My parents will sign a betrothal agreement for me in the next week."

His stomach clenched. "To whom, if I may ask?"

"Henry Casper, the Earl of Hartly," she said through clenched teeth.

Thomas jumped from his chair. "Henry Casper is old enough to be your grandfather. What are your parents thinking?"

She flinched but did not cower. "That I will be a countess."

"There are other earls in the realm."

"I am afraid that I have refused quite a few offers of marriage."

It was almost legend the number of offers that Lady Dorothea Flammel had turned down. A duke had even offered for her and reports indicated she had broken his heart. "There must be someone left other than a man who walks with a cane and can no longer hear a word spoken."

She stood and pulled her cloak back over her head. "I completely understand. You do not wish to marry or the idea of marrying me is repellent. Forgive me for taking up your time, Mr. Wheel."

She headed for the door.

He rushed over and took her arm turning her around to face him. "I am honored by your offer, Lady Dorothea, and wish I could help you, but I am only Mr. Wheel. I have no right to marry so far from my station."

Her face reddened. "I did not realize you were such a bigot, Mr. Wheel."

"Thomas."

"I beg your pardon."

"My name is Thomas."

His face was close to hers. Her warm sweet scent filled his head with nonsense, a mixture of flowers and herbs.

"I..." she stuttered. "Forgive me for the late intrusion. I am sorry."

He did not release her. "Tell me one more thing, Lady Dorothea?"

"Dory, my name is Dory," she said in a smoky voice, while looking up at him.

It took every ounce of his control to keep him from sweeping her up in his arms and taking her to his bed. To hell with society and rules. "Why me?"

"I beg your pardon."

He leaned in closer. "I am curious why you chose me for this honor. You could have gone to any number of men who would jump at the chance to have you. I would like to know what made you come here."

She pulled away from him. "You seemed the safest choice."

He laughed so hard that she flinched as the noise of it filled the room.

"I do not mean to insult you."

"I am not insulted, Dory, just surprised that you would see me as a safe choice." He continued to laugh.

She was not laughing. Her eyes were again filling with tears.

The sight sobered him. "I am sorry to laugh but I see nothing safe about me being alone with you, my dear."

She dashed the tears away. "I only meant that you would not intentionally hurt me. You have a reputation for being kind to women and you like my music. I knew you would never stop me from playing or composing."

His gut twisted. "Why would you have to stop?"

"Mother has long told me that once I am married, my music must be put aside. I have resisted marriage for the last five seasons so I can continue to play."

"Dory, I will give you two insights into men of which you may not be aware. First is that we are not all tyrants and the second is that not all men are like your father."

Sorrow coursed through her eyes like the waves in the sea. "He lives to find ways to embarrass my mother in public. I will grant you she is no treat to be around, but I think she loved him once a long time ago. He is cruel beyond reason."

"Not all men are like that."

She shrugged. "I know. I do not think you are like that. For example, when you take a mistress you will be discreet. You would never cause me undue pain. That is why you would suit so well."

Sd around her middle.

His hand moved of its own accord and reached out and touched the skin where her shoulder met her neck. It was like silk under his fingers. "What makes you think I would take a mistress?"

"All men do eventually. At least you would be kind about it." She pulled away from his touch.

"I must repeat myself, Dory. All men are not like your father."

She shrugged and waved off his comment. "Will you help me?"

How he wished he could. "What is your plan?"

Turning, she faced him. "I would like to leave for Gretna Green in the next day or two. It is best to not tell anyone. I have not even let on to Sophia and Elinor about my plans."

Sophia and Elinor had married two of his closest friends and were Dory's longtime confidants. It was incredible that she would not share something so monumental with her best friends.

"I know I can trust them, but I thought it best not to put them in an awkward position. It's not fair."

He sat on the chair near the fire. Too big for the delicate seat, he'd always hated it as it suited a lady better. He curled his long legs under, leaned his elbow on one knee and his chin on his fist. "Once we married how would we get along in this plan of yours?"

"What do you mean?"

"Would you share my bed?" He sat up and found her standing only a few feet away.

She flinched but did not run away. "It would seem the least I could do."

Laughing, he said, "Not exactly the romantic image I had hoped for."

She walked closer until she stood in front of him with only an inch separating them. "You may have me now if you wish." Her voice trembled.

His groin jumped in response to her offer, but he put his hands on her hips and leaned his head against her stomach.

She trembled, but stood her ground.

Incredible as it sounded, she would allow him to deflower her. "Oh, Dory, you do tempt me."

Tentatively, she touched his hair. "I think I heard a 'but' coming next."

He gazed at her perfect face. Her hand was still in his hair moving in tiny circles. It was an innocent touch but it felt erotic to him. Any touch from her would have had that effect he suspected.

Forcing a smile, he only wanted to ease her fear of him. "But it would be beneath both of us to make love here in my study without a marriage to make it legal."

"Are you saying you will marry me?" No joy bubbled in her voice at the notion. She sounded more like a death sentence had been averted and she would only suffer life in prison.

He took her hands out of his hair, kissed the back of one, and then the other, and stood. So she could sit in the chair he'd vacated, he pulled another from a few feet away. He sat so close, their knees almost touched.

"I hope you will forgive me, Dory, but my answer is no. I cannot believe I am saying it myself. If you truly wished to be my wife, it would make me unspeakably happy, but like this it is less than romantic. In fact, it borders on the morbid."

She frowned. "I could have come to you with lies and told you I was madly and rapturously in love with you and could not live without you another moment. Would that have altered your decision?"

"It might have."

A furrow appeared between her brows.

Thomas reached out and smoothed the wrinkle. "I am glad you did not attempt to mislead me, Dory. I wish I could help you. For the first time in my life, I wish I was a lord or a knight so I would be worthy of your hand. However, my station is to be a gentleman and yours a countess. It would be selfish of me to lower your status in society."

She let out a long sigh. "I do not give a damn about titles. I am to be married to a lecherous old man who will keep me as a trophy and perhaps allow me to play pianoforte from time to time to entertain his friends. Everything I have ever wanted tossed aside. My mother will do as she has always threatened and burn all of my music." She leaned forward and touched his face. "Everything I am is about to be ripped from me. Can you understand, Thomas?"

He put his hand over hers and kissed her palm. "You are overwrought and have exaggerated the situation. I have never heard anything violent about Henry Casper. Though he is old for you, he lives well and will provide for you in the fashion to which you have been raised."

"You are wealthy," she said.

He laughed. "I have ample funds, but I am not titled and I never shall be."

"You are a snob, Thomas. If I do not care about a title, then, why should you?"

"You should care, Dory. I will admit that my association with Marlton and now with Kerburghe has afforded me more invitations than most gentlemen of my station receive, but I fear you would find life as Mrs. Wheel very unappealing."

"Are you a man with a terrible temper?" she asked.

Surprised by the question, he sat up straighter. "I do not think so."

"Would you keep your wife from pursuing her own goals?"

"I don't believe so, as long as the goals did not put her in harm's way."

"So, if I wanted to join the fire brigade you would be opposed to that venture?" Her eyes narrowed but she did not smile.

He shook his head but answered. "The fire brigade would be quite a dangerous endeavor, and I would advise my wife against such foolishness."

"Yes," she said. "You do sound like a tyrant. I think it obvious we would not suit." Sarcasm dripped from her words. She squared her shoulders and stood.

"I do not believe you have thought this through." He stood with her.

She turned and raised her eyebrows. "You believe I am impulsive and rash?"

A small voice inside his head told him he should take care with his next statement, but he ignored it. "In this decision, you seem to have jumped before looking."

Pursing her lips, she nodded. "Do you know what it takes to play the pianoforte as I do?"

The question was so out of context, he fumbled for his answer. "I believe I do. I have tried to become more accomplished and my talent has limited me."

"Have you sat for hours at a piano to achieve perfection in one stanza?"

"I have," he admitted.

"I have not heard you play, Thomas, though I hear you are accomplished, and I have heard you say you are not. I suspect you play very well but are not gifted with that something which makes one musician stand out among the rest."

He hated that she was so accurate in her description of his skills.

"I do not mean to insult you. It is just fate that makes one person good and another great. A cruel joke, if you will. My curse is being a woman. If I were a man with the talent that God gave me, I would play to massive crowds and kings would sponsor me. Not that this is what I want really. I want to be allowed to play every day for the rest of my life. I am not the type who jumps in without looking and have been analyzing my options for weeks. I examined it as I would a new piece of music. You were not a whim of mine to get me out of trouble. I believe we could make a nice marriage."

"Nice," he repeated in the same monotone she gave her speech.

"There is nothing wrong with nice."

He closed the distance between them.

Her chest heaved.

"Nice is not good enough for me." His arm came around her waist and in spite of the twelve-inch difference in their heights his lips were on hers before she could protest. She was stiff in his arms, but she put her hands on his shoulders and did not push away. Patience kept him gentle while he wanted to thrust his tongue in her mouth and taste her sweetness. One sip at a time, he caressed her lips with his. He ran his hand up and down her side from her hip to the edge of her breast, longing to feel her flesh rather than the soft material of her gown. Not touching her anywhere too intimate strained his desires.

She softened in his arms.

A sigh escaped her lips and Thomas took the opportunity to sweep the inside of her lips with his tongue.

She gasped, and he plunged inside. Her tongue was less forceful, but she joined him in the pleasure of the kiss.

Nipping at her lips, he watched her. "I will think about everything you have said tonight, My Lady. I am also cautious and like to give a large decision my full attention before jumping in."

He released her.

Dory straightened her dress. If he had wanted to put a name to the expression on her face, he would have said she appeared confused. He thought it was not a bad start.

"May I ask why you are so hesitant?"

"Shall I be completely honest?" he asked.

"I would prefer that you were always honest with me."

He nodded. "I am very fond of you, Dorothea, and have long thought you are one of the most beautiful and talented women in London. What you propose opens you up to a rather large scandal. Elopement is bad enough, but to run off with someone beneath you in station could be something you would not recover from."

"I am not concerned with my reputation," she protested.

"Well, I am. I think not being invited to the most fashionable homes in London would make you unhappy. I would not want my wife to be unhappy."

"That is very kind of you, but I am willing to risk censure to have a life that includes my music."

Wishing she would say something more heartfelt would not make it so. "I would like a wife who wanted me for something other than my love of music. I am also concerned by your apathy toward a romantic involvement."

"So idealistic, Thomas." She rolled her eyes.

His fingers itched to pull her back against him and take all she offered, but the damned voice of reason kept his hands at his sides. "I did not realize it myself, but I find the notion of a wife whose only interest in me is escaping a worse situation abhorrent." He held up his hand to stop her from further comment. "However, that kiss we shared was not apathetic nor were you uninterested. I wonder if helping you would not also suit my own desires."

Her eyes widened. "I already told you I would share your bed."

He touched her cheek. "Oh, Dory, I wish you could believe all men are not cut from the same cloth as your father."

She shrugged.

"Perhaps in time you will learn differently." He brushed a single tear away from her lashes.

Straightening, she stepped away from him. "My parents will announce my betrothal in less than a fortnight at mother's ball."

He dropped into a low bow. "You will have my answer before then."

Tainted Bride

Foolish Bride

Desperate Bride

Also by A.S. Fenichel

HISTORICAL ROMANCE

The Wallflowers of West Lane Series

The Earl Not Taken

Misleading A Duke

Capturing the Earl

Not Even For A Duke

The Everton Domestic Society Series

A Lady's Honor

A Lady's Escape

A Lady's Virtue

A Lady's Doubt

A Lady's Past

The Forever Brides Series

Tainted Bride

Foolish Bride

Desperate Bride

Single Title Books

Wishing Game

Christmas Bliss

HISTORICAL PARANORMAL ROMANCE

Witches of Windsor Series

Magic Touch

Magic Word

Pure Magic

The Demon Hunters Series

Ascension

Deception

Betrayal

Defiance

Vengeance

Visit A.S. Fenichel's website to view her full library.

www.asfenichel.com

Writing contemporary romance as Andie Fenichel

Christmas Lane

Dad Bod Handyman

Carnival Lane

Changing Lanes

Lane to Fame

Heavy Petting

Hero's Lane

Summer Lane

Icing It

Mountain Lane

~

Writing contemporary romance as A.S. Fenichel

CONTEMPORARY EROTIC ROMANCE

Alaskan Exposure

Revving Up the Holidays

CONTEMPORARY PARANORMAL EROTIC ROMANCE

The Psychic Mates Series

Kane's Bounty

Joshua's Mistake

Training Rain

The End of Days Series

Mayan Afterglow

Mayan Craving

Mayan Inferno

End of Days Trilogy

About the Author

A.S. Fenichel also writes as contemporary romance author Andie Fenichel. After leaving a successful IT career in New York City, Andie followed her lifelong dream of becoming a professional writer. She's never looked back.

Originally from New York, Andie grew up in New Jersey, and now lives in Missouri with her real-life hero, her wonderful husband. When not buried in a book, she enjoys cooking, travel, history, and puttering in her garden. On the side she a master cat wrangler, and her fur babies keep her very busy.

Connect with Andie
www.asfenichel.com
www.andiefenichel.com

Printed in the USA
CPSIA information can be obtained
at www.ICGtesting.com
LVHW010137131024
793661LV00003B/651